PENGUIN BOOKS

US

'Only two books in my life have made me cry . . . [One of them] is *Us*, Richard Mason's devastatingly tragic, funny and utterly gripping novel. Fantastic stuff and without doubt my book of the year'
Rebecca Pearson, *Independent on Sunday*

'In his latest [novel], Mason capitalises on his early promise with this compelling tale about three friends who have drifted apart since their university days, but remain connected by the shocking death of the woman who was, variously, sister, lover and best friend to each of them. It looks set to confirm Mason's reputation as a powerful storyteller with a bright future' *Red* Magazine

'Richard Mason has created a classic with a twist with this startling novel. It deserves to win all the prizes' Geordie Greig

'Like Bret Easton Ellis and Jay McInerney, Richard Mason reveals our helplessness with the gift of a social painter. *Us* is a novel of structural virtuosity' *L'Unità*

'*Us* is a merciless portrait of contemporary Great Britain . . . This young writer ranks beside Julian Barnes, Ian McEwan and Jonathan Coe, but is no simple follower. [*Us*] confirms his place among the small group of the most interesting new British novelists' *Ill Piccolo*

'Richard Mason is . . . the most insightful investigator of the psychology of the young among the new generation of British writers' *Il Tempo*

'*The Big Chill* meets Evelyn Waugh' *The Arts Show*, BBC Radio, Scotland

Richard Mason was born in South Africa and lives in Glasgow. He has written for a number of international newspapers and magazines and his first novel, *The Drowning People*, won Italy's Grinzane Cavour Prize for Best First Novel. His work has been translated into twenty languages.

In 1999, Richard set up the Kay Mason Foundation, in memory of his sister, Kay, to help South African children receive the education they deserve. For more information, please see inside.

www.kaymasonfoundation.org

Us

RICHARD MASON

PENGUIN BOOKS

PENGUIN BOOKS

Published by the Penguin Group
Penguin Books Ltd, 80 Strand, London WC2R ORL, England
Penguin Group (USA) Inc., 375 Hudson Street, New York, New York 10014, USA
Penguin Group (Canada), 10 Alcorn Avenue, Toronto, Ontario, Canada M4V 3B2
(a division of Pearson Penguin Canada Inc.)
Penguin Ireland, 25 St Stephen's Green, Dublin 2, Ireland
(a division of Penguin Books Ltd)
Penguin Group (Australia), 250 Camberwell Road, Camberwell, Victoria 3124, Australia
(a division of Pearson Australia Group Pty Ltd)
Penguin Books India Pvt Ltd, 11 Community Centre, Panchsheel Park, New Delhi – 110 017, India
Penguin Group (NZ), cnr Airborne and Rosedale Roads, Albany, Auckland 1310, New Zealand
(a division of Pearson New Zealand Ltd)
Penguin Books (South Africa) (Pty) Ltd, 24 Sturdee Avenue, Rosebank 2196, South Africa

Penguin Books Ltd, Registered Offices: 80 Strand, London WC2R ORL, England

www.penguin.com

First published by Viking 2004
Published in Penguin Books 2005
1

Copyright © Richard Mason, 2004
All rights reserved

The moral right of the author has been asserted

Typeset by Rowland Phototypesetting Ltd, Bury St Edmunds, Suffolk
Printed in England by Clays Ltd, St Ives plc

To Benj

Me

I

Julian

It happened because I took my class on an outing to the National Gallery. In a misguided moment last week this seemed like a good idea: teenagers should get out of the classroom at the end of term, be shown things that aren't advertised in movie trailers. I thought they might enjoy the enormous portrait of Charles I on horseback – the one near the entrance, by Van Dyck I think – as a round-off to their studies of the Civil War and Restoration. It's important for kids to be exposed to art and culture, if only so that they'll see that media conmen like Jake Hitchins aren't the only artists our civilization has ever produced.

Not, by the way, that I'm bitter about Jake's success. If I could persuade people to spend thousands of pounds on my melted garden furniture, I'm sure I would. But that doesn't mean I have to present it to innocent children as art, or ascribe it 'depth' or 'apocalyptic vision'. It doesn't mean I have to talk about it at after-school society meetings or discuss it round my friends' dinner tables. Not that Jake's ever asked me to do either of these things: we never spoke much and don't speak at all now, haven't for years. When his name comes up I usually pretend we've never met, it's far simpler that way.

I wonder, incidentally, if Maggie knows about my refusal to take joy in the big con Jake has perpetrated on the chattering classes – and if so, what she thinks of it. I dream about her sometimes and in these dreams she's laughing at me, saying that everything happened too long ago to matter now; chiding me for meanness of spirit. She always took the view that there was plenty of love to go round, plenty of joy for all – but that's only because she always got as much as she needed of both. She'd enjoy the absurdity of Jake's career; she'd probably contrast it with the mundanity of mine. Certainly she'd have smiled if she could have seen me this morning, trudging through central London in the rain because our headmaster is too tight to pay for a minibus.

'It's one of the advantages of being a centrally located London school,' he told me with a straight face. 'The boys can walk everywhere. Take Miss Patterson with you and make an adventure of it.'

It wasn't exactly what I'd envisaged: me shepherding a group of unwilling schoolboys through wet streets with Mavis Patterson, the school librarian, a severe woman in her late forties with no smile lines. I'd thought more along the lines of *Dead Poets Society*: bright weather, inspired youth, young minds opening. Instead the boys were grumbling in the cold and I was relegated to the back of the line by Mavis to prevent straggling.

We made it as far as the Mall and up it okay. Mr Chalker, the Geography master, is an expert at planning routes along streets with wide pavements. From the Mall, just by the ICA, we turned left and up the set of triumphal stairs which links it to Pall Mall. The kids crowded round the news stall at the top, pretending to shelter under its awning while actually scanning the top-shelf titles, until Mavis's sharp voice got them moving again.

I was halfway up Pall Mall when I saw him striding towards Piccadilly, on the other side of the road: a small, fair-haired man who should have been in Hampshire.

My father.

Through the rain he went, with no umbrella. He walked quickly, confidently, with long hungry steps, exuding an eagerness I've never associated with him. I watched as he disappeared through the oak doors of a discreetly expensive restaurant on St James's, wondering what on earth he was doing in the city with such a spring in his step.

When he'd gone I turned to see Mavis and the boys almost a block ahead of me and hurried to join them, but something of my father's briskness stayed with me. I realized what troubled me when I was on the steps of the National Gallery, chivvying the loiterers: I associate him with measured paces and a straight back and today he looked . . . almost furtive. I stood in the foyer, supervising the checking in of raincoats and the distribution of audio guides, watching as half the class disappeared immediately into the gallery shop. I went over my weekend telephone call with my father: he hadn't mentioned coming up to London; in fact he'd said it was too cold for leaving home. I remembered that, particularly.

I looked over at Mavis, wondering if she'd cover for me. Mavis isn't known for her willingness to make life easy for other people, but she's a stickler for keeping up appearances; I sensed that she wouldn't be able to refuse a request made in the presence of half the fifth form.

'Miss Patterson?'

I tried to strike a light, frank note. She looked at me with narrow eyes.

'I've got to collect an order for text books on Charing Cross Road. There's been a problem with numbers and delivery so I said I'd pop in this afternoon. D'you mind holding the fort while I'm gone?'

Her eyes narrowed further. I could see her wondering

whether or not to believe me, deciding to give me the benefit of the doubt. It helps, occasionally, to be considered 'dependable' by other people – hardly the most glamorous of accolades, but it has its uses.

'Of course not, Mr Ogilvie,' she said at last through pursed lips.

Let me make clear that I'm not the kind of son who would normally follow his father about, but then I've never thought of my father as the kind of man whose activities might repay surveillance. I come from a long line of bystanders. While braver, blood-thirstier, more passionate members of our species waged wars in bygone times and toyed with genetic extinction, my ancestors sat, non-committal, in the safety of the shrubbery. They chose a successful evolutionary tactic and stuck to it, which explains why so many of us exist today: the mass of cosily unobjectionable people who make neither war nor peace, who abide by rules, avoid getting into trouble and lead unremarkably prosperous lives. Caution lives deep in our genes. It's the root cause of all our actions – even, oddly, those which seem least cautious.

Maggie was the exception to this rule, of course.

My father often used to joke about her being the milkman's daughter. Not seriously – at least, I *hope* not seriously – but as a humorous allusion to her difference. Where we (me, mother, father, endless cousins) are blond, Maggie was dark; where we are hesitant, she was decisive; where we are considered, she was spontaneous. She was poured from a different mould than the rest of us: she walked more quickly, shook hands more firmly, argued more vociferously than any of us. In fact, I think the reason my father caught my attention this afternoon was not, so much, the fact that he should have been in Hampshire, but the fact that he was walking like Maggie.

Outside the gallery, the rain had eased and the sky had returned to an untroubled grey. Tourists were out in force again, causing an amble jam from one end of Trafalgar Square to the other. I hurried past a group of white-socked French schoolchildren and into the little street along which my father had strode so expectantly a few minutes before. The restaurant was intimidatingly exclusive and entering it demanded a moment's clarification of motive. If all I wanted was a cosy chat with my dad, a Goodness-me-what're-you-doing-here? encounter, then I could simply ask the Maître d' to take me to Mr Ogilvie's table. The fact that I didn't do that, but asked for a table of my own, should have made clear to me that what I wanted to do was eavesdrop, not gossip; but I was too conscious of my cheap suit to pay that knowledge much attention.

It was almost 2.30 and the restaurant was emptying. It was larger than it seemed from the street and divided into velvet-upholstered booths by oak partitions. In an attempt at Edwardian luxury palm trees were scattered erratically through the room, but it didn't take me long to spot the crown of my father's balding, palely blond head at a corner alcove.

'I'd like to sit there,' I said to the waiter, pointing to the booth between us and my father's.

'Of course, sir.' Without a further word he led me to the table and asked if anyone would be joining me. Afraid of betraying myself by my voice, I shook my head and feigned rapt contemplation of the menu.

The man behind me *was* my father – no doubt about it – and his companion, whose smaller form I had not been able to see over the partition, was a woman: a woman with a high, cooing voice who laughed at his jokes. He was talking quickly, fluently; in fact, he was talking elegantly, with a well-turned poise he exhibited occasionally at the end of a successful dinner party, but which was otherwise new to me. They were discussing a mutual acquaintance, recently moved to New Zealand.

'You know what they say about New Zealand . . .' he purred, with what can only have been a sly smile.

'What, darling?' My father was having lunch with an unknown woman who called him 'darling'.

'Great fun . . . but not for the *whole* weekend.'

His companion exploded in a firework of giggles. 'Oh, Henry,' she said; and then again, as if some point needed clarification, or as if she had moved her hand to his, 'Oh, Henry.'

I sat still, adrenalin coursing through me. Then the waiter was by my side, asking if I was ready to order, recommending the specials of the day, politely disguising his surprise when I remained mute and pointed at the menu, indicating the *steak au poivre* and writing *medium rare* on his proffered pad. I tried not to think of Mavis's probable irritation. I could always blame my delay on the inefficiency of the bookshop staff, I told myself as he disappeared, leaving me alone, alert, heart thumping, ears tuned for every note of my father's hushed voice – except that it wasn't hushed.

The talk behind me ranged freely. My father and his companion seemed to know each other intimately but not extensively, and there remained certain details to be filled in. I heard him explain how easy it was to get away to London, now that he was semi-retired; how in an ideal world he'd have his own flat here. They discussed the lengths of their marriages, how quickly the years sped by.

'Timid little woman, my wife,' he said. 'But a jolly good

mother. I've no complaints.' He lowered his voice an octave. 'I've been terribly . . . discreet, after all.'

'Really, Henry?' she breathed, archly.

'Wild oats must be sowed, mustn't they, Julia?'

'I couldn't agree with you more.'

'And I've had my fair share of what I call "foreign expeditions". I've nothing to complain about – but then, frankly, neither does she. She only found out about one of them and that was years ago. We even joke about it sometimes now, between ourselves. She calls it my "youthful indiscretion", bless her.'

Why didn't I confront him then?

Because I'm cautious, I'm made that way, and cautious people do not cause scenes in restaurants, especially in the immediate aftermath of a discovery as shattering as this one about their parents' marriage. What cautious people do is wait, so I waited – though now I was sweating so visibly that the waiter came over and asked me if I was all right.

'A glass of water, sir, perhaps?' he murmured.

I nodded. As I drank it, I listened to my father's talk as it drifted from topic to topic with an urbane ease I didn't associate with him. He was impish and informed, had opinions on all the new art shows and had gone to the final dress rehearsal of the current production of *Mayerling* at the Royal Opera House. 'The director's a personal friend,' he said, matter-of-factly. All of which was news to me.

Gradually the talk returned to more personal subjects. It seemed that Julia's marriage to a modern art dealer named Alex was going nowhere.

'Honestly, Henry, if it wasn't for Clara and Jonty . . .' she teetered off, pitifully, at one point.

There was a sympathetic pause from my father. 'At least

you love your children,' he said quietly. 'And that's a blessing worth treasuring.'

Silence followed, during which an eyebrow may have been raised. Julia said: 'But don't all parents love their children?' I felt my fingers tighten their grip on the tall, cold glass in my hand.

'The answer to that question depends on what you mean by love.'

'Oh come on.' She chuckled. 'Don't pretend you don't know what love is.'

'I had a daughter who taught me the meaning of that word.'

The urbanity had left his voice now; he was talking more hesitantly. There was a pause, during which I took a hasty gulp of water and Julia – as the partition's trembling testified – lent forward and touched my father's arm.

'*Had* a daughter?' she said gently, softly accenting the verb.

More silence. When my father spoke again, I heard to my astonishment that he was close to tears. I've only seen him cry once before, and that was at Maggie's funeral, in that cold crowded church full of lilies and their sickly scent of death. Now he was close to tears again, but restraining himself.

'Yes,' he said slowly, as if taking a decisive step towards intimacy with this unknown woman. 'I had a daughter. Maggie. She died several years ago.'

I've often noticed the morbid curiosity of even the nicest people. Very few, when told of another's death, can resist enquiring almost immediately after its manner, though there may be a briefly murmured line of sympathy before the inevitable question. In Julia's case, the sympathy was transmuted to a softly sorrowful coo after which she said, as I had known she would: 'And how did she die, Henry?'

I felt my stomach tense. Nobody knew precisely what had happened, least of all my father, but only three people in the world were capable of making an educated guess: me, Adrienne and Jake. I was fairly certain of the sequence of events; I could imagine the glint in Maggie's eyes, hear her heart beating with the elation of proving herself greater than me.

'I shouldn't bore you with this,' he said gruffly. 'God, what a fool I'm being. It's been – what? Twelve, no, thirteen years now. Honestly.'

'*Tell* me.' I could almost feel Julia's eyes meeting his, touched by his sorrow, silently sanctioning release. 'We can sit here all afternoon, if you like. The children are with Mrs Norris until five.'

Children. *Children*. I glanced at my watch. Three-quarters of an hour had gone by.

'I hardly ever speak of it now. It upsets my wife too much.' My father cleared his throat and a sympathetic bit of tongue-clicking emanated from Julia.

'They say she died instantly, painlessly,' he went on. 'I'm never sure whether or not to believe all that stuff about painless dying. I can't help thinking that's just something they dish out to cheer up the relatives.'

The partition between us shook in sympathy with my father's shoulders. The waiter looked over at our tables and I saw his eyes rest for a well-disguised moment on the steak he had set before me twenty minutes before, which remained quite untouched. Slowly, not knowing what else to do, unable just to sit there, I took a hesitant mouthful. It was stone cold. Julia was now murmuring words of pity and consolation.

'At least you have your son,' she finished, softly.

My father said nothing and my shoulders tensed again. After

a moment or two he blew his nose and seemed to compose himself, and his voice when he spoke at last sounded much more like the voice he had used through most of the meal: still alien to the voice I knew, but unbroken by stifled sobbing.

'The thing about my son . . .'

'Remind me of his name.'

'Julian.'

'A *delightful* name.' She made the pronouncement with emphasis, as though signalling an important change of mood. 'And what does he do?'

'He's a teacher at a mediocre boys' school in central London. I think they give him the English and History classes and he runs a few of the extra-curricular activities. To tell you the truth, I'm not sure he's the kind of chap who'll ever come to much. Perfectly decent, of course, never broken a rule in his entire life. Remembers Father's Day and Mother's Day like a clockwork gift-giver. Not much spark, though, very little to say for himself.'

'Oh come on. No son of yours could be so insipid.' Julia was being playful now, gently praising and teasing at once.

'I think the central problem with my eldest, indeed only, son –' here my father lowered his voice and leant forward – 'I mean, this is not the kind of thing I would ever dream of saying under normal circumstances, you understand?'

'Quite, Henry.'

'Not the kind of thing I'd ever admit to in public. But something I've had to admit to myself in recent years.'

He paused, and as his silence filled the restaurant, booming and resonant, I found I could no longer hold my cutlery, my hands were shaking so much.

'The simple truth,' he said at last, 'is that Julian's . . . *excruciatingly* dull.'

2

Jake

I stare at myself in the bathroom mirror, wondering what time of day it is. Gaunt face, tired eyes, skin like death. My eyes are so red I look like a badly taken photograph. There's a big red scratch down my back. My dick's covered in some dry brown substance which may or may not be blood.

The girl who might tell me is still slumped over in bed. Breathing, thank God, but lost to the conscious world.

My limbs ache. I can feel the joints in my knees. I walk slowly to the shower, stand underneath the hose, turn the temperature gauge to warm. One of the few benefits of fame is improved plumbing. As I turn the tap vague memories of last night begin to stir. A bar. A laughing girl. Some eco-babble . . .

The water's painfully cold. My heart lurches from the shock but a second later the temperature rises.

Aaaahh.

Pleasure before Pain. I don't know how long I stand there. Shaving seems too great an effort. My hair's matted with sweat and some weird sticky stuff. I've got no idea what it is. I think of washing it. I even raise my hands above my head, but my arms are too weak. I feel like an arse-about-face version of Samson, powerless *with* his hair. When I've stood so long my knees are about to go, I turn off the shower and step out of it. This is the crucial part of my day's beginning, the moment I know I must be brave and endure.

On cue the nausea comes.

Its explosive force ricochets through my intestines and I resign myself to spending the next ten minutes kneeling on cold white tiles, head in the toilet bowl. As I'm vomiting a strand of hair falls across my face. The stench is almost unbearable. I consider coming up for air, but know that chances are I'll vomit on the bathroom floor.

As I can't be bothered to clean anything up, and since I'm almost sure this isn't a day for my cleaning lady, I abandon the idea.

Eventually it's over. The nausea subsides. It doesn't disappear. It gave up disappearing a year or two ago. But it subsides to the manageable levels I have learned to call normal. I pull myself up by the towel rail and consider taking another shower. I haven't been clean, properly clean, in what seems like months. But warm water regularly makes me ill, and I'd rather go dirty than risk another ten minutes with my head down the loo. So instead I splash ice-cold water from the basin all over my face and neck. Then I look at myself again in the mirror, marvelling at the link between self-abuse and pragmatic decision-making.

I still look like shit.

'For someone who's spent two an' a 'alf hours in the bathroom,' she says when I go back into the bedroom, 'you look like shit.'

I try to think of a witty comeback, an interview phrase. Unfortunately, I stopped being able to think of anything clever to say around the time the nausea became permanent. 'Honestly?' I ask instead, mock-impressed by her acuity. 'And would you mind confirming that Tony Blair is, in fact, a Tory?'

To my horror the girl giggles. What in the name of hell is her name? She stretches over, exposing a nice little body, a bit on the thin side but with firm breasts, hairy under-arms. So she is the eco-warrior, I think, registering a slight relief. At least I've succeeded in placing her, which already makes this morning better than most.

'What were you doing at the Groucho Club if you're an eco-warrior?' I ask, almost genuinely interested.

'A what?'

'An eco-warrior.' More and more of our conversation is coming back to me, but patchily.

'Sorry?'

She looks hesitant, uncertain. I see her hope I'm joking and wonder if the eco-warrior was perhaps someone else. Another girl, another night, another morning-after begun with dread. 'Just kidding,' I say, for no reason at all. I've definitely got past the point of minding too much whether or not a girl realizes I don't know who she is, but that's not the same thing as courting such disclosure.

'Aren't you going to make me some coffee?'

Definitely not the eco-warrior, then. Feminists and environ-mentalists only let you make them coffee on the third date.

'Sure,' I say, glad for a reason to turn my back on her.

I walk slowly into the kitchen, measuring my paces. It's full of gleaming surfaces and old newspapers waiting for the recycling man. My housekeeper Josefa's a bit of an eco-warrior herself. Maybe . . . But no. The eco-warrior I'm thinking of may not be the girl currently sprawled over my bed, but she's definitely not Josefa either. I don't usually go much over thirty, occasionally thirty-five. Josefa must be a good thirty-eight if she's a day, and older women don't tend to put up with my particular brand of bullshit.

Everything's so fucking clean I don't want to touch it. Briefly I consider taking a shower now that I'm feeling a bit better. Then I remember I'm not feeling that much better and decide not to. Deliberately, belligerently, I lay a clammy hand on the shining stainless steel handle of the coffee pot. It leaves a perfect palm print that disappears magically as I watch it.

Phenomena like this have the power to entertain me for hours on end in certain moods.

Right now, though, I'm a man with a mission in mind, because I've just felt sufficiently at ease in the intestinal region to know what would help me get through the next hour or so. Humming to myself I open the door of a stainless steel cabinet and take out some cups. They're bone china, white with thin purple stripes. I have no recollection of buying them.

I fill the kettle, hands shaking slightly as I hold it under the tap. I'm careful to make sure the water's cold before it touches my skin, as I don't want to risk a reversal in steadily-declining nausea levels. When the kettle is boiled I make a cafetière of coffee for the woman previously known as eco-warrior. For myself I brew a swilling infusion of camomile tea, really swirling the tea bag to get the full flavour.

Half a teacup hot water, half a teacup vodka. The launch pad of my day.

Since further sex is out of the question for someone in my condition, it's time to engineer a parting with non-eco-warrior. This is a shame, in some ways. She's not bad-looking. There's something sweet about her smile, something seductively fuck-able about the way she's sitting with her legs pulled under her when I go back into the bedroom. She's probably a nice enough person. I hand her a cup of coffee, thinking.

'Ta very much,' she says.

The trick in these situations, by the way, is to act like you're desperate for the girl to stay. There's nothing less sexy than desperation. Nothing more guaranteed to send any self-respecting woman off in search of a cab. 'I know we've only just met,' I tell her hoarsely, watching her eyes widen, 'but I don't think there's any point in playing games, not when the heart's involved.'

She smiles at me, warily.

'That conversation we had last night.'

'What conversation?'

'The one where you . . . It was so incredible, how we just clicked like that.'

Her smile falters.

'It just seemed like you understood me, like you, I don't know, just got me straight off.'

'But . . .'

'It's the connection we have together.' I force myself to stare meaningfully into her eyes. 'Kindred spirits, whatever they call it. I mean, we haven't known each other long, granted . . .'

'About nine hours.'

'Yeah, but there's time for all that. Don't you see?'

I consider telling her we've got our whole lives ahead of us, but you've got to draw the line somewhere. I'm losing concentration because the other thing that arrived with the nausea was the voices. One voice, actually. Mine. Everything I do, everything I think and feel, from the most frivolous to the most toe-tinglingly profound, is turned almost immediately into words. It takes a moment for the sentences to form, so they're always just behind my absolutely present reality. They're then read aloud, in my own voice, with a monotonous regularity that has made me want to kill myself. If I concentrate, I can make one voice louder than the rest. I can listen to the slightly delayed live broadcast of whatever I'm primarily doing or feeling. At other times the channels all play at once. A dialogue between the itch on the heel of my left foot and the zit just under my collar. An impassively delivered update on the continuing pain in my knee. Round-the-clock reporting on my alcohol consumption.

As I go through the steps in the dance with non-eco-warrior, my head's so full of sound I can barely think what I'm supposed to do next. Is this my prize for having a high IQ? The voices deliver everything they say smoothly. Indifferently. Not very loudly *rabbit face*, *dog tits* but very regularly and very quickly. At the moment, for example, one's telling me I should ask her where the blood came from before she leaves *lip's bruised from a kiss, a bite, a fright in the night* while another's describing the tantalizing seduction of the itches in my scalp, iridescent pinks in a sharply major scale begging to be scratched *raw ribs, bright bite, up for a fight* and a third's saying that I've put, am putting, this poor girl through enough.

You'll see why it's not always easy for me to stay 'on message'.

As non-eco-warrior pulls a tight, thin sweater over her tight, thin torso, clearly about to leave, the voices fade. They don't stop, they never stop. But they do get quieter now, easier to ignore. The vodka's hitting the spot.

One voice won't shut up, though. It's the one reminding me that I haven't thought about Maggie since waking up with non-eco-warrior. I know from experience that it takes a lot of vodka to silence this little demon, so I'm able to compare pain with gain and conclude that silence at any price is not my philosophy.

Believe me, it's not because I think I should think about her. It's been thirteen years, eight months and six days since she died now. It's not that I think Maggie would want me to think about her, either. I don't even think she'd want me to think I should think about her. It's just that I always do. Sooner or later. Eventually. Not a day goes by without my being reminded. Without the voices describing the brown, greying hole she has left behind.

Not that memory's always helpful or clear. Would it be more satisfying if it were? Not really. We forget things because we know instinctively how much we can deal with. Why fuck with a survival strategy as old as the species itself?

It has its disadvantages, though. I find it hard, now, to remember details I never thought I could forget. Stupid things, like the way she used to smell when she woke up or the look on her face as she played Chopin. The smooth sheen of her voice or the throatiness of her laugh.

I'm not sure I haven't half-invented her laugh, to tell you the truth. Can anything produced by a real person have been so lovable? So perfectly and intricately full of joy and colour, with flashes of magenta and silver exploding in the distance behind it? That's what worries me. I've made a monument of Maggie – and if she knew she'd never forgive me.

Non-eco-warrior's dressed now, and for a second the sight of her firm bum in a tight skirt turns me on. I know my limits, though, and don't do anything. Instead I sit on the bed, watching as she picks up my clothes, folding them over the chair. Without looking at me, she takes my wallet out of my trouser pocket and selects four crisp scarlet fifty-quid notes.

'You know that deep 'n' meanin'ful chat we 'ad last night?' she says when she's at the door. I don't really know what she's talking about anymore, but nod for effect. 'Well, we never 'ad it.' She looks at me coldly, disgustedly. 'By the time you found me you was totally out of it. Could barely cum, let alone talk. Stupid fuckin' ponce.'

She opens the door and lets herself out. In the corridor she pauses and turns round. 'I only went wiv ya 'cause it was fuckin' freezin' on the street.'

3

Adrienne

Beep, beep, beep.

I don't know why I'm even trying to call Julian – it must be midnight in London, or later. What's the point after all these years? It's been a long time since that day in the rain when he sauntered out of my life, quietly parcelling up his grief and his anger and strolling off, looking around just once at the corner. I wonder if he thinks of me, ever. Did he think of me when he heard from Jake?

Sitting by the phone I remember his big white teeth and awkward hands that day, and the timid, half-hearted attempt at a wave he gave me, not meeting my eyes.

I take a deep breath, replace the receiver, pick it up, and press redial. *Beep, beep, beep.* I'm about to go through the procedure again when I realize there's no more time for it – people are arriving in, let me see, an hour and a half and I'm not even dressed. Maybe Julian's become a closet phone addict (possible) or maybe he has a new girlfriend who's a closet phone addict (definitely possible) or maybe his number's changed without him telling me (probable).

Breathing calmly, slowly, just like the doctor said, I sit still for a moment, running it all over in my head:

- Jake's letter: at the bottom of my lingerie drawer.
- The caterers: in the kitchen with the party planner.

- The DJ: setting up in the dining room.
- Tip for the doorman: check.
- Flowers: check. (Why lilies? I hate them. They remind me of funerals.)
- Momma: in her bathroom, getting ready, under control.
- Baby: not showing yet.
- Vegan dinner for the general's daughter: check.
- Hair: check.

I get up and walk slowly around Spencer's den, straightening a picture frame or two (he looks great in the one with Laura Bush). I have a successful husband, a prestigious apartment, a fabulous chef, I tell myself calmly. Thank *God* for André. Momma was right. I'm thirty-two years old, still a size four, still with great legs, hair, nails. Everything's perfect. When I've repeated this fact ten, maybe fifteen times, and all the picture frames are straight and I've plumped and re-plumped the cushions on the armchair, it seems true – or true enough to last out the evening, which is all that matters.

In the hallway I check my eyes, which are red but rectifiable. My hairdresser did a great job, I notice, and I stand for a moment in front of the mirror, practising my smile, trying to get my eyes to shine and sparkle. You've got to project happiness, Adrienne, confidence. I guess I'm hoping this self-instruction will produce an on-demand glow, and when it doesn't I remind myself there's always make-up.

I own a lot of make-up.

With this thought to calm me, I head down the corridor, past the locked door to the fourth bedroom, past an enormous bowl of lilies. Flowers of death, Julian used to call them, but they're impressively expensive in mid-winter. In the kitchen I hear André's shrill voice fussing over the oysters, which is vaguely reassuring. By the time I reach the door to our bedroom I'm not shaking so much, am steadier on my feet.

At the last minute I don't open it.

I can't.

Spencer's in there, and his manic energy won't calm me. He's planned tonight with ruthless precision – the food, the guests, the theme, the decor – and he'll be tapping frenziedly at his Palm Pilot, barking at me because I'm not dressed yet. He'll also be nervous and trying to disguise it, which means he'll be horny – and that's something I can't face right now.

So I head back to his den, where I intend to sit calmly for a few minutes, collecting myself.

I'm not even going to think about calling Julian, so I go and look out of the window, down to the traffic on Park Avenue, and watch the hordes of caterers and waiters streaming through the service entrance. A cab races up and before it's even stopped a man gets out in tight white shorts and a tank top, and even from here, ten floors up, I can see enough to wonder momentarily if a brief but passionate affair would restore my interest in men. To my surprise he hurries through the service entrance too, and I realize he must be one of the statues.

Nonchalantly I wander across the room, readjusting the already perfect alignment of the picture frames, consciously experiencing the deep shag pile of the carpet on the soles of my perfectly pedicured bare feet in a very Buddhist way. Maybe I'll spend a moment checking out some magazines, I think. A nice, calming, *normal* activity. So I sit down on a sofa, trying not to worry about having spoilt the perfect plumpness of the cushions, and pick up a copy of *Variety*.

Leafing through it, I see an article on Spencer subtitled 'Hollywood's Midas: the man whose touch is box office gold', which lists all his films and their box office takings above a photo of him on the set of *Mother of All Battles*. A few pages on is an ad for his latest venture, *Heroes*, a reality TV show about life in the military in which real people fight real wars, featuring a close-up photograph of Tom Buckley with mud all over his face, eyes blue and brave, jaw set, in a desert somewhere.

I'm sitting with the magazine on my lap, taking long deep breaths, when there's a knock on the door. It's Martha, my assistant, a skeletally-thin woman who could be thirty or sixty and who wears a look of constant surprise (the result of too much surgery around the eyes) which is misleading. I'm a little afraid of Martha and what she knows.

'Hi, Martha,' I say, playing it cool. Martha comes into the room and gently removes the magazine from my hands, like I'm a troublesome child who's played too long with a toy I might choke on.

'How're you feeling?' she asks brightly.

It's a question I've learned to dread because it's never possible to tell the truth in reply, never possible even to begin to share what my life is really like. I stare at her, thinking that I can't let Spencer down, even if he does donate heavily to the Republican party, so I just say, trying to mean it, wishing as I open my mouth that I'd chosen some slightly more convincing response: 'Great.'

'Good.' She smiles at me kindly, eyes wide open and big and blue like some larger-than-life antique doll in a museum. 'Because your mother'd like a quick word.'

'Adrienne?'

I hear her voice from the corridor, coming through the door to the main guest suite, which is open a little. A heavy wave of scent, some sickly Thierry Mugler concoction she's begun to wear in her struggle to be young, hits me as I poke my head through the doorway, taking a second to realize my mother's prostrate on her bed, perfectly made up and stark naked. She's been dyeing her pubic hair again, I notice.

'Hi, Momma,' I say.

'Adrienne, honey. Come sit by me.'

This is the beginning of an old game which hasn't varied much since I was five or six years old, since before my father left. I go over to the bed, trying to concentrate on the heavy pile of the carpet, trying to remember how fortunate I am to have a mother who loves me so much, trying not to wish she could be put on pause.

'How're you feeling, sweetie?'

From Momma, somehow, the question is even more difficult to answer than it was from Martha, because the salary gap that protects me from my assistant doesn't exist with a parent.

'Great, Momma,' I say decisively, knowing from experience that the only way to avoid an excruciating heart-to-heart is to begin talking quickly and refuse to stop until it's time to finish getting dressed. 'It's so exciting tonight's finally here, so exciting to have *you* here, with us,' I tell her, sitting down on the bed, a few feet from her dyed pubic hair. (What's she trying to do? Prove that older women get laid too?) 'I don't know what I'd do if you weren't here to—'

'You never were very good at managing on your own, were you, honey pot?' says Momma briskly, cutting me off and swinging two athletic legs over the cashmere blankets and standing up. She moves over to where her dress – mad, bad, and dangerous to wear – is carefully laid out on the chaise longue Spencer bought because it once belonged to Rita Hayworth.

I know what Momma's after, but I'm a seasoned player too – and before she can continue I'm on a roll. 'Honestly-Momma-you-worry-too-much-I'm-*great*-just-a-little-nervous-that's-all-oh-my-God-look-at-that-dress-you-look-fantastic-it's-beyond –' and at the same time I'm moving towards the door, telling her I'd better get going or I'll never be ready in time, repeating how incredible her dress is, dreading the inevitable parting shot which flies after me when I'm halfway down the corridor again.

'. . . because you're *so* like your father, dear.'

There's no alternative now but to bite the bullet, so I take a deep breath and walk boldly into the bedroom. *Our* bedroom.

Spencer's sitting on the bed, wearing socks and boxer shorts. For a moment the veins on his forearms revolt me, but I subdue that and he looks up. Since he turned fifty he's made it a point of honour to keep his dimensions the same they were when he was twenty-three, but his face is leathery and his skin looks too old to be stretched so tightly over his rigorously worked-out body. His Palm Pilot's lying on the bed beside him and as I thought he would, without looking up, he reminds me of the schedule for tonight.

'People are arriving at eight for eight thirty,' he says. 'I want to make the welcome speech at nine.'

'Sure.'

He lifts his chin and smiles at me. We both know how to play Husband And Wife Before A Party. I can tell he's feeling horny, so I go over to him and he pulls me onto his lap and the way he's looking into my eyes, anyone who didn't know us would think we had a functioning relationship – which, of a kind, we do. His mouth tastes clean, of peppermint, and his skin is soft but taut over the muscles of his back. Over his full head of hair, I see the open door to the dressing room and the walk-in closets with their drawers. Jake's letter is in the bottom one, lurking. Spencer's sliding his hand over my thigh, but I really haven't got time now or I'll never get dressed – so I disengage and murmur something about wanting to look my best for him.

This isn't how the scene goes in Spencer's mind, though. 'Martha's scheduled to do the final checks, Adrienne. You've got to learn to delegate.'

Since there's no answer to this argument, I just look at him sweetly, thinking that sex now would be disastrous for my hair. He's smiling up at me, confidently expectant, and so I resort to compromise and go down on my knees and pull his boxer shorts down. His cock, which is not as big as Julian's, is hard but tastes clean in my mouth. I moan a little, since this is our anniversary, but when he tries to put his hands on my head, controlling the rhythm, I reassert myself, moving them away and saying, between strokes, 'Careful of my hair, honey' – which Spencer's respectful about, because *my* hair's a symbol of *his* success.

4

Julian

When my father met me at the station this morning, his aura of unobjectionable normality had returned and even as I watched him shamble across the car park I thought how different he was from the person who had bounded up St James's a few days before. He seemed to have shrunk; his voice was thinner, less exuberant than it had been.

'Ah, Julian,' he said. 'Welcome.'

We shook hands, both of us wondering whether the gesture would develop into a hug, both of us shying away at the last moment. My father, so tactile with Maggie, is not at ease with me; I sensed it in the stiffness of his grip.

'Good to see you, Dad.'

As he led me to the Volvo I tried to remember his conversation in the restaurant; I tried to picture what his face must have looked like, as he spoke about my mother and me.

'Mum well?'

'As well as usual. School going well?'

I thought of my return to the National Gallery and Mavis's cold eyes.

'Very well.' I couldn't find anything else to say: the only real conversation we might have had was the one we couldn't possibly have, under any circumstances. I watched him as he reversed carefully out of the parking space; I had watched him reversing out of parking spaces for thirty-two years. It seemed for a moment that the events of a week before were so unlikely, so easily forgotten that maybe they could be.

We drove on in silence, through the town and out beyond it into fields and winding country lanes. The light was failing, though it was barely half past four.

'And what have you been up to?'

The question was a standard one in my father's repertoire, but now it seemed to be tinged with subtle derision, as though he didn't expect me to have been up to anything much. I thought over what I'd been doing in the month since we had last seen each other: two trips to the movies with friends, one alone, a week of frenzied marking of mock exams. By comparison with the discovery that he was regularly unfaithful to my mother and thought that I was a waste of space, nothing much seemed worth retelling. I felt, suddenly, as though I were back at school, with Benedict Chieveley asking me dismissively whether I'd gone anywhere 'interesting' in the holidays. (The answer, of course, was always no, since Brittany was about as exotic as my father's choice of family destination ever got.)

'I've been out so much I've hardly slept,' I lied.

My father took his eyes off the road to look at me and I saw his eyebrow twitching to raise. 'Really?' was all he said; but it seemed to me there was some challenge in his tone and I began to invent crazily, telling him of wild parties, a club opening, a midnight roller-blading expedition through central London.

'Sounds like you'll need a rest in the country,' he said as he pulled into the drive.

The house was just as it's always been: rambling and thatch, hidden from the road behind a screen of impeccably pruned hedge. There was smoke coming from its chimneys and its windows were glowing with light, the picture of domestic bliss. Walking through the kitchen door I was confronted by the old smell: of sweet seasoned logs, my mother's cooking, freshly-cut flowers, well-stuffed cushions.

'Your mother's upstairs, lying down,' said my father, shuffling off to his study. 'Help yourself to tea or anything you want.'

I waited until he had closed the door and left me, and then I did what I always do when I come to this house now: dismiss the reality of the present and summon the visions and voices of the past. So little has changed, you see. The climbing frame my father built for Maggie and me (and which my mother preserves for my children) is still at the bottom of the garden, still redolent of excitement and adventure. The hedges still abound in secret passages, though they are barred to me now, indeed to anyone over four foot tall. The piano is still in the sitting room, its lid still open as though about to be played. Walking down the hall I sniff the air, catching the scent of dust and polish and warm fires on winter nights, trying to settle myself as completely as possible in the past – as if, blessed with success, Maggie might come bounding down the stairs at any moment.

None of us plays the piano: that gift was another symbol of Maggie's uniqueness. But the instrument is kept tuned, as though for her ghost; and I sat down at the stool and played the first bar of a Mozart sonata, a trick Maggie once taught me by rote. What would she say if she were here now? If she, with me, had overheard our father in that palm-filled restaurant?

Every inch of this house is full of her. Without her, the whole place has become a mausoleum, a child's playground preserved in tender yet macabre detail. As though anxious not to sever our links with a past now lost, my mother has kept the place exactly as it was when we were children. Tin soldiers and steel trucks still decorate the mantelpiece in my bedroom; and Maggie's dolls, long disused even when she died, are still piled on the pink and blue eiderdown in hers. Maggie's cupboards remain full of her clothes, though they're folded more scrupulously than they ever were when she wore them, and somehow, beneath the stench of mothballs, it's still just possible to trace the lingering remnants of her smell, so powerful in the months after she died and drifting slowly towards extinction now.

The house puts a brave face on its sadness and would look cosy to an outsider. Only those who live in it know that it is as easeful as a much-loved spaniel, returned from the taxidermist's and placed by the fire – curled up and sleeping for eternity. My mother has taken our childhood and had it stuffed: the image is preserved but the essence is gone, and where there was once so much, there is now so little to say.

I try not to think of Jake ever being here. I try not to imagine him in Maggie's bed, straining on top of her, under that eiderdown. I try not to imagine him watching her play, or bathing in the bath she and I used to share as children.

5

Jake

When non-eco-warrior has gone I go back into the kitchen and pour myself some neat vodka from a bottle I always keep chilling in the freezer. My hand makes its mark on the bottle just as it did on the coffee pot. This time, though, the ghostly image disappears at twice the speed.

As the last trace of the tip of my index finger disappears, I wonder whether I should kill myself today.

I know, have known for some time, that I'm heading for death sooner or later and probably sooner. This is something I have in common with humanity. I'm okay with it. Only rich Americans like Adrienne's mother are obsessed with living for ever. We all die. It's just that in my case I'd like to speed up the process a bit. Cut through the formalities.

The telephone rings. I hear my voice. Not a voice in my head but a digital recording of my voice played to outsiders as well as me. It's saying tonelessly that I'm unlikely to be in a fit state to return anyone's call in the foreseeable future, so would they kindly either call back or sod off. I find it's best to be frank about messages, because it's not like I never answer my phone. Sometimes I do. It's more that I never, *ever*, call anyone back.

The person speaking is a journalist I dimly remember agreeing to have lunch with at some indeterminate moment in the past. Today is the day of our meeting, apparently. She's at the restaurant already and she likes my message, it really makes her laugh, but she hopes I'm not being serious. She purrs over her Rs. She's ordered Bellinis, she ends pleadingly, sensing perhaps that she's lost her catch.

The phone goes dead.

I'm just beginning to feel the need to piss when I hear my own voice again telling the outside world to sod off. It's Hank, my (art) dealer.

'Jake you prick,' Hank is saying. He's an irascible New York queen whose mood swings make mine look like amateur work. 'I know you're in that shithouse, and I mean house of *shit*, you persist in calling "home". "Hell" might be a better name. You should think about it. Get it engraved on a little brass plaque and hang it outside your door. *Hell. No Flyers or Junk Mail.* I know you're in that semen-stained bed of yours, paying two quid a minute to have some bored housewife with three kids listen to you jack off. Hang up the cell and pick up the landline, goddammit.'

I sit tight on the sofa. He waits. I win.

'Okay you little fuck. I can't believe I'm being nice enough to tell you this. Particularly since you're obviously too fucking wasted to even *register* the fact that Christine Seignier, an in no ways un-major feature writer for a small magazine you might have heard of called French *Vogue*, is currently getting pissed off waiting for you to show your sorry ass in the bar of the St Martin's Lane Hotel.'

I take another gulp of vodka and settle back to enjoy the show. When Hank's on a roll there's no stopping him.

'I don't know how much tape your machine has,' he continues, reading my thoughts, 'but I could go on and on and, frankly, *on* here. I mean, let's take a look at the big picture, the "career" aspect of the issue. You haven't had a major exhibition in three years. You haven't produced a single sale-able piece of work in more than two years. I don't count that phial of piss Valentine Serle bought, by the way – he did that as a favour, to help you out.

'Because I'm the kind of innocent idealist I am, I still believe in you. Which means I've thrown my guts into organizing your new show at my top end, and that's *top end*, gallery – even though I'm still waiting to see a single fucking piece of new work. But it's not just me who's in the mood to help you out. Delightful Mademoiselle Seignier is prepared to write gushingly about you in the kind of magazine the people who buy your art *read*. She's even throwing a little session with a make-up artist into the bargain, so you won't look as dead as you feel in the photographs. Isn't that *nice* of her? D'you think she *wants* to be talking to a reeking alcoholic no-hoper who prefers jerking off and watching daytime TV to injecting his career with some much-needed publicity? D'you think *she* wants to? D'you think *I* want to be talking to his *answer* machine? If you don't get your sorry little ass out of your cum-soaked sheets and into a cab pretty fucking quickly . . .'

I can sense he's heading for a rhetorical climax. This gives me the energy to pick up the phone and put it down again. Two nil to me.

I don't even move when it rings a third time. Hank continues, uninterrupted, in mid-flow.

'. . . I'm going to get you gang raped by a group of fero-ciously endowed black construction workers who won't take no for an answer. Do you understand? Fuck *you*.'

The line goes dead.

I breathe a sigh of relief and take another sip of vodka. Then I decide on second thoughts to down the remainder of the glass. Maybe I could try shooting some gin up my nose with a water pistol. I'm just about anaesthetized to pain by this point in the morning and the kick is unique. By the time the answer machine clicks on again I've almost forgotten about Hank.

'Jake, you goddam mother-fucker. You wanna *talk* to one of the gentlemen who's gonna be takin' care of you if you don't get your *butt* in a fuckin' *taxi*?'

The line goes dead. Immediately the phone rings again. He has me on his speed dial list. Hank knows that to get me to do anything requires enormous patience and perseverance. He's also discovered my Achilles heel, which is a certain sensitivity to threats of enforced buggery.

'Because I'm goin' out *right* now to get one of those meaty black construction workers . . .'

I have no choice now but to pick up. One of the irritating things about drunkenness is how limited your options seem at any given moment. I should learn to take my phone off the hook instinctively in situations of siege.

'Get your fuckin' *ass* into a cab right *now*!' Hank screams, a dangerous note of looming triumph in his voice. He knows that getting me to pick up the phone is an important victory. 'You have no fuckin' *idea* what I'm gonna . . .'

'*Okay!*'

There's silence. It's two-one to me but Hank's won the battle that counts.

'I'm sending a car for you in ten minutes and I'll sweet talk mademoiselle in the meanwhile.' He pronounces 'mademoiselle' with a lingering Z. 'If you don't get into the car, or if you screw this up in any way, my black buddies are standing by.'

The line goes dead.

6

Adrienne

I'm in the hallway, fully dressed and waiting for people to show up, while Momma fusses over Spencer's cravat and feels his shoulder muscles as she straightens the braid on his coat. Since I have nothing to say to Momma or Spencer, I pretend to readjust one of the vases of lilies.

'Careful of the pollen, dear,' Momma breathes, not even looking at me.

'Sorry, Momma.'

Briefly I wonder if my life is going to continue like this indefinitely.

There are fifty people coming to dinner and two hundred arriving after them to be photographed dropping ash on expensive-to-replace carpets. Even though everyone knows everyone – that's the point, after all – Spencer absolutely insisted on having an announcer, so for the next forty minutes or so a pompous voice calls out the names of the people my husband most wants to impress tonight.

I beat it to the kitchen, telling myself I'm legitimately checking on things. Waiters are hurrying backwards and forwards through the swing doors, carrying boxes filled with red velvet on which the canapés have been arranged to look like jewels. The theme of the night is Empire and Spencer and I are Napoleon and Josephine, his choice, while most of our guests have dressed as American imperialists. The waiters are liveried like imperial Russian footmen and were hired by the casting director who did the staff for Ian Schrager's hotels. Only some of them speak English, but they all have excellent bone structure.

'Oh my God, Mrs Crawley . . . I can call you Adrienne can't I, now we've been through so much together? You look . . . *beyond* fabulous.' It's the party planner and the casting director, both of whom speak at once. They're shiny Chinese-Americans who could be lovers, it's hard to tell, and by this stage I'm past caring anyway. I wonder briefly if I should sneak into my bedroom and try Julian from there. No, I decide, too risky in too many ways. 'Where are the statues?' I ask, instead, remembering the man who got out of the taxi. 'I should check on them.'

'Ohmy*god*, you're going to *adore* them.'

They're leading me towards the service elevator and the building's fire escape. Behind a white curtain there are sounds of movement and conversation and the casting director disappears behind it, I'm imagining to check everyone's decent.

'*Voilà!*'

Standing in front of me is a group of Roman gods and goddesses, basically naked, wearing silver loin cloths and carrying lightning forks. In such a seething mass of physical perfection it's not easy to spot my man. Everyone has been dusted white, to look like marble, and a make-up artist is squatting patiently in the corner, adding a scarily realistic crack to someone's supposedly weathered torso.

'Hi,' I say.

'Hi.' There's a bubble of greeting and then everyone ignores me. The sensation is profoundly relaxing. For a while I stand there, just listening, but then Martha's tugging at my arm, asking me where I've been, Spencer wants to make the welcoming speech – so with a regretful look over my shoulder at the tantalizingly honed bodies behind me, I follow her, remembering to thank the casting director and the party planner as I leave them, making my way back through the kitchen towards the crowd.

'Where were you, sweetheart?'

Spencer puts a hand lovingly, authoritatively, on my shoulder. His eyes are narrow in his square, lined face and I know this is because I'm behind schedule, but I also know he won't provoke me, not tonight. I enjoy the sensation of having him in my power like this, because the success of this event depends on my compliance and he knows it. It takes two to play wedded bliss.

'I was checking on the statues,' I tell him.

He speaks gently to me, as though I might break. 'I just wanted to make sure you were ready for the speech.'

'Sure I'm ready.'

'Of course you are.'

He keeps his hands around my shoulder and leads me down a corridor, towards the hall. He's handling me carefully, like a delicate commodity. *Heroes* was made with the full co-operation of the defence department and as the Pentagon's chief fixer in Hollywood, Spencer's keen to be seen as a loving family man, respectable enough for politics. This is why we're celebrating our anniversary for the first time in six years, in front of a hand-picked audience.

He leads me into the room, towards a specially constructed podium. Since it's a good two feet off the ground and I'm wearing high heels, he lifts me from behind, right on to it. For a moment I stand there by myself, which is excruciating, but then he leaps up boyishly beside me. The room goes silent.

'Kings and queens,' Spencer begins. 'Ladies and gentlemen. *Friends.*'

Breathe calmly, Adrienne, hold your husband's hand, look happy – that's it. He waits for our guests to take us in and I look over them and see the statues climbing into position in the dining room. The decorative theme for dinner is ancient Rome, the food is imperial French.

The irony of being Josephine to Spencer's Napoleon hasn't occurred to me before now. Suddenly it makes me want to laugh. Only Spencer could choose two great lovers from history who got *divorced*.

'We've got you all here tonight,' Spencer's saying, 'to share a very special moment.' He puts a strong hand around my waist and draws me to him. For a nauseating second I think he's going to kiss me in front of everyone, but instead he stares lovingly into my eyes. 'Because tonight's the night of my tenth wedding anniversary to this incredible girl, who's about to make me the happiest guy on earth.' He pats my stomach as he says this, speaking in an intimate whisper which a mike hidden in his lapel broadcasts to the room. He sounds weirdly snakelike, amplified like this. People cheer, flashbulbs go off.

I'm placed at dinner between a three-star general, who's advising Spencer on technical aspects of *Heroes*, and Tom Buckley, the star of the show, who's been given a week's leave from the marines to do the publicity. Neither of these companions is my choice, though since I haven't invited anyone to this party except my mother, that's hardly surprising. I try to think of who I'd *like* to be talking to, but have difficulty in coming up with a single name.

'Great to see you again, Mrs Crawley,' says Tom, shyly.

Tom's actually quite sweet. At least, it's sweet that he has a crush on me, and he's less unbearable than the other guests at this party – mainly because he hasn't been important for as long as the rest of them.

'How are you finding things?' I ask him, as trumpeters signal the arrival of the first course.

'Well hey, you know, it's pretty wild,' he offers. Spencer picked Tom because he spoke, he said, like a cross between a frat jock and the public's idea of the perfect, gruff marine. The fact that he's the personification of the All American look and has a body to match didn't hurt his chances either. I smile at him, wondering what it's like for a farm boy from the Midwest, who only ever wanted to go into the marines like his dad, to be on the cover of next month's *Vanity Fair*. I'm tempted to ask him, directly, but in the end I don't because it might sound patronizing.

'Are all the girls throwing themselves at you?' I say instead, watching him blush. It's sweet that he still blushes.

'Well, hey . . .' He can't quite meet my eyes. 'The thing is, ma'am . . .'

'Call me Adrienne,' I tell him.

'Adrienne.' He swallows and I watch his Adam's apple bob up and down his strong, bronzed neck. 'Let's just say I'm looking forward to getting back to the line of duty.'

No one says 'line of doody' quite like Tom.

'Don't you find it distracting, trying to track down terrorists with TV cameras all around you?' It's the girl on the other side of Tom, an actress who slept with Spencer expressly for the chance to sit next to his new protégé tonight. She was briefly on *Beverly Hills 90210* and has done a few movies, none of them wildly successful. She's clearly been advised that what her career needs is a celebrity boyfriend, and Tom Buckley is the moment's celebrity-boyfriend-of-choice. He can't cheat on you because he's fighting a war. You can check up on his movements twenty-four hours a day, on line. What more could a girl want?

'You get used to them,' Tom says. 'And, hey, they're not really there all the time.'

'No way,' she drawls. 'But I thought the whole, like, *point* was that, like, this was reality TV.'

'It is,' Tom patiently explains. 'But there are times when what I'm doing is sensitive, so we film a lot of back-up footage. If I need to take a break, or run a mission or something, they just play the back-up tapes.'

'Oh my *God*, that's so *coool*.'

The general leans over, breathing right into my face. 'Shouldn't be tellin' the pretty lady the secrets of the trade, Tom.'

'Oh sir, I'm . . .'

'Your secret's safe with me,' whispers the girl, bringing a long scarlet fingernail to her bee-stung lips.

7

Julian

There were people coming for dinner. I suspect my mother thinks these weekends at home must be a little dull for me, since she usually makes a point of inviting some nice family from the village to make the numbers up. Or perhaps she's afraid that we, just us three, left alone without Maggie, will run out of conversation in some embarrassingly unavoidable way.

Tonight's social sacrifices were the Johnsons: Mr, Mrs and Miss.

'Goodness me, Julian, but it's been a long time,' said Mrs Johnson as she walked in. 'What is it? Five years, six?'

It might well have been longer than this; I thought how little wish I had to see her again as we all shook hands. Mary Johnson, now a corporate financier, and evidently also on an enforced weekend at home with her parents, smiled at me with dread and excused herself to take a mobile phone call. She's my age, possibly a few years older, but 'still single', as her mother confided in a hushed whisper as soon as she had left the room.

'Where do you go to meet nice girls, Julian?' asked Mrs Johnson as soon as she had a gin and tonic in her hand, leaving me a moment to consider the four or five embarrassingly short-lived romances I've had since Adrienne. 'Your father's been telling me you lead an extremely active social life.'

I looked over at my father, pouring drinks on the other side of the room, and thought he'd probably know more about where to meet women than I did. Something about the way Mrs Johnson was leaning towards me suggested she actually expected me to answer her question, but Mary's return provided a diversion.

'Something soft for me, please,' she said quietly when I offered her a drink.

'Oh, come *on*, Mary.' It was her father, a robust man in his mid sixties who swears he owes his constitution and enduring health to a bottle of gin a day. 'All this no-drinking, organic nonsense you young people dream up nowadays. Can't drink, can't smoke, won't touch a carrot that hasn't been offered a therapy session. You miss all the fun of life.'

Mary looked at me and raised her eyebrows slightly, as much as if to say, *Do yours treat you like this when you come home, too?* But even as I smiled in implicit acknowledgement, I thought that my parents never treated me with this kind of easy informality.

'Shall we eat?' asked my mother brightly.

When we were at the table, smiling politely at our poached salmon terrines, Mrs Johnson asked whether anyone had seen any interesting 'shows or what not' in London. As the only resident Londoners present, all eyes naturally turned to me and Mary, and I found myself repeating the lies I had told in the car.

The point of the exercise, as it had been earlier, was to demonstrate to my father that, far from being 'excruciatingly dull' I was, in fact, an individual radiant with social desirability who could hardly find a moment for himself or his work in the endless round of parties, exhibition openings and first nights that made up his life.

'Jake Hitchins is an old friend of Julian's, you know,' said my mother proudly, not long after I had begun. 'From school and university. Such a *nice* boy. He's even troubled to send him an invitation to his new show.'

This was news. Since when has Jake Hitchins been asking me to his openings?

'It arrived last week,' she went on. 'I knew you were coming down, so I didn't bother to send it on.'

'Shame about the art,' boomed Mr Johnson, ignoring both of us. 'My wife and daughter made me spend an hour in a gallery once looking at a lot of laminated dust and I decided I never needed to see another Hitchins show again, thank you very much.'

'Just because you think Victorian watercolours are the acme of civilized taste . . .' murmured Mary.

'Oh, come on,' interrupted her father. 'If other people want to pay good money to have dust – or garden furniture, for that matter – collected for them and dumped in their own homes, that's fine. But don't drag me off and expect me to gawp over it.'

It's precisely to avoid conversations like these that I usually pretend never to have met Jake.

'My father's a bit of a reactionary,' whispered Mary, disguising a smile. Her face, I realized, was strikingly formed, and if not attractive in the conventional sense, it was at least the kind of face you could talk to. She had a strong jaw, pale skin, freckles and auburn-tinted hair. For a moment I wondered what she'd look like naked, but the thought of the gossip her mother would generate if we ever did anything together stifled my nascent libido. 'He's so rude about art dealers, you wouldn't imagine,' she was saying.

And that's when I had my idea.

'Speaking of art dealers,' I began, 'I met a hilarious one this week, at a show at –' I searched for the name of a respectably trendy gallery – 'at the White Cube.' The table looked at me smiling, expectant. 'Not the most discreet man I've ever met, but then that's often the way in the contemporary art world, isn't it?' I managed to squeeze out a little chuckle as if at the memory.

'If art is life, then life is art and everything is performance,' said Mary, helpfully.

'His name was Alex Something,' I said pointedly.

If I had expected a high energy reaction, I didn't get one. My father didn't even blink, but sat methodically portioning the salmon on his plate and taking dainty bites, as though wary of fish bones.

'What was he saying, dear?' asked Mrs Johnson. 'Though of course I never understand the humour of the young.'

I smiled, as though remembering a private joke. 'I shouldn't be telling you, I suppose,' I began, 'but since you don't know any of the people concerned . . .'

'Tell us at *once*. You can't dangle London gossip before impressionable country folk and then refuse to divulge.'

'Well, he was telling me about a pretty awful situation he found himself in the other day, but he was being so damn funny about it.' I looked round the table to make sure I had my audience's attention. My father was still studying his plate with intense interest. 'You see, he'd just been meeting the curator of the Royal Academy and decided to have a bite to eat at a little place on St James's.'

Still my father sliced the salmon.

'You know the one I mean. Just off Piccadilly. Full of palm trees and ageing dandies.'

All three Johnsons nodded.

'He'd just sat down and ordered his food when he heard a voice that was pretty familiar to him talking at the table just behind. There are wooden partitions dividing the tables, so he couldn't see who was talking – and neither could the person talking see him. But he could hardly not have recognized the voice, since it was his wife's. Julia's. And would you believe it, she was with another man.'

'*No!*' exclaimed the Johnsons in unison.

'Yes,' I replied, getting into my stride now, even beginning to enjoy myself a little. 'And not only was she with another man, but she was calling him darling and listening to him drone on about his family and kids. They were obviously having some kind of illicit tête-à-tête.'

'So what did he do?' This was Mary, brown eyes wide and lips curling in anticipation of a smile.

'Well, he just sat there for a while, listening. Apparently they were having the most *excruciatingly* dull conversation. His wife and her lover. That's what really hurt. Alex said he wouldn't have minded if his wife had chosen to deceive him with someone interesting – or even just someone younger. But she was with the most horrifying old bore who seemed to think he was a Renaissance man just because he'd once been to a dress rehearsal at Covent Garden.'

I glanced round the table to check the progress of my anecdote. My father was still exhibiting a scrupulous interest in his poached salmon; my mother was looking at me and smiling, a little wanly I thought; and the Johnsons – *père*, *mère* and *fille* – were agog for more. I was thoroughly satisfied.

'So anyway,' I continued, 'he sat there for a bit until he couldn't bear it any longer. He just had to see what the chap she was with looked like, you know, because he was so soul-destroyingly uninteresting he hoped his wife was at least getting a certain physical pay-back from the whole sordid enterprise. Eventually he got up and went to the other side of the restaurant, as though he were going to the loo. He said the whole thing was ridiculous because he had to hide behind palm trees and what not, but of course he couldn't let his wife *know* he'd overheard her in the act of seducing a geriatric. He wouldn't have embarrassed her like that, he said.

'Finally he got to a spot where he could clearly see her table. Apparently the fella she was with was old enough to be her grandfather and –' I looked at my father's thinning blond hair – '*and* he dyed his hair some kind of ghastly straw colour. Poor Alex was laughing so much he had to be careful not to draw attention to himself. He said it was so undignified, having to compete with a maquillaged waxwork for his wife's affections.'

Mr Johnson was laughing heartily and took a large slurp of red wine which gurgled merrily down his throat. 'I don't know,' he chuckled. 'I rather think, good on the old codger. Chasing after a filly twenty years younger than him. Shows he's got *balls*, at least. What do you say, Henry?'

But my father had excused himself to go to the bathroom.

8

Jake

I'm sitting on the sofa, waiting for Hank's driver. It seems like the only sensible thing to do is panic-drink my way through the remainder of the bottle of vodka – which I do, hoping it will eliminate my anxiety. What Hank doesn't know, because I've refused to tell him, is that the sum total of my preparation for my new show consists of a black plastic bag full of smooth pieces of bone I bought from an abattoir a year ago, thinking they might come in handy.

I've told him I don't want to show him anything until all the pieces are made. He accepted that – which bought me some breathing space, but not much. The date of the show has been set for three months' time. The press machine has ground into action. The only problem is that the point of conceptual art is the 'concept', and I haven't been able to think anything through for at least two years.

Against my better judgement, I get up from the sofa and stumble towards my studio. It's at the back of the house, a state-of-the-art space with twenty-foot ceilings and a glass roof. I don't let Josefa in here, or anyone else. I don't come here myself that often anymore. The floor is honed ivory sandstone. You can see my footprints in the dust when I walk. Sparks fly round me as the motes catch the sunlight. In the corner is the only unsold work in my *Apocalypse* series. It's a piece of fake lawn, with two plastic deck chairs on it by a plastic table that holds a plastic cocktail glass with a plastic cherry in it. The ensemble has been torched and is eerily melted. The deck chairs have sunk in on themselves. People – smart, rich people – have paid six figure sums for stuff like this.

The emptiness of the room makes my heart rate rise. I feel resentful of Hank. Who asked him to take it upon himself to make me an artist? I never trained as one. I can't draw or paint or sculpt. I don't understand perspective. I hear him telling me that none of this matters anymore, that 'art' parted ways with 'skill' a long time ago. I see him as he was ten years ago. Leaner, enthusiastic, less sweaty. He didn't leave messages on my machine about black construction workers then. He didn't threaten and whine.

Maybe because he didn't have to. Making this stuff used to come naturally to me. It was a trip, being able to smash things up or burn them or slice them and then sell them. I never thought it was real, any of it. I never bought into it. It was nice not being poor anymore. I enjoyed the improved plumbing. I found that I didn't need to try very hard with other people, because no one ever takes offence if you're a celebrity. I didn't pretend to be a genius. I never asked to go down in history.

It's paralysing, having to think when you can't. For two years I've been working on a new show and all I've succeeded in doing is buying a bag of old bones. I try to remember the last time the voices were quiet enough to let me think. The problem is that the only thing that shuts them up is vodka, and when I've drunk enough to muffle them I can't really move.

I go back into the house. The light in the studio depresses me. I go into the kitchen and take another bottle of Absolut out of the freezer. I remember the journalist from French

Vogue, waiting for me in a restaurant. It occurs to me that I'm in no state for an interview. I open the bottle and pour some into one of the white china cups with the purple stripes. I take the cup back into the sitting room, then change my mind and go back for the bottle, too. I tell myself that I'm going to sit quietly and wait for Hank's driver but I know that, realistically, the chances of my leaving home today are slim to none.

Remembering my earlier mistake, I make sure to unplug the phone.

9

Adrienne

It's later. I'm on the dance floor with my husband and the band's playing our song, which is actually Spencer's song, something I hear him singing in the shower practically every morning. Cole Porter's 'You're the Tops', from *Anything Goes*. I imagine him looking at himself in the mirror, shaving maybe, singing it at the top of his lungs to his own reflection, but I can't think about Spencer too much right now because I'm seeing him too clearly. It's getting more and more difficult to pretend we're the couple the night demands us to be.

What would Maggie say? Or any of them? What would Maggie do if she discovered I was having the child of a man famous for producing 'big guns, tight buns' movies that glorify violence and conflict? How would she react to the fact that my husband has masterminded a reality TV show set in a war zone, a *variety* of war zones? As though war was about *entertainment*?

When the song is over I make my way into the corridor, where people are smoking and talking to each other about diet regimes and personal trainers. I hear one woman mention the word 'homeless' as I pass, but realize she's not talking about people but fashion houses since she's an important realtor who specializes in relocating high-profile companies. As I'm walking to my bedroom I see Lucy Farrington, this girl I knew at Oxford who always tells people we're 'old friends' and who I include in my parties as though we were.

'*Sweetness!*' she shrieks. 'How *are* you? Enjoying your special night?'

'Loving it,' I say, with what I hope sounds like fervour.

'A marriage made in heaven, lucky girl. And what are us singletons to do, now that people like you have snapped up all the most promising men?'

Being single is the main topic of Lucy's conversation, and she discusses it at length with any one of the thirty or so influential women who are her 'closest girlfriends'.

'Come on, darling, send some fab guy my way. Be a poppet, won't you?'

She's looking at me almost pleadingly, through large round eyes that used to, I'm sure, be brown, but which are now the electrifying blue of a coloured contact lens. She's wearing a vintage Edwardian dress, turned inside out so the seams show, by (I'm guessing) Alexander McQueen, and a small but dazzling tiara. Looking at her expectant face, I have an idea.

'Come with me,' I say, taking her hand. And when we've threaded our way back down the corridor and through the hordes on the dance floor and I've yelled Lucy's name above the music into his ear, I leave her with the general, wondering if an action so gratefully received can really be considered malicious. Then I'm in the corridor again, determined not to meet anyone else's eyes, and soon I'm in my bedroom, in the quiet of a space full of crisp Egyptian cotton. I know I'm about to start crying, so I lock the door and go into the bathroom and lock that door too, and then burst into tears.

Jake's letter is still in my lingerie drawer and I consider, briefly, taking it out and looking at it, but then wonder what that will achieve. I know what it says. Reading it again will only make me take longer to calm down and force me to consider accepting – which is something I've already decided I can't do. I can't go and I won't go, and that's fine. And final.

So I sit down on the edge of the bath, trying to get myself together, but the bathroom smells strongly of Spencer, specifically of Spencer's aftershave, and I know I can't stay here much longer. Really concentrating on composure, I go over to the basin and focus on the damage my tears have done to my eye-liner. Extensive but rectifiable. Otherwise I look how I always look, which other people describe as 'gorgeous', so ten minutes later I'm ready to face the world and I make sure to practise a smile or two before unlocking the bathroom door, then the bedroom one.

More and more people are arriving, the after-dinner crowd, and the corridor is jammed with glowing shoulders and jagged cheek bones and jewels. It takes me twenty minutes to make it back to the dining room, but by the time I've arrived I've told so many people I'm having a *great* time that I almost, weirdly, feel better. And then I see my statue. He's standing on a plinth by the door and has a body that makes Spencer's look like he's trying way too hard – which, essentially, he is. My statue's tall, with broad shoulders, a narrow waist, beautiful definition. He doesn't, unlike Spencer, look like he's had the balloons from a children's party inserted surgically in his upper arms and his nose is straight and a little big, but that's okay because he's tall and has . . . *presence*, I guess. He's standing totally still, earning every cent of his hundred bucks an hour, his little silver loin cloth tied tightly, teasingly, over his hips.

Looking at him, I wonder again if a brief affair might be what I need, a little sampling of the freedom Spencer takes as his natural right. It seems absurd that a woman of thirty-two, who might have had so many men, has only had two.

You're beautiful, I tell myself. Desirable. What's the point in being miserable at your own party?

Moving purposefully across the room, not quite sure what I have in mind but sure I'm going to do something, I head in the direction my statue's staring. As I walk through the crowd I'm accosted by more people, so it's a good ten minutes before I'm standing in the far corner, still not sure what I'm going to do but kind of excited. I see Lucy Farrington deep in conversation with the general at a table in the distance, and when she sees me and waves I wave back. She leans forward to whisper something in his ear and just when her head's too far back for him to see, mouths '*bliss*' at me. Unable to think of anything better to do, I give her a second wave and bare my teeth in what I hope is a photogenic smile.

Somewhere to my left a flash goes off and I congratulate myself on being alert.

When I'm finally standing in the corner the statue's looking at, I see he's not staring out of the window at all, at least not anymore. He's looking further down, as though at a person, and there's something so intense about his gaze and the rigidity of his body that I sense silent communication. All the hot ones are gay, I think sadly, looking to see if I can see who he's seeing. But there are too many people standing around me and the person, whoever he is, is sitting down, so I spend a moment looking at my statue instead, feasting my eyes on the best flesh money can buy.

Then I notice . . . *No.*

There's an unmistakable bulge in the tight silver loin cloth.

Trying to act as though I haven't seen anything I risk another glance, including him for safety's sake in a long sweeping panoramic of the room. It's as though I'm looking for somebody, and when Lucy Farrington waves again I wave back again, hoping she won't notice how ragged my smile is this time. Tom Buckley's been cornered by the actress, who's leaning towards him, whispering something into his ear.

There is definitely something going on in that loin cloth.

Even as I look, the bulge bulges and gradually the whole outline of his, well his *dick*, becomes clearly visible for anyone to see. And although he carries on standing still there's the faintest trace of this incredibly sexy fuck-me smile around his lips and I'm suddenly obsessed with finding out who he's staring at, so I clock the direction he's looking again and make my way boldly through the crowd.

This time I move more quickly, trying not to catch anyone's eye. I'm not far now, scanning the tables filled with flowers and small groups of expensively dressed people getting slowly drunk and raucous. I'm getting closer all the time, I know it, and my statue's erection's getting ever more ridiculously visible. Now he's smiling quite obviously, this big sexy grin of chalked lips and white teeth.

Suddenly I know, just *know*, he's staring at someone sitting at the table in front of me. I move to the side, smiling ferociously and making my way through another group of people, another round of scrupulously hygienic, non-contact kisses. And then I find the table I'm after, the table my statue's staring at, and it's totally empty, except for . . . my mother, who's staring at the statue, my statue, and – I move around the table to get a better look at her face – licking her lips. My sixty-year-old mother who dyes her pussy is making *my* statue get a *boner* just by licking her lips.

This is too much.

No more breathing calmly for me. No more *nothing*.

I think of Jake's letter in my lingerie drawer. With a total

clarity I'm not used to, I see that I don't need to speak to Julian
– or Spencer, or Momma.

Jake asked me, and I'm going.

10

Jake

'We had to break the fuckin' door down, Jake. You were so out of it you didn't hear the bell or the phone.'

Hank's sitting on the end of my bed. My head's exploding.

'You could have died,' he says gruffly, smoothing down the bedclothes.

'So?'

'Don't get smart with me, you little Britfuck. You're lucky to be here.' Opening my eyes a crack, I try to work out where 'here' is. It seems to be a small white room with a single bed and a basin and a chair and a vase of daisies on the window sill. There's an anxiety in Hank's expression which I'm used to, but a sympathy that scares me. He's talking about the show, telling me to take my time, that most of the work's already done. He's saying I should put my energies into my recovery.

From somewhere a half-forgotten line comes back to me. Something Julian used to listen to at school. A song.

'The show must go on,' I say.

When Hank's gone I meet my counsellor, John. The first thing he tells me is that he's a recovering alcoholic – as though that should immediately make me feel better. He's also a recovering crack addict and so is presumably even more fucked-up than me. From the first I can tell I'm going to dislike him intensely. He has a shock of throbbing ginger hair which casts a weird fluorescent light over the room. He's looking at me calmly, like he's seen it all before. When he speaks it's with a totally classless accent, which is the one thing that makes him easy to be around. He doesn't remind me of Benedict Chieveley.

'No napping now,' he's saying briskly. 'It's time for group.'

'Sex?'

'*Therapy*,' he replies firmly, leading me out into the corridor.

Then I'm in a big airy room full of sunlight and daisies and a lot of fucked-up posh people. Everyone is very pale and well-dressed apart from me. Some of the girls are actually quite attractive. I wonder if fraternization is against the rules.

'This is Jake, everybody,' says John.

'Hi, Jake,' they chorus.

John suggests everyone help themselves to coffee before we begin. I find myself standing in line for the big tin Thermos with the kind of girl Julian used to go for before he met Adrienne. She's tall, with dyed blonde hair cut in a bob. She's obviously got money and she's wearing a small string of pearls over a pink Ralph Lauren shirt and jeans.

'Hi,' she says to me, putting out her hand. 'I'm Camilla. Camilla Boardman.'

'Hello Camilla Boardman,' I say. 'Jake Hitchins.'

'What an atrocious place to meet a man,' she says, grinning.

'Oh I don't know, it'd make a good story if we married and had kids.'

She looks at me like she's half forgotten what flirting's like. 'My counsellor told me I couldn't look after a pot plant last week, so it'll be a while before I get round to babies, darling.' She smells sweet and expensive. Not usually my type, but who can afford to be picky in rehab?

'What's your tipple of choice?' I ask.

'Oh, please. *Too* boring. It's like arriving at university and being asked what A-Levels you did. I've only been here a week and already the conversation's driving me crazy. Can't you guess?'

I look at her, appraisingly. 'English, French and History of Art?'

'Very funny.' She smiles. 'Have another go.'

'Cocaine?'

'Spot on, baby. I'm the life and soul of the party, me. At least I used to be. Nowadays the biggest party on the social horizon is group therapy, which isn't quite what I'm used to, shall we say?'

We reach the Thermos and I pour out two Polystyrene cups of cheap instant coffee.

'When you remember how much this place costs,' whispers Camilla in my ear, 'you'd think they'd supply us with vaguely decent hot drinks, wouldn't you? Is a properly ground coffee bean *too* much to ask?'

As the days pass it becomes clear to me that Camilla's the only person it's even vaguely worth talking to in here. After 'group' we often walk through the excessively landscaped gardens of this asylum for rich people. I like her because she's so uncomplicatedly herself. She really doesn't give a shit and I appreciate that. I find it admirable. She's also never heard of me, which is a relief. She likes the arts though, at least she says she does. And she always wears freshly ironed shirts, which remind me of something. Something good and permanent.

She knows Benedict Chieveley, of course. Everyone who talks and dresses like Camilla knows Benedict Chieveley. That's the way posh England works. They took Scottish dancing lessons together as children. I'm guessing they snogged at a Christmas party when they were sixteen or something, but she hasn't confirmed that. She has her dignity, which is another thing I appreciate about her.

I find myself telling her things on our walks. Not to 'own up to my problem' or any bullshit like that. Just to pass the time. To give some shape to the blurred contours of the days which morph tracelessly into one another here.

'Was he really such a bastard, darling?' she asked when I first told her what Chieveley did.

'Is this a refuge for fucked-up members of the moneyed classes?'

'I had no idea. He seemed so sweet when we were, let me see, fourteen. I suppose people *are* sweet at that age.'

'People like him are sweet to people like you, whatever their age. It's people like me they have a problem with.'

'I suppose so,' she said, lowering her eyes.

I haven't had a drink since before leaving my house. According to my day count I've been sober for seventeen days, but that figure doesn't have much meaning for me. Hank was whispering this morning about my getting better in 'no time at all', but I don't trust his prognosis. There's something weird about Hank lately. He's stopped being his queeny aggressive self and become something much . . . *sicklier*. He calls me up all the time and never swears now. Maybe he's having a nervous breakdown. Maybe he should be in here.

He keeps on telling me to stop worrying about the show and 'acknowledge my condition' – which is just where he misses the point.

I'm not your average junkie-in-denial. I chose to become an alcoholic. It was a rational weighing of alternatives. On balance I decided that being sober all the time was too painful to consider as a lifestyle choice. So I use alcohol as an emotional analgesic. If it makes me pass out occasionally, so what? So what even if it kills me? It only saves me the trouble of doing the job myself.

I spend some days in my room, in bed. I try not think of my empty, dusty studio. I find myself thinking about it obsessively. I imagine Hank hounding me for work I haven't yet made. He may be playing good cop now, but there's no guarantee that'll last. Sometimes I close my eyes and pretend to sleep. Sometimes Maggie seems close to me. She flits through my day-dreams, calming the voices. If I close my eyes and concentrate, I can see her face. It's not always easy to tell what she's thinking. I try putting her in the places we knew together, but this only generates fragments of her. Her fingers curling, rolling a joint. The corner of her mouth, downturned, as she reads a book. Once I see her eyes as they were that last night, bright with anger.

I wonder what Maggie would think of this place. What she'd make of John. I think she'd feel more sympathy for him than I do. There's something fragile in his cheeriness which she'd warm to. I think she'd laugh at the institutional furniture and approve of the daisies. Is she glad I'm here? Probably.

I wonder if she'd be surprised that Camilla Boardman knows Benedict Chieveley. Probably not. I wonder where Benedict Chieveley is now, what he's doing. I wonder if he's heard of me, seen my work in the Tate Modern. Wouldn't admit it if he had, the bastard.

I love the fact that he met his match in Maggie.

Lying in that white, bare room full of daisies, I have the first idea I've had in nearly two years. It takes me by surprise.

I hear Maggie laughing. Would she find it touching? What would Julian and Adrienne say? It would be entertaining, at least, to see the look on Chieveley's face. To have him know it was us.

For the first time in weeks I feel strangely uplifted.

Then

I

Jake

Picture the scene. It's an overcast afternoon in Fareham in 1978. The rain has stained the concrete playground a dull black. Someone's scratched *Israelis out of Lebanon* on the slide, which is too wet to play on. The swings are rusting on their cables. The merry-go-round still works but it's the bigger kids who get to sit there, not me. In dry weather they squat on it, talking and smoking. Going slowly round and round. Stumbling off occasionally to vomit if they've been drinking. On a day like this one it's empty. Hinges rusting in the rain. Paint peeling. On the bus shelter flaps a damp poster for *Midnight Express*.

I'm eight years old.

What this means is that I'm even skinnier than I was later. Stick insect thin, with snappable legs and an arm that someone did snap. In a fight on the stairwell of the housing estate. Not that we live on the estate, mind. We have our own house, with its own lawn, own terracotta figurine in the back garden. Everything.

My arm's in a cast, pristine and white. Recently set and inviting attention. I'm walking home, trying to keep out of people's way. My mum says that's the best way to stay out of trouble. Don't make eye contact and learn to run. Good advice in certain circumstances, but not if you're walking towards a group of gigantic fifteen-year-olds, smoking under the bus shelter.

Don't look at them, don't look at them.

I don't. Which means I don't see when one of them starts following me. I don't catch him looking back over his shoulder at his friends, winking and smiling. I don't see him until his arm's round my neck and my head's pushing into his stomach. No time to run now. No way to escape.

I let myself be led back to the bus shelter. Someone puts a cigarette in my mouth. 'If 'e can smoke that,' she says, 'we'll let 'im go.' She's a big, tall girl with breasts already. Round, podgy face. Evil eyes. 'If you start crying, you're gonna get it,' she tells me. Smiling. Friendly, even.

I try to inhale. It's like filling your lungs over an erupting volcano.

'Have anuvva go,' the girl suggests helpfully. Menacingly.

I try again but know even before it's in my mouth that it's no use. My eyes have started to stream. I can feel my lip trembling. I'm eight, remember. An eight-year-old doing what eight-year-olds do: crying.

'Fuckin' ponce,' someone says. Sneeringly. There's laughter and then I'm being held again. From behind. Lifted off the ground. Put on someone's shoulders. A thick-set fifteen-year-old enjoying his new-found strength. More laughter. From the corner of my eye I can see the girl rummaging in a tatty leather handbag. A cast-off from her mum, or else found in the bin of one of the posher mock Tudor houses on Veryan Lane. Then she's waving a black marker like a talisman. I'm being put down, held down. Someone's sitting on my chest. Someone else on my face. I can hardly breathe but know the less I say or do the easier it will be.

I'm scared they're going to hurt my arm again, scared because once was enough, thank you very much. Soft fingers are pulling at my fingers. Holding them down. I try not to struggle, try not to wonder, from under an unknown bottom, what's going on – or what's going to go on. There's the scratch of marker on plaster. Several scratches. More laughter. Then there's light. No one's sitting on me anymore. I'm lying on the ground, in the wet.

'Just piss off, won't you?' the girl says.

2

Adrienne

My maiden name's Finch, as in those Finches – the banking dynasty, the record alimony payment, the sex scandal. Maybe you read the *Vanity Fair* piece on Momma, announcing her divorce? It wasn't one of her finer moments, but the cuttings still turn up from time to time – they even (almost) made a movie about us, *Finch vs. Finch*, but Spencer managed to get it killed in development.

Momma still blames me, secretly, for the break-up of her marriage, even though she's the one who spilled the beans to a magazine. She used to tell me all the time when I was a kid that if I'd just come along earlier, everything would've worked out fine – as though her infertility's my problem. That's typical Momma for you.

My parents spent five years trying to conceive me, about the same amount of time they stayed married after I was born. Jerry told me the first time Poppa held me in his arms he knew he had to get out – out of his marriage, I mean. I guess I was living proof he could have his cake and eat it, and there wasn't much point in dealing with Momma anymore, though he didn't have the balls to tell her so for a few years.

I used to blame him for that before I knew better. Now I admire him for putting up with her for so *long*.

One of Momma's other gripes is how long she had to push before I came out. She loves to tell people she wouldn't have an epidural in case it was, you know, bad for me or something. So the fact she endured eighteen hours of agony to bring me into the world is again my fault, like I should have clawed my way out of her uterus or something. You can't win with someone like Momma, and that's something you've got to get used to if you're related to her.

The truth is, she's hung up about where she comes from – not that she'd ever admit it. She's learned the Park Avenue Princess role pretty well but she'll never feel really secure in it, so she needs to *dazzle* everyone all the time. Almost to show them why Poppa would've married her, to explain why he would've bothered turning a Midwest college student, studying catering at Iowa State, into a Manhattan celebrity.

Poppa used to say it was because Momma looked a lot like Bette Midler when she was younger.

She was a cook when she met my dad, paying for her travels around Europe by getting employment on people's boats. As she told it to *Town and Country* magazine at the time, the whole thing was pretty romantic. My dad was cruising with the Rothschilds down the Amalfi coast and she happened to land the job of *sous-chef* in the boat's galley, and he saw her dishing up vegetables the first night, and she saw him and . . . they fell in love. That's the magazine version, anyway, and there's no getting the real story out of her now. Momma likes the refuge of a good anecdote.

When I was a kid the *Town and Country* spread was framed and hung on the wall of a guest bathroom in our house in the Hamptons, as if to remind anyone spending the night how lucky they were to know us. Momma was always very careful to tell the story first, to make a big joke of it. She was always going, you know, 'Oh, Tom picked me out of nowhere!' and when she was drunk she used to say Poppa had plucked her from the gutter, the Rothschilds' gutter. It was like she wanted to be the first person to mention it and laugh at herself before anyone else could.

Momma's always said that there's nothing about you other people won't forgive if you're beautiful *as well as* rich. Just being rich isn't enough, and beauty on its own without wealth to display and augment it is nothing – so she's spent her life making sure she's got ample supplies of alimony to fund the necessary surgery, and Society has welcomed her with open arms.

The problem with my parents' marriage wasn't really me, though. The problem was that by the time one of my father's sperm had fussed its way through the resistant wall of my mother's egg, all they had in common was an obsessive interest in other men.

3

Jake

It's only when I'm round the corner, out of sight, that I see it. Someone's written *Cunt* on my arm. And underneath someone else has added *Faggot*, with a few erect phalluses thrown in for good measure.

First I try to get the plaster off, but it feels like my arm's breaking again. It's too hard for me in any case, too solid and strong. But I've got to do something. I can't go home like this. My mum'd never let me go to the playground again, I know that. It's starting to rain heavily. I'm getting soaked through. The only advantage? You can't tell my tears from the rain water.

So I'm walking in the rain, wondering what to do. Should I run away? Should I try to break the cast off? How'm I ever going to get dry again? Or warm?

There's only one person who might help me. Simon. He's my friend from down the street. His family's also got a house, but it's not as nice as ours. It doesn't have a terracotta figurine or a garage. But it's a house, which is why my mum lets me go and play there. She doesn't like it when I go onto the estate. She thinks the kids there're too rough. I told her I broke my arm falling off a swing in the park.

On the way to Simon's, I pick up little stones along the street. By the time I get there my pocket's full of them, so I climb over the side fence and into the alley that runs down one side of his house. From here I've got a clear view of Simon's window, and if I calm down and concentrate I should be able to throw the stones at it with reasonable accuracy until he hears me.

Let him be in his room. Please let him.

He opens his window. A shinny down the drainpipe later, and he's standing beside me. Simon's the kind of kid who's good at shinnying down drainpipes.

'Fuck,' he says, as his feet touch the ground. He's only eight, but he talks like a grown-up. He's small and wiry, like me – but tougher, more fearless. 'At least they didn't break it again,' he adds, helpfully. And then: 'Come with me.'

This is why I like Simon. For his ability to cut to the quick of every situation. To know what to do and how to do it.

He takes me to his dad's tool shed at the back of the garden. There's a stove in here and it's warm and dry. Simon's dad needs somewhere to get away from Simon's mum and this is it. The shed's full of little drawers and scraps of news-paper. Simon's dad is passionate about the horses and the walls are covered with tips on racing and form. He's also keen on DIY, so the drawers are full of wire, picture hooks, nails, string. Pens.

'We need a magic marker the same as the one they used,' says Simon, quietly efficient as always. 'Help me look.'

He starts at one end of the shed and I start at the other. Rummaging through boxes and drawers full of strange smells and weird, rusty things. Because I don't want to be a wimp, when I prick myself on a nail and cry out, I pretend I haven't. Simon's not fooled, though. He's staring intently at the blood, impressed despite himself. The nail went in deep and the wound's bleeding freely. 'Here,' he says, passing me a scrap of paper. 'Wipe it up. Wrap this round it and see if the bleeding stops.' Simon has an eight-year-old's professional interest in other people's pain.

The paper's small and rectangular and I don't know how much good it's going to do. But I haven't got anything better so I hold it against the prick left by the nail. Red oozes through it, discolouring a word I don't know. *Ain*-something. I suck my finger a bit and the bleeding stops. I put the paper in my pocket, to throw away later.

My mum's surprised to see I've decorated my cast to make it look like a zebra, but she accepts the explanation when I give it. Once Simon and I had found a marker and coloured over the words *Cunt* and *Faggot*, not to mention the drawn-on penises, we decided it would look suspicious unless we made the splodges part of a larger decorative scheme. The zebra motif was, predictably, his idea, and my mum does what she does with all Simon's ideas – she buys it.

'Go'n watch some telly with your father,' she tells me, 'and I'll bring your tea in. But you'd best get out of those clothes first. And have a bath.'

I'm in the bath when the doorbell goes, bringing the news that will change my life. I'm lying in five inches of tepid water, trying to keep the plaster dry and wash with the other arm.

4

Julian

I should say at once that I don't know the full story of what happened to Maggie, not strictly speaking. I know what happened in the end, of course; I heard Adrienne's breathless account on the clammy morning that followed. What I mean is that I don't know exactly why it happened, exactly why Maggie thought it would be clever, or funny.

Jake was with her; he's the only one of us who knows what she said, what she was thinking. I can, however, take a shrewd guess; and if asked to, I'd tell you this: that my sister died laughing, exultant.

Maggie's problem was that of any fundamentalist. The world, for her, was divided into black and white, good and evil. In addition to this she had a complicating fetish for the weak, an addiction to the righting of perceived wrongs. You can't understand how redundant the words 'interest' and even 'passion' are in describing what it was she felt for any creature not strong enough to defend itself. Maggie was 'interested' in sixteenth-century literature; she was 'passionate' about Beethoven and Leonard Cohen; but she was fetishistic only about those who lacked justice, and the means to its distribution.

Many children experience something similar, perhaps a twinge of what animated Maggie; it's a phase they go through. Maggie's was no twinge or phase. Hers weren't the transitory fits of tears with which kids express their dawning distaste for the world, or seek to avoid the awful truth – which must one day be acknowledged or ignored – that all around there is evil and pain and sickness and cruelty and nothing to be done about it.

You know about the kids who start crying when they see a run-over dog and kick up a fuss unless they're allowed to bury it themselves, in their own back garden, with their own hands? Maggie had no patience with such dilettante altruism. She wasn't one of those cradle-born egoists whose sympathy for others is but a cloak for their own deep concern with a pain they feel for themselves and which, though eased occasionally, will not go away: the pain, heavy on inexperienced shoulders, that is the price of consciousness.

Maggie had an obsession – a deep, unfaltering urge which proved unsusceptible to the shallower arguments of practicality and reason. You can see it in the photographs of her as a toddler, in the fierceness with which she clings to the teddy bears and fat, plastic cubes which surround her in her playpen. Even at two and a half, Maggie is sovereign of all she surveys; she sits forward, stridently assertive, clutching a stuffed squirrel called Jazbo – though perhaps 'clutching' is not quite the right word. Maggie, I suppose, is *cradling* her toy, but with a firmness that chimes with the light in her eyes.

In the background, a sunlit lawn and apple trees; in the foreground, the plastic bars which mark the limit of this toddler-queen's dominions. In the centre of it all, Maggie herself: a tubby, jolly baby with dimpled knees and rosy cheeks and flashing curls of a glittering near-black that spark red and brown and gold in the sunshine.

From the moment she could crawl, Maggie dominated our childhood games – though it was I, as the older one, to whom the role of leader should have fallen, if you believe what the psychologists tell you. I, who could walk and talk and count (and count in French) at least eighteen months before she could, nevertheless played second fiddle, right from the start.

Why? Because I wanted to, because Maggie made me want to. That was the thing about her, the quality that stopped her from being infuriating.

She was enchanting.

She had a way of taking the lead and making people love her for it; and our parents, so reserved and formal with me, were helpless in the face of her ardent warmth. She delighted in making me laugh in inappropriate situations – at family drinks parties, in church during the sermon – and she could always keep a straight face, which made my descent into giggles all but inevitable.

As she grew older she was quick to puncture pomposity and to mimic it: the self-satisfied strut of one of our father's stockbroking friends or my godfather's habit of pronouncing his Rs as Ws. 'Be wespectful,' she'd whisper in my ear as he arrived for lunch, leaving me unable to meet his eyes and dreading the first time he declared that something or someone was 'widiculous'.

5

Jake

Fifteen minutes later I'm in my pyjamas and walking down the stairs. Simon's dad is in the sitting room talking to my dad. Screaming, really. In a state of 'some alarm', as Julian would put it.

(Not that Julian's ever been to Fareham. Not that he's ever even thought of Fareham – except vaguely, maybe, as the Place Jake Comes From. He couldn't, for example, spot it for you on a map, the posh bastard.)

Simon's dad is Italian, a Neapolitan. Mr Quintavalle. His English is excitable and uncertain and now, more than ever, incomprehensible. He seems the odd one out of the trio, since Simon and his mum are both English. So English. But I like Mr Quintavalle. He sometimes lets me and Simon into his smoke-drenched shed to play with the nails and bits of string and torn newspaper cuttings we find there.

I stand on the stairs, listening. It's impossible to tell if he's crazed with rage or sorrow. He's in the grip of something I haven't experienced. Something stronger than my fears and desires. I feel for a moment the child's strong yearning for adulthood, but I'm also a little afraid of it. Afraid of what grown-upness can do to people. Of what grown-upness is doing to Mr Quintavalle.

I hear my own dad's soothing voice, the tone he uses

sometimes when Mum gets in one of her moods. A gentle, reassuring sound.

In the kitchen, Mum's dishing up fish fingers and peas with lashings of ketchup. My favourite. Done really crisp, just how I like them. I soon forget about Simon's dad. I'm happily prepared to go on with my dinner, looking out over the tidy back garden. When my dad comes in to read me my bedtime story I remember to ask what's wrong with Mr Quintavalle. He ruffles my head and smiles at me. 'Hear him go off on one, did you Jakey?' I nod. 'Well, it's grown-ups' business, at least for now. You'll find out about it soon enough.'

'Soon enough' comes sooner than my dad intended, about half an hour after I've switched off my light. My parents are still up. I can hear them creaking around downstairs. Talking urgently. Moving between rooms. Once I hear my dad laughing, my mum telling him to stop, but with laughter in her voice, too. As though a great big joke's taking place. A great big joke in the grown-up world which only grown-ups can understand.

A pebble hits my window. First one, then two. It's Simon, standing in the alley. Face white, voice hoarse and trembling. He's never come round to my house this late. I wonder if Mr Quintavalle's sick or something. Is he going to die? If not, what's all this about? I signal to Simon to climb up the drain pipe and soon he's beside me on the sill, panting. He's been running.

'Fuckinell!' is what he says. He's got big news, but it takes him a moment to catch his breath. 'I know all this,' he tells me when he's calmer, 'because I heard me mum havin' a go at me dad last week when she found the slip in his pocket. Fuckin' furious, she was. Said he was a drunken wop, couldn't be trusted with money, wastin' it on the friggin' horses.'

'What's a wop?'

'Never mind what a wop is. The thing is, he's totally freakin' out.'

'About what?'

Simon looks at me, pityingly. 'About the bettin' slip, bollock brain.' Simon enjoys the look of confusion on my face. 'You ever heard of the Grand National?'

'Yeah.'

'Well, they raced it this afternoon up at Aintree, didn't they?'

'So?'

'So, me dad put a twenty quid treble on three races.'

'What's a twenty quid treble?'

'It's a kind of bet. He put twenty quid on May Mornin' to win the 3.10, Lightnin' Dance to win the Grand National, and Rosalie to win the 4.20.'

'Yeah . . . So?'

'*So*, dipshit, the reason me mum called him a drunken wop is that the odds on May Mornin' were sixteen to one. Right?'

'Right.'

'Only thing is, May Mornin' won.'

'Cool.'

'Better than cool,' says Simon. 'Because when May Mornin' won, me dad made three-twenty on top of his twenty-quid stake, which makes . . .'

'Three hundred and forty quid? Fuck.' I have a go at this new word, wanting to show how impressed I am. To make so much money for doing nothing seems pretty impressive to me. What's Mr Quintavalle so upset about?

'That's not the half of it,' says Simon mysteriously. He's enjoying himself now, because he likes being knowledgeable. 'A treble covers three races, right? So me dad doesn't get the three-forty straight off. It gets put as a bet on Lightnin' Dance, to win the Grand National. And Lightnin' Dance's odds are twenty-five to one. So when he wins, Dad makes . . .'

But I'm not bad at maths myself. 'Eight thousand five hundred plus three-forty – that's eight thousand, eight hundred and forty quid!' The sum is the largest I have considered in my short life.

'That's right,' whispers Simon. 'And . . .'

'And that money gets put on, what was the other horse's name?' I'm getting the hang of this now.

'Rosalie, to win the 4.20. And you know what the odds on Rosalie were?'

'What?'

Simon waits, choosing his moment carefully.

'Come on.'

'All right then.' He pauses, impressively, before saying: 'Odds on Rosalie were ten to one, right? Which means . . .'

It takes a moment to compute the enormity of this. When the moment's passed, we both know what Simon's going to say next – only neither of us can believe it. The figure hangs in the air between us, like rumbling thunder. We can barely imagine it, let alone say it out loud.

I find my tongue first.

'So your dad's . . . Your dad's . . .'

'My dad's won exactly ninety-seven thousand, two hundred and forty quid, to be precise my dear Watson,' intones Simon proudly, giggling at the same time. He's been reading *The Hound of the Baskervilles*, as instructed by his mother the English teacher.

'So what's he freakin' out about?'

'He's lost the ticket,' says Simon simply. And then, from nowhere, the fatal news: 'You've got it.'

6

Adrienne

My parents' divorce was fairly amicable – at least on the surface, at least to begin with. They needed time to explore being themselves, Momma told me vaguely one afternoon by the pool. Poppa didn't even attempt an explanation, but took me out to lunch more often than usual for a few months.

Since I wasn't the only five-year-old girl I knew with divorced parents, things didn't seem too unusual. In fact, I didn't even think about it that much – not until, a year or two later, Momma told *Vanity Fair* my dad was a fag. Photographed by Helmut Newton just after she'd had her tits done for the second time, in a Halston dress practically cut to the waist, she told everyone everything – the cosmetic surgery, the yearning for pregnancy, the debilitating discovery of her husband's sexuality.

You want to know what I think? I think Momma was pissed off. She'd have preferred to lose my father to another woman – to anyone, pretty much, but a balding Englishman in his early sixties with a developing paunch and a serious brain. Jerry's very existence invalidates my mother's devoted hours of gym time.

She was the one who got custody of me (wanting it marginally more than Poppa did, I guess) and she set about defiantly creating a magazine-perfect scene of domestic bliss, as if to show him what he was missing. She liked the trappings of motherhood, I think, the posing opportunities, the shopping trips and birthday parties. It was never quite clear whether or not she liked me.

The person I was closest to, growing up, was Jerry. He was the first adult ever to behave consistently as though I was worth spending time with, as though I had opinions of my own that might deserve attention.

As Momma's still fond of pointing out, he isn't a handsome man. He isn't very tall and he eats such greasy food Poppa's always worrying about his cholesterol. He's older than Poppa too, but is still going strong despite the bacon rolls and aversion to personal trainers. That's the English for you.

Jerry sort of shambles around the place, always in the same old clothes, always looking at the world with a kind of merry cynicism. He used to be a don at Oxford, an historian at St Botolph's in fact – ages ago, in what he refers to as 'my previous life'. That's how he got me in there, even though I'd missed the official application date. He'd thought for a long time that emergency measures were required to get me away from my mother, but he only said so once, on an autumn afternoon when I was seventeen.

7

Jake

Thank God for Simon. He's always up for a challenge. Especially one that's going to net him a cool ninety-seven thousand,
two hundred and forty quid. The answer to our problem's
simple. We have to find the betting slip and return it (covered
in my blood) to Mr Quintavalle, without him noticing any
thing. Easy, right? Except that the slip's in the pocket of my
trousers, which are currently downstairs in the laundry basket.
If they get washed, so will it. If my mother checks the pockets,
she'll find it.

'We've got to go down and get it,' says Simon simply, as
soon as I've explained things. And then, as if I didn't know
this already: 'Before she puts it in the machine.'

He's willing to risk it, but honour compels me. He doesn't
know the geography of our house. The squeaky boards on the
stairs, the creak of the airing cupboard door. I know these
things. I have to be the intrepid one. So Simon gets into my
bed and puts a pillow over his head, in case my parents check
on me, and I open my bedroom door and creep to the top of
the stairs. Mum and Dad're still in the kitchen, still talking.
Their voices are less urgent now. More matter-of-fact. I hear
them discuss who's going to do the shopping and hear Mum
tell Dad something about Mrs O'Donnell, who lives up the
road. She's been complaining about the noise from the playground again. That woman.

The conversation carries on as I walk down the stairs. Taking my time. Armed only with my own wits, which I do my best to keep about me, heart pounding. The boards only creak twice, which isn't bad going. I can tell Simon they never squeaked at all, because already this has become a story, something to be told and boasted of. An adventure like the ones I read about obsessively in Hardy Boy books. A tale sold in paperback with a lurid drawing of a fifteen-year-old boy holding a torch on the cover. Except that fifteen-year-old boy is *me*, and I am eight.

I feel fifteen at least by the time I'm downstairs.

The airing cupboard, where the laundry's kept, is between me and the kitchen, down a long narrow passage from which there's no retreat. Thrilling with self-pride I creep towards it. The passage is dark, so I have to feel my way – but I know where I'm going, what I'm doing. Every inch of this house is my territory. Familiar as the back of my hand.

This is why I don't expect the unexpected, which takes the form of a large terracotta pot, left in the middle of the passage to be carried outside. A large terracotta pot which makes a dull, resonating *thud* when I stub my toe on it, which in turn makes the kitchen voices stop. There's a grating of chairs and I see my dad's shadow through the frosted glass of the kitchen door. It's a split-second choice between retreat and advance. Only the thought of Simon makes me carry on. The airing cupboard's the only place to hide in.

The door's just shut, closing me in damp wetness, when I hear my dad in the corridor.

'Nothing here,' he says at last. 'False alarm.'

Dad mustn't open the airing cupboard. Dad mustn't open the airing cupboard. Dad doesn't.

'I'm ready for bed.' It's my mum, she sounds sleepy. 'I'll just put the washing in before I come up.'

'Not now, Bev. Makes such a ruddy noise on its spin cycle. Can't you leave it till the morning?'

There's a moment's hesitation – but Dad sounds weary and so does Mum. 'Okay,' she says. 'But you put it in tomorrow before your shift starts.'

'Deal.'

Five minutes of anxious searching later, I'm back in my room with Simon. The ticket, stiff with dried blood, is on the carpet between us.

'Maybe we could rinse it,' says Simon cheerfully.

Except, as we discover, you can't rinse blood. Soon the ticket's on the carpet again, still red. Now moist and fragile.

'Fuck,' we both say together.

8

Julian

When the autumn came and traps were set for mice, it was the six-year-old Maggie who got up in the middle of the night and went into the cold kitchen to set the springs and liberate the cheese – which she left by the trap, in the middle of the floor, confident that it would be gone by the next morning. It was a solemn duty, this deactivation of mouse traps; as she used to whisper fiercely, late at night, creeping into my bed for warmth, humans had quite enough to share, and how could anyone tempt another creature to its death with food? It seemed a wicked trick, worse by far than anything dreamed up by the mysterious Taxman our father was so fond of complaining about.

So every night that traps were set, Maggie didn't go to sleep – in case she didn't wake until morning. And every night that traps were set I'd hear her, once my parents were safely in bed, creeping down the stairs and into the kitchen; and then, in the stillness of the house, the sharp *click* of the coiled springs as, one by one, she set them off. Later, when she was seven or eight and more used to her own powers, I (aged nine) would be co-opted into these midnight skirmishes with evil; and, though older, I would follow her instructions meekly, a little anxious at the possibility of being discovered, or of losing a finger – eventualities which never seemed to enter Maggie's head, so fervent was her concentration on the task.

My father used to say he had no idea how the mice did it, that we must have an unusually brainy sub-species in residence, the Einsteins of the mouse world; and Maggie and I would wink at each other in complicity against the cruelties of adults, before setting ourselves the task of finding and removing the bright green pellets of poison which my father laid when the traps, time after time, were found empty in the morning.

One night, however, when traps lay strewn over the kitchen floor, Maggie did go to sleep. Perhaps my parents stayed up later than usual, or perhaps they made less than their usual noise in coming up the stairs to bed. I don't know because I, lying in wait for the anticipated clicks, heard them clearly enough, if more gradually than usual – though I pretended not to have done when Maggie woke me before dawn, tugging at my sleeve, tears in her eyes.

'Come look, come look,' she whispered urgently.

It was 4 a.m. and the dark night was turning murky, its blackness dissolving into a swirling grey, shot with pink. The house was freezing and we crept through it in our pyjamas. Maggie was crying, but holding back the tears, as though in my presence (though I was the one who could count in French) she needed to put a brave face on things.

'Look, Ju,' was all she said, as she pushed open the door to the kitchen and surveyed the devastation before us.

Of six or seven traps, all had sprung, and every one of them contained the stiff brown body of a field mouse, collared in blood. Unable to do anything but stare, we stood there dumb, uncertain of how best to cope with this massacre.

'My fault,' said Maggie quietly. 'My fault for going to sleep.' And with that simple phrase she left the room and I heard her run, heedless of noise, up the stairs and into her bedroom, from where the first sounds of sobbing were soon audible from behind her angrily barricaded door. I was left standing in the middle of the kitchen in my dressing-gown, surrounded by bodies, and there was nothing for it but to go back to bed, hoping my sister's explosive cries wouldn't wake our parents.

Maggie's sobs that morning were not, though I did not know this then, simple outpourings of pity and sorrow, though she felt both. Their source was more complex than mere sympathy; and they, themselves, were richer and rawer, more rasping and enduring, than the cries I felt obliged to produce in chorus. Try though I might, I could find nothing as sincere within me as whatever it was that drew from my sister the wails that came from her room. And perhaps because I could sense the comparative feebleness of my own feelings, I gave in to the tempest brewing above, accepted it and did my best to emulate it, trying all the while not to feel outshone by the fierce little creature who was already, as she would always be, the centre of everyone's attention.

Maggie possessed none of our mother's graceful ability to ignore unpleasant truths, to undo what has happened by pretending it away. She couldn't let go of things, couldn't wean herself from the need to change all that is essentially unchangeable about human life: the dominion of the strong over the weak, the large over the small, the old over the young. And accordingly – though I only tested this years later – she was insulated in her passion from the calmest, most carefully constructed arguments.

She was also, or rather, she could also be – how should I put this? – a stubborn little bitch.

9

Jake

Then Mr Quintavalle comes up with his Idea, and does it for my future. The next evening he invites the whole street round. Everyone goes because no one can resist an Event. His lounge is full of people drinking coffee, eating sandwiches made with anxious care by Simon's mum.

Mr Quintavalle has a plan. He wants to make someone rich.

Not that he tells the whole street everything. Only Mr and Mrs Quintavalle, me and Simon and my mum and dad know what's really going on. When everyone has stopped catching up, Mr Quintavalle tells them a few things. He's lost a betting slip. He must've dropped it somewhere between his house and the bookies'. It looks like this. For a moment my heart stops, then he produces another ticket. Just like the one currently drying out under my mattress, only not red.

He's being calm and considered. He speaks slowly, showing hardly any emotion. Except, as Simon whispers in my ear, for his right eyebrow twitching the whole time. Which means that something Big is happening inside Mr Quintavalle, only he doesn't want to let on to other grown-ups.

'And, ah . . . ah . . .' he says. 'For the person first to find it, and give it to me back, I pay ten per cent of the winnings.'

It's a simple idea, a good one. But it sets in motion a sequence of events far beyond Mr Quintavalle's reach.

Simon's generous. 'I told you to take it,' he reminds me

gravely. 'It wasn't your idea. You didn't steal nuffin'. You should get the prize.'

We've started calling it a prize, because the whole thing has become a thrilling treasure hunt. With one important difference – which is that we, *we*, know where the X marking the spot should be. Us and no one else. Under my mattress. Nine thousand, seven hundred and twenty-four quid, waiting to be claimed. Tucked between the bed frame and the undersheet.

How could I have refused Simon's offer?

Or his advice? Which was to soak the ticket once more. In a puddle. And then bring it home in triumph. Which is exactly what I did, the very next afternoon, when excitement in the street was at fever pitch and spreading onto the estate. I took the ticket outside in my pocket and found a muddy puddle and this time it emerged more brown than red. I took it back to Chiltern Walk, holding it delicately.

When Mrs Quintavalle opened the door her face went white and she reached for the knocker to steady herself. Before saying: 'Lorenzo.' Weakly, quietly. Unable to believe the evidence of her own eyes. This miracle bestowed on her by God, through the agency of this skinny boy with a plaster-cast covered in thick black lines of magic marker.

10

Adrienne

I'd spent the morning shopping with Momma, acting out a little ritual that always began in the same way – she'd look me over at breakfast, taking in every detail of my badly chosen outfit, and say, 'Oh my . . . *God*,' stretching the sentence till it snapped. Then she'd suggest a 'mother–daughter day', which meant her leading me from store to store, undressing and discussing me in front of frighteningly elegant sales assistants who treated me like I wasn't there – because the person paying was Momma, and she never let anyone forget it.

I was standing in the private room of the lingerie department at Barney's, with Momma and her favourite sales assistant, trying on bras. I don't know if you've ever been an unconfident seventeen-year-old semi-anorexic with fried eggs for breasts, but I have and I can tell you that showing lingerie off in public just isn't fun.

'Miss Finch, are you okay?'

The voluptuous bitch of a sales assistant could see I wasn't okay – partly because the bra I was trying on was ridiculous, just so much white lace drooping off my chest like it was hung up to dry.

'I'm fine,' I told her.

'Is something wrong with the stock?'

I looked at myself in the mirror and at Momma standing behind me.

'Nothing's wrong with the stock.' I tried to smile as I said this – but I knew that if I touched another piece of lace I'd start screaming, so I moved over to where my clothes were hanging and picked up my jeans. I watched in the mirror as Momma nodded at the sales assistant, who scooped up a pile of bras and left the room.

'Now, sweetie . . .' she said, coming over to me and curling her fingers over my shoulder. 'You can't go blaming your breasts on the sales staff.'

Things got very bad after that. Momma said I was an ungrateful little *bitch* who'd turn out a deviant no-hoper just like her father if I didn't learn some manners. I said *she* was the bitch and told her I wasn't going to be her dress-up doll anymore. I don't know where the words came from, or what effect they had once I'd said them, but I had the first taste of the way Maggie would later make me feel in that carpeted little cubicle.

'Since you're so good with sales people, why don't you see if you can get a refund for *me*?' I screamed, bursting out of there and into a small crowd of shoppers and assistants who'd taken time out of their day to listen to us. As I ran through them I heard the whispers start – 'Oh my God, that's Adrienne Finch. Really? *Those* Finches?' – and I didn't stop running until I was in the street.

A tearful phone call and half an hour later, I was sitting opposite Jerry in a booth at his local diner, looking into his pale blue eyes and trying not to think about what was going to happen to me when I got home.

'You should start thinking about an English university,' he interrupted, before I was even half way through telling him what had happened. 'I rather thought it might come to this, eventually. You should start this coming Michaelmas too, if possible.' He smiled at me, kindly, patting his pockets. 'Now where on earth is my diary? There are some numbers that might come in useful.'

I'd missed the application date for Oxford by about nine months and hadn't gone to a single interview or anything, but Jerry proved that in England, as elsewhere, it's not what you know, but whom. Since I knew Jerry and Jerry himself had been a don, which is what they call college professors over there, I guess they took his personal recommendation seriously and I got a letter accepting me to study English Literature, under Professor Macklethwaite of St Botolph's College, about a month after that lunch.

'They've only just started taking girls at St Botolph's,' Jerry told me when the letter arrived, 'which means that one of the last bastions of single-sex tertiary education has fallen. A cause of mourning to some, but of celebration to you, eh?'

And he raised his glass of sherry and suggested we both drink to my future.

II

Jake

Old man Quintavalle was as good as his word – prompting my granny to remark that there was at least *one* Catholic you could trust. After a triumphant walk to the betting shop to register his win, he sat down and wrote me a cheque. In front of all the street, he sat right there on the couch in his lounge and wrote me a cheque – or rather, he wrote my dad a cheque. All he asked of us was not to cash it till his prize money came through, which made my mum laugh and say it was the least we could do.

You might have read something about it in the papers at the time. Just the kind of heart-warming story people like.

My dad wasn't too sure about accepting the money. 'Jakey only found the thing in a puddle,' I heard him saying to my mum in the kitchen, after I had gone to bed on The Night Mr Quintavalle Wrote The Cheque. 'And Lorenzo's a friend of ours . . .'

'Which is exactly why we can take it, Barry,' my mum said fiercely. She had something new in her voice. Something determined. I tried to think of how she'd look. My easy-going mum, usually so mild and warm, sounding like a knife.

'The deal's fair and square,' she said. 'Lorenzo's already written the cheque, for God's sake. It's almost ten *grand* Jakey's won. You know what that is?'

'It's a lot of money,' said my dad.

'It's an *education*, Barry. D'you honestly want Jakey going to the local comp and ending up a builder like his father? Taking drugs with those rough kids on the estate? D'you honestly *want* that for him? You know he's bright, you know how far he could go with the right education. This money's his. He earned it. We've no right to take it away from him, now the cheque's been written and everything. It's his future, that money.'

And so my future it became.

My therapist, the fiery ginger John, asked me this morning if there's 'schizophrenia in my family'. He says it's important for a therapist to know as much about his patients as possible. Meaning: *he* wants to know as much about *me* as possible. As if a recovering crack addict could offer meaningful advice to an alcoholic-by-choice if only he knew his 'family history'. Well I don't have a family history. As I explained to him, 'witheringly', my equivalent of what Benedict Chieveley calls ancestors didn't see many doctors. They died as they lived: uninvestigated.

'Only the rich get fancy diagnoses, because only the rich own words,' I told him, surprised to find that I meant what I said.

Without knowing it, Mr Quintavalle gave me words. Or at least a visitor's card to the institutions that control them. He didn't tell me what else I'd need besides the card. He couldn't have done. He didn't know. Neither did my parents.

Neither did I, until it was too late.

Fast forward five years to a cold, dark afternoon in early September. I'm wearing, for the first time, a set of entirely new clothes, with emphasis on entirely new shoes. We – Mum, Dad and me – are in the Ford Cortina, freshly cleaned and gleaming for the occasion. The car looked flash in Fareham, definitely upwardly mobile. Here it looks flash too, but less desirably so. Just like music becomes suddenly cringeworthy if you listen to it with the wrong person, so something happens to the car as we turn on to a long gravel drive. It becomes shameful.

When I realize the Cortina's the only new thing in sight, it dawns on me (on all of us, perhaps) that it's the worst kind of recently-old new. It's been cleaned to *look* new, which immediately makes it stand out here. Here nothing's new, or meant to look new. The place has a calm permanence I'm not used to. My house, the drainpipe Simon used to climb up, the playground full of rusty swings and graffiti, all this seemed permanent enough – or used to. Now, however, immediately, shimmeringly, even as my dad stops the car, these landmarks from my past begin to dissolve. How can they hold a candle to the permanence of these buildings which represent my future?

We're in the gravelled courtyard of Botesdale (pronounced 'Bushel') College. All around are pillars and cobblestones, coated in the hush of centuries of quiet study and wealth. A *lot* of wealth. The kind it takes centuries of niggardliness and penny-pinching to accumulate. Qualities that declare themselves in the scuffed lino of the entrance hall. In the ugly strips of fluorescent light that sear their ways across panelled ceilings, gloating painted crests.

'Wow,' says my dad, feelingly. 'If you wouldn't call this place posh, I don't know what you would.'

We're in a world of cold large rooms and scuffed lino and cantilevered vowels. We're at a New Boys' tea party where my mother's careful hair and fashionable trousers scream inadequacy. Where my father's freshly pressed brown suit provokes . . . attention. Certain politely raised eyebrows, expertly hidden. Fanning out from him to the furthest corners of the room. Giving me a taste, my first, of Things To Come.

People are standing in groups. Tidy women wearing pearls and fond expressions. Slouching men in old suits, but good ones, and smart shoes worn so often they've become comfortable. Not like my shoes, which are chafing the back of both heels and squeaking on the parquet as I move. With each smiling couple stands a boy, in a suit slightly newer than his father's but just as good, wearing shoes as smart as mine but far more comfortable. The children in the room are the only guests who seem anything less than perfectly at ease – but even now it's clear to me how well-drilled they are, how experienced they've become at hiding weakness, at brushing awkwardness away, pretending anxiety out of existence. Because although one thirteen-year-old boy can smell fear on another at a hundred yards, there's nothing obvious about the nerves of these half-adults. They stand straight, they shake hands, they smile enthusiastically, occasionally brushing a strand of long, clean hair from a frequently tested eye.

Everyone seems to know each other. At least the grown-ups do, and there are cries of recognition and welcome.

'I *remember* Charlie's performance in the Summerfield's Father–Son match. So you'll be after a place in the Eleven, will you, old chap?'

'Jeremy starting already? It seems like only yesterday I was getting sloshed at his christening.'

'On my first day there wasn't anything as lush as New Boys' tea. Just the standard bog wash, then off to bed . . .'

When my parents speak, they speak differently from these people. They speak differently from themselves, too. They've lost the quality children prize above all others in their makers:

a sense of self-ease. In Fareham, in the Quintavalles' lounge, my mother sounds different from the woman standing next to me now. She moves differently too, more straightforwardly. Here her voice is higher and she's less keen to use it. Dad stands next to her, smiling loudly, saying nothing.

12

Julian

The chickens were my father's idea, to begin with.

At some point in the mid- to late-seventies, when even the English middle classes eating poached eggs round Hampshire breakfast tables spoke with dread of war with Russia and the consequent nuclear fallout, of the dangers of our increasingly decadent dependence on others, he had an idea. This wasn't the kind of experience that happened to my father every day, or the kind of experience, once undergone, that he was easily capable of forgetting. It sprang from a friend's passing remark about the benefits of self-sufficiency. We had land, after all, though not, admittedly, very much: two or three acres, with enough room for a horse or two and an orchard of apple trees. But we had land, and land can be cultivated and made to bring forth of its goodness the bounty of the earth. Not so?

His first attempt was vegetables. With an industry and enthusiasm quite alien to his usual, measured energy, he sowed lettuce, French beans and courgette in the spring; tomatoes in the summer; and he would, he confidently assured us, have planted leeks, turnips, swedes and Brussels sprouts in the autumn, if the first crop of the aforementioned hadn't emerged from the earth, shrivelled and disease-ridden, and damped the flames of his ardour.

Undeterred, he decided to move to a whole new level of home cultivation: livestock. We would have eggs; and since the idea of eggs leads, inevitably, to the idea of hens, he appeared one day with two fat specimens under his arms, squawking and wriggling and shedding feathers.

Maggie was ecstatic.

Hens, my father said, were less dependent on the season than vegetables; and besides, they added to the back garden a hint of farmyard delights, did they not? Our hens would lay enough eggs to feed the whole village in time of crisis; and in the meantime their clucking and scuffling and strange, jerky gait made them into a kind of neighbourhood attraction for the local children – who, though country dwellers, had been scrupulously fed on packaged food all their lives and had seldom, consequently, had the opportunity of inspecting a real, live hen before.

We built them a coop of gracious proportions in a corner of what was now called the 'kitchen garden'. Maggie personally supervised the installation of the wire fencing, and for a week the hens lived there in joy and ease and obligingly began to lay large, whiteish eggs, like globes. We called them Boadicea and Mathilda, and spent much time anxiously discussing their well-being and ministering to their wants.

One morning, however, two rather terrible deaths took place. I was woken early, at six or seven, by a commotion in the kitchen garden: a confused cacophony of squawking hens and barking dogs and the sound of Maggie's voice, raised high in fury. Leaping out of bed, I saw a fluttering of feathers from the window and a flash of pale gold: our neighbour's Labrador, Poppy, whose gentle compassion Maggie was wont to praise to the skies.

Hurriedly fastening my dressing-gown and putting on my slippers, I ran down the stairs and out of the back door, to find Maggie in tears. In her arms was Boadicea, still clucking, but missing large patches of feathers. Of Mathilda, the other guardian against cholesterol shortage in the village's diet, there was no trace, save a few bloody drops which led to the hedge. From a distance came the sound of loud and joyful barks.

'I'll get Poppy,' I assured my sister, already well-drilled in the exacting of retribution. 'I can't believe she—'

'It wasn't *Poppy*,' screamed Maggie. 'Poppy wouldn't hurt a fly. You know that. How—'

'So who was it?' I asked, anxious to divert this torrent, adding quietly the corrective 'Or rather, what was it?' since I was, after all, a twelve-year-old schoolboy and quite familiar with my interrogative pronouns.

'It was a fox,' said Maggie shortly, as though this should have been obvious to me. 'I heard poor Mathilda squawking and ran outside and saw him, dragging her off through the hedge. I've sent Poppy to get him back.'

Her face was flushed; her breaths were quick and sharp. I looked at her awkwardly, thinking that though my little sister might have a certain way with people, it really was ridiculous of her to think she could order animals about – at which point Poppy appeared at the hole in the hedge. Clamped and twitching in her mouth was a young fox with a mouthful of feathers.

'Good dog,' said Maggie approvingly, picking up the shovel that leant against the wall of the hen coop as Poppy laid the fox at her feet. I thought she intended to find and bury Mathilda and prepared myself to join in the solemn celebration; but Maggie wasn't yet in mourning. Sensing his last opportunity, the fox lay still for a moment before springing to life, intending presumably to make a dash for it – though Maggie was too swift for him. Like an angel meting out heavenly justice, she brought the shovel down on his neck in a sharp blow that ended in a crunch, and the fox moved no more.

'*There*,' she said, with tearful satisfaction.

13

Jake

'Ah, Jake. Good to see you again.'

A man in his forties is striding towards us, rudely healthy, with a round face and full cheeks and triumphantly age-defying black curls. I've met him once before in a brief and terrifying interview and I know that his palm when he shakes my hand (which he does vigorously, enthusiastically) will be damp. So it is.

'Good to see you again.' He looks at me penetratingly, with a twinkle in his eyes that may be kindness or amusement and is probably both. He's my new housemaster and parental stand-in and his name is Joshua Palmer-Jones.

'And Mrs Hitchins. How lovely you look this afternoon.'

Mum blushes. Dad doesn't know what to say. In Fareham you don't tell someone's wife she looks 'lovely', whatever the time of day. In Fareham you don't put your hands on someone's wife's shoulders, as my new housemaster is doing, and kiss her firmly on both cheeks. My mum doesn't know where to look or what to do. So, since she can't avoid the kisses, she tries to offer a hug in return, but just as she's putting her arms round his neck, Mr Palmer-Jones withdraws. My mum's left lurching awkwardly over him and before she can correct herself, my dad has said (louder than he's said anything else): 'Careful, Beverley.'

It's not exactly that there's silence after this. People

carry on talking and Mr Palmer-Jones covers things up as best he can. But nothing escapes the radar sensitivities of a thirteen-year-old and I've noticed the smile of a boy standing a few feet from my dad. It's a delighted smile, a surprised smile.

Something, something which can't be spoken of now, is indescribably amusing.

'I hear your mother's name is *Beverley*.'

It's later. Mum and Dad have gone. The Ford Cortina no longer litters the gravel. I'm in a long, low room lined with steel-framed, severely blanketed beds. The air's electric with the desperate generosity of thirteen-year-olds out to make friends. Tuck boxes are being opened, chocolate spread exclaimed over. A sticky copy of *Playboy*, culled from an older brother's collection, is doing the rounds, being ogled over nervously. Anxiously.

'I *hear*,' says the voice again, speaking slowly, clearly, with emphasis, 'that your mother's name is *Beverley*.'

The person speaking is a slender, dapper fourteen-year-old in the year above.

'Er . . . yes,' I say.

'Does she use the full name? Or does she prefer some kind of diminutive?'

His voice glints like glass in wintry light. I've never encountered the word 'diminutive' before, but it sounds expensive, an appropriate accessory.

'Er . . . yes,' I say again.

'Are you capable of saying anything other than "Oh yes"?'

'Er . . .' But I know I've been tripped up. 'Yes.'

He smiles at me, but coldly. He's a cut-out from a 1930s magazine, with quietly glowing cheeks and a high forehead. He's taller than me, and broader, but not thick set.

'Oi!' someone yells from across the room. 'Check out the tits on this one.'

The boy looks at me again, appraisingly. His eyes take in my new suit and new shoes and narrow a fraction. My shoes abruptly go the way of the Ford Cortina. There's suddenly no conceivable reason for a self-respecting person to be seen dead in them. They're black and shiny slip-on loafers with leather tassels. A little tight.

'Like the shoes,' the boy says.

His eyes remind me of the eyes of the girl at the bus stop in Fareham, the one who told me to shut up and smoke a cigarette. They're full of amused anticipation and accepted authority.

Then he says: 'Give my regards to *Bev*,' and walks away.

14

Adrienne

How do you think Momma's likely to react to my father's boyfriend's suggestion of my going to his old college? I mean, we're talking Oxford, *England* here – it's a long way from Iowa.

That's pretty much my analysis, too, so you'll understand why I don't tell her anything until the day before I leave.

She's in bed, lying stretched across the middle of the mattress with her hands falling loosely at her sides, having a migraine and wearing a peach silk negligée – not a good sign. The sounds of a daytime talk show drift through a seventeenth-century Flemish tapestry hanging between the windows, which conceals the widescreen TV and VCR equipment.

'Momma?'

'Sweetie?'

What do I say? You only need to flick through a certain back issue of *Vanity Fair* to see that Momma has a real talent for fucking things up for other people. She's not a predictable person – even when you've known her all your life, there's no saying what she might do in a rage one day and laugh about the next.

Watching her in all this peach silk I have a vision of her calling the authorities at St Botolph's and, you know, telling them I've got a criminal record or something, or I'm psychotic.

That would be just Momma's style, and in a year or two she'd be talking about whatever it was, telling it like it was some hilarious anecdote.

So I say: 'Nothing, Momma. Just wanted to check you were okay,' and she gives me a limp wave and murmurs that I'm a very special little girl.

A few hours later, I try again. I mean, it's not like I can just leave the apartment at nine o'clock tomorrow morning without saying goodbye – or can I?

'Momma?'

She's still on her bed, eye mask cast aside this time, staring straight at the ceiling through wide unflinching eyes.

'Momma?'

She gives no indication of hearing me, but slowly, gracefully, brings her hand to her face and covers her eyes. She sighs.

I wait.

'I feel like death,' she says.

I just wanted to let you know, Mom. I'm going to college tomorrow, in England. The words ring out in my head and my blood sugar levels nosedive, so when I open my mouth to speak all I say is: 'Can I get you something?'

'A revolver and a bottle of vodka,' says Momma.

It gets to the point where if I don't tell her in the next fifteen minutes that I'm planning to move to the other side of the world, I'm going to be forced to deal with the guilt of her worrying about where and why I've disappeared, not to mention the possibility of her contacting the authorities and the media once I've been gone a couple of days.

We're sitting in the kitchen of her new apartment, sipping the two cups of boiling water flavoured with lemon slices which Amelia, Momma's maid, has just handed us. A Lincoln town car's waiting outside to take me to JFK and I'm trying to figure out the best way to tell Momma this.

'I'm going to England today, Momma,' I say quietly.

'Did you hear Lulu Mellon's having her tits done again?'

'On the daytime flight, which leaves in about three hours.'

'This must be at least the third or fourth time. It says so right here, look.' She waves this morning's Page Six at me. 'Amelia! Could I get some more melon, please?'

'And I won't be back till Christmas.'

'How many breasts can a woman want? Can't she make up her mind? The second pair were lovely, just gorgeous . . .'

'*Momma!*'

'What, Adrienne?'

'Momma, I need to—'

'Interrupting was one of your father's most irritating habits.' She looks up at me, kind of vacantly, from behind perfectly made-up eyes – but I've just walked out of the room.

'Come right back in here this *instant*, young lady!'

But I just go into my bedroom and get my bag and start walking out of the apartment.

She catches up with me as I'm waiting for the elevator.

'I tried telling you earlier, Momma.'

'Tried telling me just *what* exactly, earlier?'

'I'm going away.'

'*Away?*'

'I'm going to England. To college. I tried telling you earlier.' The mahogany doors of the elevator slide open and I step through them, wheeling my case behind me. Totally unable to believe I'm actually doing this, I press the Close Door button. 'Bye,' I say, firmly.

'Just one little minute, princess.' Momma slams a polished

fingernail on the button on her side and the doors leap open again.

'My car's waiting. I've gotta go. We can talk from England.'

'From *England*? What in God's name are you *talking* about, Adrienne?'

'I . . . I tried telling you earlier, Momma. I'm going away to college. To Oxford.' She just stares at me. 'Which is, you know, in England.'

'You're going nowhere of the sort, young lady.'

'Yes I am, Momma.'

She looks at me through freakily narrowed eyes. 'Your father put you up to this, didn't he?'

'No.'

'How're you going to *pay* for it if he didn't?'

But of course Poppa was paying for everything. He'd even bought my ticket. What could I say? 'I tried telling you earlier.'

'Don't *give* me this bullshit, Adrienne.'

'Momma, I . . .'

'It was that butt pirate, Jerry. Wasn't it?'

'I . . . No, Momma, it was . . . *my* idea.'

Slowly, almost ostentatiously, Momma takes her finger off the button. 'You've never had an idea of your own in your life,' she says emphatically as the doors begin to close. She's standing in front of me, cool as a glacier, and she doesn't try to stop me again. It's bizarre, you know – I'd expected her to freak out and when she doesn't I find it scarier than if she had done.

15

Jake

The chatter of holidays and prep. schools carries on around me. Politely unraised eyebrows when my turn comes.

'So Fareham Primary's in . . . ?'

'Fareham.'

'Oh yes.' Pause. 'Don't think we played you at anything, did we?'

'No.'

The where-were-you-befores. The who-do-you-knows. Sizing each other up. Wondering who's to be leader, who led. Endless social computations, purring through air electric with ambition. The fourteen-year-old boy, who seems to be in a position of authority, is still on the other side of the dormitory. He's taller than the others around him, saying something about one of the women in the magazine which makes everyone laugh. The nervous, high-pitched cackle of ingratiating adolescents.

Unexpectedly, he looks up and his eyes meet mine. He leaves the group of thirteen-year-olds, which gradually disintegrates, and moves slowly towards me again.

This time he smiles more warmly.

'Settling in all right?'

'Yes, thanks.' I'm so pleased with myself for not stammering this time, I grin inanely from ear to ear.

'I'm here to help you new boys settle in, so if you've got any problems, I'm the one you should come to.'

'Okay.'

'You seem like a decent bunch, your year.'

He looks round at the room, full of undressing boys, and smiles. Perhaps he's forgotten my mother's name. I make a mental note to look up 'diminutive' in the dictionary before going to bed, just in case he asks again tomorrow.

'Lights out is at 9.30. I don't mind terribly if you stay up longer, just make sure Parmesan doesn't catch you out of the dorm.'

'"Parmesan"?'

'Sloshed Parmesan. Otherwise known as Josh Palmer-Jones, depending on how pissed he was when he introduced himself to you.'

'Right.'

'I bet he gave your mum a big smacker, didn't he?'

I nod hopefully, remembering the awkward tussle in the house dining room. I want to share a joke with this older boy. I want to be included in his laughter. Our eyes meet and two sharp blue discs shred me like paper as he takes me in – head to toe. 'He always does that,' he tells me, 'with your type of parent.'

More silence.

Then, abruptly: 'What's your name, anyway?'

'Jake.'

'Not your Christian name.' He sighs briskly, bored by my innocence. 'You won't be called by your Christian name by anyone here except close friends in your year. Older boys like me will always use your surname, and you must use ours unless we ask you to call us by our first names. That's how things work.'

'Er . . . right.'

He looks at me steadily. 'So?'

Like the Ford Cortina and my dad's suit and my mum's Christian name and my shoes, 'Hitchins' becomes instantaneously unmentionable. How have I got to the age of thirteen without realizing this before? How come the unrepeatability of my own surname has never occurred to me? Everyone here's got names like 'Devereaux' and 'Knox-Cartwright'. No one here's called 'Hitchins'.

'It's not a trick question, you know'.

I can't think of anything to say. Nothing seems suitable. The longer I delay the less I feel able to tell the truth. For a moment I think nostalgically how comparatively simple it was at home, having my arm broken in the stairwell of the council estate. At least you knew what you were in for, at home. At least you knew you had a pretty good chance of getting away. Here nothing's certain, and one more false step might have explosive consequences.

In this moment of weakness, behind the glossy head facing me, someone throws a book into the air for someone else to catch. It moves slowly because time has come to a near standstill. I can hear the blood thudding against my chafed heels. I haven't read the book but I saw it once serialized on telly. The programme was full of people like the grown-ups downstairs, moving easily around places like this. A name leaps out at me.

'Mulcaster,' I say.

'Glad we got *that* over with. Well, how d'you do, Mulcaster?' A firm hand is stretched out, to be taken by mine. And then the ominous-innocuous words I haven't yet learned to dread: 'My name's Chieveley.'

16

Julian

God, what a long time ago all this seems. It's not easy to remember your pre-pubescent self; nor is it particularly gratifying. I was quite short for my age and not very good at games (though better, at least, than Jake). I was clever, but not, as it transpired, exceptionally so; certainly I was not as clever as I had seemed to the masters of my prep. school. I was an unassuming, slightly plump, fair little boy with – and this was my cross – a voice of pure, unbroken treble, which belligerently refused to break.

If you've ever been a boy approaching adolescence, you might remember what it's like: the nightly scrutiny of your body, the silent hoping and praying. It's a time of furtive dreaming and fervent masturbation and all you've got to get you through it is a blind faith in the transforming powers of Mother Nature.

'Do you know any grown-up men with unbroken voices?' my mother asked the summer before I went to Botesdale, after finding me in my room with a suspiciously red nose and wet eyes. 'It's inevitable, darling. It happens to everyone, without exception. It'll happen to you, too, I promise. Trust me.'

Trust me, trust me. I tried to trust, I was willing to trust; but no matter how much I trusted, or whom, my voice refused to break. My complexion remained stubbornly unblemished as, with secret envy, I watched my classmates squeeze the first proud spots of nascent puberty. Day after day I stood in front of the bathroom mirror, anxiously scanning for signs of greasy redness: to no avail. While the boys in my form grew silent and awkward and took to having conversations that stopped, abruptly, as I approached, I remained unnervingly pre-pubescent.

At prep. school the tardy state of my physical development was bearable; there were others, too, whose hands remained in proportion to their bodies and who could still reach a high C with tear-inducing ease. It was obviously not terribly *desirable* to be excluded from the showers which, by tacit consent, were given over to the boys whose groins already sprouted luxuriant evidence of prompt virility; but it wasn't socially unthinkable, either. At prep. school, where pre-pubescence is the accepted norm, I didn't stand out sufficiently to have my inner, private anxiety exacerbated by public ridicule.

Botesdale, I knew, would be different, and this was where the challenge lay. If only my hormones would use the summer holidays profitably, exploiting those endless weeks of sun and freedom to break my voice and conjure up a few spots, then all would be well. It didn't seem very much to ask.

I tried gargling with vinegar and going in the afternoons to a far-flung field, to sing and sing until I was hoarse. A rumour had done the rounds of panic-stricken twelve-year-olds at school that a voice could be *forced* to break: if you sang high enough for long enough, you might just catalyse the inevitable.

I took careful control of my diet, too. Popular wisdom had it that chicken skin contains female hormones, which delay the onset of appropriate development. Oestrogen became a spectre in my inner life: a vague and shadowy presence, which might drag me at any time, kicking and screaming, to some dark region beyond the liberating reach of testosterone. I ate red meat diligently, gorging myself on steak and chops and rejecting any but the most manly of vegetables.

Needless to say, I ended the summer exactly as I had begun it: still short for my age, still spot free, my voice still capable of an effortless soaring which frustrated me to the depths of my soul.

The night before I went away to Botesdale I was in my bedroom, gargling with vinegar and trying to sing at the same time. It seemed self-evident that two methods, combined, were more likely to succeed than one; and although, as I warbled, inevitable sips of neat vinegar slipped down my throat, I felt this sincerely to be a price worth paying.

I was concentrating so hard on the task in hand that I didn't notice my father's knock – or see him as he entered the room and eyed me quizzically from the doorway. It was only when he coughed that I became aware of his presence, and then with a jolt that made me swallow half a mouthful of vinegar, which in its turn set me coughing and spluttering and retching.

With characteristic circumspection, my father said nothing; he just watched and waited until I had rinsed my mouth out and dried my face and turned towards him.

'I've got something for you,' he said, simply. 'Something my father gave me the night before I started school. You should probably have it now.'

He was holding a small parcel in his hand, the size and shape of a thick book. 'Think of it as a survival manual,' he said, placing it on the edge of the bed and straightening the eiderdown. 'You'll find that the most useful passages have been underlined for you. Feel free to add any markings of your own.'

17

Jake

Why, why, why, why, why, why, *why*?

Time has abruptly accelerated, from a slow crawl to twice its usual speed. Why did I tell such a stupid lie? How did I ever think I'd get away with it? As Chieveley moves away from me, languidly telling everyone to get to bed, I know with bowel-clenching certainty he'll find me out.

He leaves the room and flicks the light. Everything's dark and silent, but only for a moment. Soon there's more noise than before and soon after this boys are leaving their beds and then pillows are whooping through the air. I can't move. I can't speak. I'm what Simon would call well and truly *fucked* and I know it. I can taste the knowledge of how fucked I am. It has a bitter, acrid quality, like smouldering electric wires.

All I don't know is exactly how long I've got.

The answer turns out to be eight and a half days, because that's how long I manage to keep out of Chieveley's way. My luck runs out at a quarter past eleven on the morning of the ninth. I'm walking back to the house after a Latin lesson (which I've learned, by now, to call 'sesh', because that's what lessons are called here) when, from nowhere, Chieveley taps my shoulder.

'I'll be coaching you through your Tits' Test, Mulcaster,' he says quietly. 'Meet me outside the house at four o'clock.'

By four o'clock nausea's gnawing deep in my belly.

I've heard about the Tits' Test – Botesdale's answer to the Spanish Inquisition. I know I've got to learn the lore of this place, its traditions. I wish I didn't have to have them explained to me by Chieveley, in the company of people who know my real name. In fact, I've seriously considered running away to avoid facing this gauntlet, this incitement to fate to Make Something Happen. All that has stopped me is the thought of my mum's face and her disappointment. 'This money's an *education*,' she has said, eyes shining, to my father. How can I spoil the story she so looks forward to telling? Especially now, when it's hardly begun?

I can't.

Which is why I'm here, listening intently, taking care to keep up. If only I don't lag behind and don't ask any questions, I'll be all right. If I take care not to give Chieveley a reason to say my name, or what he thinks is my name, and if I don't talk to anyone who knows my *real* name, the Inevitable might be put off for a bit longer.

18

Adrienne

Jerry and Poppa are waiting for me at the airport. They're both giving me hugs and saying how much they're gonna miss me, how proud of me they are. None of us can believe Momma's just let me go like this and Poppa tells me (only semi-sternly) that I should've told her before, a long time before. Since we all know what would have happened if I *had*, we also know it wasn't much of an option, not really, so I tell him I'm sorry and ask him to look after Momma for me.

'Someone's got to,' he says wearily.

We all hug and I wave them off, watching them go, not able to believe I'm alone and free. I'm about to go through passport control when two men wearing jeans and baseball shirts come up to me and ask me if I'm Adrienne Finch.

'I'm afraid there's been a problem, ma'am. If you'd just come with me.'

They lead me to a dark little room somewhere off the Arrivals Hall and introduce me to a fat sixty-year-old woman who briskly tells me to take my clothes off. 'Yes, please,' she says when I hesitate, like she's bored or something. 'Bra and pants, too.'

This is *much* worse than Barney's. Much worse than getting undressed and exposing my undeveloped tits to a personal shopper. It's cold and I've got no idea why I'm here, or what's going on. Plus, the only light's fluorescent, so not only do I resemble a twelve-year-old anorexic, my skin looks lousy to boot. The old lady just nods at my chest, like she's not very impressed with it or something, before saying: 'All you skinny girls are flat, aren't you?'

Like *that's* why I'm being arrested.

19

Jake

I trot anxiously behind Chieveley. Not too close, not too far. If I catch up, he might talk to me. If I lag behind, he might call to me. I have to stay where I am, at a neutral distance, avoiding any conversation with the boy nearest me. I have to listen. So I do as we move from cloister to chapel to library to playing fields. So much more is rounded in this world than in Fareham. The square houses and ruler-drawn streets I'm used to haven't prepared me for colonnades and domes and horseshoe staircases, all in time-darkened stone.

We make it to the chapel without anyone using my name and then we're lost in its luminous darkness. High above, pale winter light filters gaudily through stained glass. The flagstones are uneven, worn down by generations of leather-soled school-boys. Tattered banners hang still as pictures above us and the air's sweet with incense. It's difficult to be terrified in a space like this and I wonder briefly what would happen if I hid in the organ loft and didn't leave with the others.

Chieveley would ask where Mulcaster is. That's what'd happen.

So I brace myself for the light as Chieveley leads us through the north door and back into the anxious reality of being a thirteen-year-old among thirteen-year-olds. He's filling our heads with facts and figures. Foundation: 1322. Founder: Edward II ('The homo king,' says Chieveley). 1400: Chapel completed. Ballards' Bunker: a cricket pitch. The Shah of Persia's Garden: an oasis of hothouse flowers, endowed by an ex-student who used to be an emperor but isn't anymore. Fellows' Field: barred to all but the Upper Sixth. Umbrellas: to be left unfurled by all except Titans. Titan: Prefect. Charlatans: the school tuck shop. School dress, formal change, semi change. Varying degrees of formality throughout the day. Demi change: civvies. Only collared shirts to be worn in the High Street. No shellsuits.

Round and round and on and on. Up staircases which appear magically from nowhere. Along flagstoned corridors. Under haughty portraits. Over stiles. Through gates. Lower Boats Colours: magenta, turquoise, lilac, with crossed oars in black. Upper Boats Colours: magenta, turquoise, tangerine, with crossed oars in white.

'Can anyone tell me what happened to Edward II?' asks Chieveley later, turning to face us. We're in a far-flung quadrangle of Elizabethan brick. The afternoon's drawing in. It's almost dark.

A small, plump, blond boy raises his hand. I've hardly noticed him until now. He's got goofy white teeth and overlarge feet.

'Please, Chieveley,' he squeals. His voice hasn't broken yet.

'All right, Ogilvie. Share your erudition with us.' Chieveley's tone is tinged with sarcasm, but otherwise unthreatening.

'Please, Chieveley . . .' The little boy pauses and looks round at the group. His eyes are wide with daring. Then, after a deep breath: 'He was murdered, on the orders of his wife's lover.'

'How was he murdered?' asks Chieveley.

The little boy hesitates. He seems torn between conflicting emotions. 'By . . . By . . .' he says. And then: 'By having a red-hot-spit-shoved-up-his-anus.' This comes out in a tumble, as a single, bizarrely elongated word.

'Bang on,' says Chieveley. 'And serves the little faggot right, too. Doesn't it, Mulcaster?'

'Who's Mulcaster?' asks the tubby blond boy.

20

Julian

The book in the package was an old edition, published in 1860, bound in brown leather tooled in gold. It smelled old, faintly peppery, and its pages were of almost invisible onion skin. It had a well-thumbed look about it; or rather, it looked as though, at some point a century or more past, it had been well-thumbed. The creaking spine told me that it hadn't been opened for years, but it didn't prepare me for the neatly printed names on the fly page: Horace Ogilvie, 1864; Edward Ogilvie, 1894; Julian Ogilvie, 1925; Henry Ogilvie, 1957. It had been bought for my great-great-grandfather, presumably on the eve of his departure for Botesdale; and it had been passed on, father to son, over four generations, to arrive in the hands of a boy with an unbroken voice who had just swallowed half a mouthful of vinegar. I felt a pang of curiosity as to whether or not their voices had already broken when they read this for the first time and I made a short-lived mental note to ask my father if his had been.

The book in my hand was one I had vaguely heard of, though I couldn't quite remember where or in what context. It had a long title, which was shortened on the spine to *Leviathan*, but printed in full on the cover: *Leviathan, or The Matter, Forme & Power Of A Common-Wealth Ecclesiasticall and Civill*. It was by a man called Thomas Hobbes, and was full of funny spellings and a long ʃ which seemed to stand in for S. The facsimile of the original title page, reproduced at the front, announced that it had first been published in 1651, *Printed for Andrew Crooke, at the Green Dragon in St Pauls Church-yard.*

Wondering whether to call Maggie, I sat down on the bed, holding the volume in my hand. As old books sometimes do, it fell open on a much-read page and my eyes were drawn to a line, underscored in faint pencil. The phrase, which might be the Ogilvie motto, leapt from the page with the grace of an undisputed truth: 'Much Experience is *Prudence*'. (Hobbes' italics, not mine.)

Sitting up under the covers, with the light on into the small hours, I discovered that the book had a curious property of self-generated communication. In its well-thumbed days the thumbing had been selective, and as a result the volume opened naturally, of its own accord, to the passages that someone (my grandfather? my great-grandfather?) had once considered instructive or illuminating. When allowed to fall open by itself, the book almost invariably opened on a page which had been painstakingly annotated in precise pencil: neat, careful letters whose calm and deliberate artistry seemed a reassurance against the perils of the unknown that awaited me the next day.

Being thirteen years old, I had never come across any political philosophy until my father gave me the book, but it didn't take me long to see that whatever Hobbes may or may not have known about the establishment of just societies, he knew a great deal about the forces that govern the dark world of an English boys' boarding school. A passage I read that night has stayed with me ever since, and seems to explain at least a part of what happened later. Hobbes writes:

In the nature of man we find three principall causes of quarrel. First, Competition; Secondly, Diffidence; Thirdly, Glory.

Benedict Chieveley was ardent in his pursuit of glory; that much was clear to me the moment I first saw him, at New Boys' Tea on my first day at Botesdale. He was taller than us, wearing a well-cut tweed jacket with leather patches on its elbows, slightly frayed. He was older than us, too, the head of the form above; and the jacket he wore had clearly belonged to his father, possibly even to his grandfather. It lent its new wearer an authority redolent of the elder statesman and I thought how confident he looked in it. Here was a person whose voice had obviously broken – probably ages ago.

In the corner of the room, tall and thin, a little haughty, was the future 'idol of the contemporary art world', Jake Hitchins. Like the rest of us he was with his parents, but he didn't seem to need to cling to them as we needed to cling to ours. I don't know how I'd have survived that first day without my mother: she introduced me to the children of her friends, also joining the school; she discussed my name tapes expertly with Matron; she charmed old Parmesan nearly out of his pants. My future housemaster could only salivate and tell her how he'd always mistrusted the results of the Common Entrance. The really clever boys, he said, winking at me, almost never showed their true colours until later.

I could barely move.

Sustaining a conversation with somebody else involved opening my mouth, which in its turn involved betraying the as-yet-unbroken state of my voice. I had no desire to display my unfortunate shrillness, but my mother nudged me towards the tall boy in the corner. 'Go and talk to him,' she said. 'He doesn't look too frightening, does he?'

Goaded by this maternal mind-reading, I moved slowly across the crowded room; but as I drew near the boy in question, Parmesan bulldozed his way through the talking groups and started salivating over *his* mother. She was the only woman in the room wearing trousers: tight, white jeans with a repeating pattern of island palm trees, in lime and pink. She was tall, with brassy blonde hair, and I don't think I'd ever seen nails like hers: so long she had to keep her fingers straight to hold her tea cup, smooth and pink and buffed to a high sheen.

Parmesan was talking to the boy now, who was replying quietly – but deeply. His voice had progressed far beyond even the quivering stage: it was well and truly broken and seemed to have been so for many months.

Tail between my legs, I made my way back to my mother and from that first day resolved to keep my mouth shut if at all possible.

21

Jake

Chieveley's staring at me across the darkening quadrangle. For a moment I think he's going to hit me and I brace myself for it. Maybe he'll just punch me and all this will be over.

But he doesn't punch me.

He smiles.

Everyone else is watching. Waiting their cues.

Gently, like an old friend giving a piece of thoughtful advice, Chieveley whispers something in my ear just loudly enough for the others to hear. 'If you can't remember your own name, you haven't got much hope of passing the Tits' Test, have you?' His eyes glow in the gathering darkness. 'Now we can't have that.'

He looks around him and raises his voice to normal volume. A moment's pause. Then: 'What would . . . *Beverley* say?'

Nobody says a word to me as Chieveley leads us back to the house. It's dark now, and cold, but it's only five o'clock in the afternoon. Tea time. Inside, the air's slippery with melted butter. 'I'll deal with you tomorrow, after prep,' says Chieveley quietly.

No one talks to me in the dormitory that night, or at breakfast the next day. The small, smug, blond boy doesn't meet my eyes. When the meal's over and the others are leaving the table, he looks over his shoulder and comes up to me. 'Tough luck, Hitchins,' he says falteringly, then stops.

Whatever more he was going to say, he thinks better of and walks away.

The day passes much too quickly. When the bell rings that evening for prep, I feel sick to the pit of my stomach. I've got a Latin test tomorrow. I try to concentrate on the words. *Ludicum, ludicri*, neuter: public show. *Ludificatio, ludificationis*, feminine: ridicule. *Ludificator, ludificatoris*, masculine: mocker. The words smile slyly from the page. *Which modern English word derives from ludicer? Ludicer, ludicri*, adjective, I write. Meaning: playful; theatrical. Root of modern Eng. word: ludicrous.

I'm in a long panelled room full of bent heads and dandruffed shoulders. The floor's an olive green lino, laced with brown and white. Chievcley's in the distance, head bent over his desk. Smiling at someone. Exchanging a confidence, a look. Both turn round to look at me. A silent laugh.

Everyone is at home in this strange world of old stone and plastic flooring.

I can't think, or write, or move. The bell rings. Prep's over. Chievcley catches up with me at the top of the staircase. I feel his hand on my shoulder and know who it is without turning.

'Don't flinch, 'Itchins. All this is for your own good, you know.'

'I'm sorry, Chieveley.'

'Don't snivel. You're here to learn how to be a man. Look at you. Look at the state of you.'

I can't meet his eyes, because I know if I do I'll start crying. Not even I'm stupid enough to start crying now.

Chieveley's hand remains on my shoulder, fingers tightening. Not painful, just present. There. Guiding me. The hand of judgement descending, its right thumb in the groove of my left shoulder. Tread trudge, laughing boys, cracked wood, lino.

The door to the common room swings silently open at our approach.

22

Adrienne

'*Baby!* Are you okay?'

It's Momma. She's waiting for me when I come out of the dark, little room. The fat old lady lost interest in me once she saw me naked and the two guys in baseball shirts are giving me back my bag. 'Sorry for troubling you,' says one. 'And sorry you've missed your flight,' says the other one. 'We're trying to arrange for the airline to have you go out on the next plane. You'd better speak to them in person.'

'*What* has happened?'

Everyone looks at Momma.

'What on earth are you doing to my daughter?' she demands. 'Do you know who she is? I'd like to have a very sharp word with your superior, young man.'

'I'm his superior,' says the other guy in a baseball shirt. 'Sorry to have inconvenienced your daughter, ma'am, but we got a tip-off from a caller and we have to take these things seriously.'

'Someone tipped you off? About *Adrienne*? Oh baby.'

She's pulling me towards her, enveloping me in a scented hug like we're a mother–daughter bonding act in a pro-motional video for pension plans. There's not a whole lot for me to do except let her and I'm still a bit freaked out by the experience, so I submit. She pushes my nose right into her cleavage, which smells of *Must de Cartier*.

Eventually I come up for air. 'Momma,' I say, 'I've got to speak to someone at the airline. I've got to get on the next plane. Classes start tomorrow.'

'Don't you worry about a thing, precious angel. Everything's gonna be just fine, now Momma's here.' She's leading me to the American Airlines desk, practically hyperventilating. 'Did they hurt you, baby?'

I'm increasingly concerned to talk to someone from the airline, because I know the chances of my making it to Oxford in time for my first class are getting smaller and smaller. Momma won't stop talking, won't stop asking if the men *did* anything to me – what does she want? was I meant to get raped? – but I just keep telling her everything's fine, I'm totally calm now, totally under control.

Obviously it's not and neither am I and Momma senses this.

'My daughter's just missed her flight,' she says loudly when we get to the desk. Ignoring the fact there's a long line, she storms right to the front, waving to attract the attention of the attendant. 'My daughter's just missed her flight!' she yells, like she wasn't heard the first time. Everyone's looking.

'Yeah, and so have the rest of us, lady,' someone growls behind us.

'Momma . . . *Please.*'

Eventually we go to the back of the line, but Momma's in a rage now because she can't bear to be made to wait for anything. She's talking at the top of her voice about how she's gonna sue and how someone's gonna pay for this and obviously the other people in line are getting kind of impatient with her. I'm so embarrassed I consider leaving, just running out of the airport and getting into a cab – anything to stop her. The thing is, I know she'll have won if I do that. I know Momma's betting on me not being able to handle the public shame of being related to her, but she's forgotten I've got a lifetime's training behind me.

You think this is the first time Momma ever embarrassed me in front of hundreds of people?

23

Jake

There must be at least twenty people inside. All of Chieveley's
year and all of mine. Chieveley stands between me and the
door. Eyes crisp. Shoulders tense with exhilaration. I stand in
the centre of the lino, throat aching with held-back sobs. No
voice. Vision blurred.

Waiting.

'So you can't even remember your own name, 'Itchins.'

I stand there, not knowing where to look. Chieveley walks
over to me and circles, inspecting. 'It's pretty obvious to
everyone in this room that you're a deceitful little brat, and
common to boot. Would you call that a fair assessment of
your general character?'

Twenty pairs of eyes stare at me, goggling, breathlessly
excited.

'I *said* . . . Would you call that a fair assessment of your
general character?'

'Um . . .'

'It's a simple question, 'Itchins. You're free to answer it as
you wish. All your reply will tell us is whether or not you're
aware of the extent of the instruction you need.' Chieveley
circles once more. Then, calmly, measuredly: 'We're waiting.'

'I . . . I suppose I . . .' What are the rules? What am I meant
to say?

'Very well. If you find the question embarrassing, we'll

move on. We're only here to help you, 'Itchins. As your future lifelong friends we have – how shall I put it? – a certain . . . duty towards you. You're a vulgar little boy on the threshold of life. Your fragile shoulders must bear the immense weight of your parents' social ambition.' An icy pat on the back of my neck. 'And they must be *terribly* ambitious to have bothered sending you to a school like this, where you're so obviously out of place.'

He looks at me, smiling gently.

Then, abruptly, exultantly: 'Hold him down, someone!'

24

Julian

Hobbes makes clear the danger of offending those covetous
of glory and her sister, reputation; and Benedict Chieveley
seemed to me not only to desire, but to deserve, the kind of
glory to which I could never aspire. His eyes flashed prowess;
his movements suggested a dawning sense of his own unchal-
lenged importance. Everything about him screamed a superiority I had no desire to test; and I feared (as Hobbes had
intended I should fear) his use of violence

. . . for trifles, as a word, a smile, a different opinion, and any other
signe of undervalue, either direct in (other) Persons, or by reflexion
in their Kindred, their Friends, their Nation, their Profession, or
their Name.

The 'direct in (other) Persons' bit was me to a tee; and I wasn't
to know, then, that Hobbes' point about names applied, with
crazy literalness, to the tall, thin boy oozing aloofness in the
corner. My main preoccupation was myself; and I was a small,
rather chubby boy with an unbroken voice. Clearly a word
out of place could have unpredictable, possibly disastrous,
consequences. My best bet would be to keep my pre-pubescent
person out of the way as much as possible; and I thanked my
father silently for thinking to warn me of possible perils.

That you're a thirteen-year-old boy with a fluting treble, at a school full of other boys, most of whose voices have broken, is enough to destabilize your assessment of reality. To me, the most remarkable thing about Jake was that he was a head taller than me, with an indisputably broken voice. This alone made me anxious in his presence; and his habit of ignoring me did little to still such unease.

Despite what Maggie later implied, I don't feel responsible for what happened to him, I should make that clear now. I hardly even realized what was going on. Empathy's as dangerous at a boarding school as it is in adult life; it breeds gentleness and sympathy and various other qualities that expose you to the mercy of others. The best thing to do is keep your head down and look firmly in the opposite direction. Never commit yourself, never defend anyone incapable of defending you in return, never offend someone stronger than you.

It's a question of simple pragmatism.

25

Jake

'Speaking frankly, 'Itchins,' Chieveley's saying, 'if we're ever going to make a self-respecting Old Bushel out of you, we're going to have to start from scratch. Again.'

It's months since the Tits' Test. Months since the game of inter-house rugby in which Chieveley 'fell' on my leg during the scrum. Months since he and the rest of the team stood round, laughing, telling me to get up, to pull myself together, as I lay in the mud trying not to cry. Christmas has come and gone and I'm back in this place of cold stone and scuffed lino. I'm back in the common room and another crowd has gathered round. It's not as big as the crowd that first watched me. Some people have got bored of the spectacle and moved off in search of new blood. But it's still a crowd, and it still laughs and whoops as crowds do.

Chieveley hasn't got bored. He slackened off until my leg was out of plaster, but the amnesty didn't outlast the injury.

'We'd better help you start speaking proper,' he tells me.

It's got its own name now, this little ritual. People call it Civilizing 'Itchins. It happens once a week on average, sometimes once a fortnight. It's difficult to know exactly when I'm due for a lesson, though there are tell-tale signs. If Chieveley smiles at me at breakfast, my number's probably up. If his eyes meet mine across the chapel and linger meaningfully, it definitely is. Sometimes he even tells me, directly: 'See you in the common room at eight o'clock.'

'Today's lesson will be on correct usage,' he says.

There are titters in the background, but not all the crowd is paying attention. Civilizing 'Itchins is an old joke, a little past its prime. Some prefer to read the newspapers or watch television, throwing in an occasional comment for good measure.

'I want you to think of a typical scene at home, 'Itchins. I want you to place yourself, imaginatively as it were, back in the sordid semi you were dragged up in. Forget us. Forget everything about Botesdale. Answer *truthfully*. Is that understood?'

'Yes, Chieveley.'

'Very well then. Let's imagine you've finished your "tea". Now you'll remember from our lesson last week what civilized human beings call the evening meal, don't you?'

'It-is-common-to-refer-to-dinner-as-tea.'

'Absolutely right, 'Itchins. Very common indeed. Well done.'

An onlooker, perched jauntily on the sofa arm, giggles.

'Now let's imagine that *la famille* 'Itchins has eaten its eggs and chips. What do we say about eggs and chips?'

'It-is-common-to-eat-chips-with-everything.'

'*Very* good. Now, presuming you were minded to move rooms, to take your instant coffee elsewhere . . . ?'

We don't ever drink coffee at home at night. It keeps mum awake and she doesn't like it. Should I tell Chieveley this? No. I know from experience that the fewer details I volunteer, the better. He's already found out enough about my home life. I was caught reading a letter from my mum at the end of last term, so Chieveley knows she's a beautician. There's no point in doling out any more information than is strictly necessary. You never know what's dangerous and what isn't.

So I just say: 'Yes, Chieveley.'

'What do you call the room you might drink your after-dinner coffee in?'

Julian Ogilvie puts down a newspaper and furtively begins to watch the show. Popular feeling is that it sometimes takes Chieveley a bit long to warm up, but once he's going he's worth watching. In the background, a football match is being discussed with mechanical enthusiasm.

'I'm sorry, Chieveley. I don't know what you mean.'

Chieveley smiles. Suddenly, dangerously, he's gentleness personified. 'Let's phrase it a different way, 'Itchins.' He's apparently eager to clarify things for me. An elderly school-master, benevolent in the face of blank ignorance. 'Forget what I said about dinner and coffee and what not. Tell me, simply, what you call the room wot 'as va telly innit.'

Despite myself, because I Should Know What's What by now, I feel relieved at the simplicity of it. Thank God, I know this one. 'We call it the lounge, Chieveley,' I say quickly, stumbling over myself in my desire to get the words out. For this whole thing to be over.

There's no reaction from the crowd. Everyone's watching Chieveley.

'And the piece of furniture you throw yourself on to, just before *Dallas*?' he goes on, smoothly. Gentle again. Blue eyes coaxing, considerate.

'What, a chair?'

'Well, you might throw yourself on to a chair, 'Itchins.' The same gentle, coaxing voice. 'But what if you wanted to sit next to someone? To your mum, the celebrated beautician, for instance. I bet she thinks J.R.'s a saucy old devil, doesn't she? What would you sit on then?'

'Well, um . . .' Play it carefully. Slowly. I try to think of a posh word. 'The . . . settee, Chieveley?' We call it the 'couch' at home, so that's definitely not right.

There's silence in the room. For one perfect, breathless instant, it seems that maybe, just maybe, I've escaped.

Then someone whoops delightedly. Julian Ogilvie starts sniggering. Chieveley's eyes are radiant with pleasure.

'I feared as much,' he says. Standing over me, looking at me, examining me. 'Oh dear, dear, dear 'Itchins. After so many months of instruction, you still choose to sit on the *settee* in your *lounge*. I'm beginning to fear that taste will never become instinctive in you.'

More catcalls.

Chieveley's smiling, moving away from me, going to the desk in the corner of the room. 'Hold him down, someone,' he says quietly. And then: 'A tip for the future, 'Itchins.' He looks right into my eyes, smiling sharply. 'Civilized people call it a *sofa*. A sofa may be found in the drawing room, the living room or the sitting room – but never, and I repeat never, in the *lounge*.'

26

Julian

There is one small confession I should make, but only one. If you really must know, it was me who alerted Benedict to the fact that Jake's name wasn't Mulcaster. That's all I did – or almost all I did – and it was done quite by accident as he showed us round the school on a smoky autumn afternoon, preparing us for the fabled Tits' Test.

Benedict Chieveley was an authority on the place: his father and grandfather had both been School Captains (as he, himself, would one day be) and he prided himself on the extent of his knowledge of school history. So, as it happens, did I. The history of Botesdale is one of my father's few passions and stories of its bloody past took the place of fairy tales through my childhood.

Perhaps you're already aware that Botesdale, against the odds, is pronounced 'Bushel', as in thing you hide a lamp under: a little trick for the tourists, devised centuries ago; a devious little *jeu* calculated to exclude all those who have no business talking about the school at all. This is an old technique of the English upper classes, by the way, this wilful mangling of pronunciation. As Jake once asked me, many years later, how can a person be expected to pronounce names like Cholmondeley ('Chumley') or Cecil ('Sissil') correctly, unless born with the requisite knowledge?

How does the unsuspecting applicant to Bridwell College,

Oxford, know that he or she is in fact applying to 'Briddle' – and that if they don't say it right in the interview, they're screwed? The answer, of course, is that they can't, which is precisely the point of these names. They are invisible markers of social gradation, like the strands of hair spies place in the hinges of doors to tell them if anyone enters a room in their absence.

As with most institutions considered august, Botesdale's origins are murkier than the authorities would have us believe. Endowed as a refuge for eighty poore scholars in the year of our Lord thirteen hundred and twenty two, the school was founded (with its sister institution, St Botolph's College, Oxford) as a semi-religious educational establishment, intended by Edward II to train boys and monks in the saying of masses for his soul.

Edward could not, presumably, have known how soon these masses would be needed, for within five years of the beginning of the chapel's construction he was in the dungeons of Berkeley Castle, king in name though not in fact, the prisoner of his French wife and her scheming lover. Marlowe made him famous three centuries later in *Edward II* (which Mr Symmonds considers too violent for a schoolboy audience), but on 21 September 1327 the drama of Edward's life was all too horribly real.

As Raphael Holinshed puts it in his *Chronicle* of 1587,

. . . they came suddenlie one night into the chamber where he laie in bed fast asleepe, and with heavie featherbeds or a table (as some write) being cast upon him, they kept him down and withal put into his fundament an horne, and through the same they thrust up into his bodie an hot spit . . . of iron made verie hot . . .

Masses were never said for Edward in the chapel he ordered to be built, and which Benedict showed us round that chilly afternoon. While the choristers for the abbey were being chosen, their founder was being tortured; and while Benedict was filling our heads with facts, I made what Maggie would later call a 'nasty, mean-spirited, cowardly' decision: I opened my mouth.

27

Adrienne

Finally we're at the front of the line. The woman serving us is small and pretty and kind of nervous looking. She's obviously been hearing everything Momma's been shouting and since Momma's wearing a leopardskin coat and diamonds she probably thinks Momma's in a position to carry out her threats – which, of course, she is.

'Can I help you?' asks the woman, anxiously.

'My daughter has missed her flight,' says Momma, like it's a declaration of war or something, like it's this particular woman's personal fault. Being Momma, she ignores the fact that the whole of JFK knows I've missed my flight by now.

'I see, ma'am,' says the attendant politely. 'May I have her ticket?'

'Show her your ticket, Adrienne.'

I show her my ticket. 'It's a bit more complicated—' I begin, but Momma just shouts over me.

'*Quiet*, sweetie, this lady's looking things up just as fast as she can.'

'I'm afraid all today's flights are full in First Class,' says the attendant apologetically.

This is just what Momma's been hoping for. 'Oh baby!' she cries. 'Oh baby, what an awful experience this has been for you. You know what I'm gonna do? I'm gonna take you to the *spa*. It's the—'

'I'm fine, Momma,' I say, steadily. The thought of spending time in a spa with my mother, naked, gives me the confidence I need.

The attendant's tapping her keyboard diligently. She looks up, still worried, and says: 'I'm afraid there's not even a seat available in Business Class. All we have left are one or two spaces in Coach on the next plane, which leaves in forty minutes. You'll have to run.'

'Listen to me, sweetie,' says Momma, and she's already trying to lead me away from the counter, pulling me towards her and smiling fiercely over her shoulder at the attendant and everyone else. 'Let's go home, have a nice lunch, talk a little. God knows we've got enough to talk about. You can take the first flight out tomorrow morning, or maybe one in the afternoon so we have some time to—'

'I can run,' I tell the attendant.

'But you'll never sleep in Coach, and you want to be fresh for classes, don't you, honey pie?' Suddenly Momma's voice has that hard, brittle quality I know to fear. She seems to have dropped the glossy oh-my-god-how-close-we-are act, and she's looking at me with freaky eyes again.

'Honestly, Momma,' I say, half-pleading. 'Coach is totally okay.'

The lady behind the counter smiles at me, taps her computer, and there's the sound of a ticket printing.

'I think you should take a flight tomorrow,' Momma says, quietly.

I can't look at her, but I know what I've got to say. 'I'll be late for my classes if I go tomorrow . . .' I begin, but I never get to the end of my sentence because Momma's turned around and is walking, Olympic-paced, away from me. The crowd parts for her, because she's the kind of woman crowds part for, and this means that when she turns to face me, as she eventually does, there's no one in her sight line.

When she yells, she does it loudly enough for everyone in International Departures to hear her. 'When I fell pregnant with you,' she screams, holding up two ringed fingers about an inch apart, 'I came *this* close to having an abortion!'

'I'll put you in an exit seat, so you've got some extra legroom,' says the attendant, sweetly.

28

Jake

Maggie and I meet on a summer's afternoon, as young lovers should. On a day when it's easy to forget – and Botesdale could make you forget. The lichen-covered walls and green baize lawns, the benevolent clock tower with its cheerful bells. On an afternoon of high summer when the air is heavy with buzzing life, Chieveley doesn't seem real. He's far away on the cricket pitch. A dappled, sunlit figure, very white against the green, smiling at a clap from the crowd.

It's Founder's Day. A sacred day in the school calendar. A day of celebrities and celebration. Champagne and girls, unsteady on their feet. Volvos disgorging hampers of salmon sandwiches and quails' eggs. Bands. Photographers. People's parents.

Not my parents, obviously.

Chieveley has made it clear he's looking forward to seeing my mum and dad again. 'I'm just *itching* with curiosity, 'Itchins,' he has said.

Certain precautions have been required. For a start, I haven't told my parents about the match. I haven't told them about the school open day or the picnics or the champagne. I haven't told them about any of these things for two years and they haven't known to ask. All I've told them about is the weekend's leave, thinking that by the time they've arrived to collect me, everyone else will have gone home.

These precautions mean freedom from Chieveley. More importantly, they mean freedom from worry about Chieveley. He's playing in the match, as the youngest member of the Eleven. After the match he, like the rest of the school, will go home for the long weekend. For three whole days in a row, nothing will happen.

I've forgotten that nothing hardly ever happens.

Maggie's sitting behind the Art Schools, arms over her knees. A tall girl with promising breasts in a tantalizing dress. Her hair spins out from her shoulders and her eyes are dark. She's frowning and staring out over the fields. Ignoring the match, intent only on her own thoughts and on the quiet warmth of the afternoon sun.

I don't know how long I watch her. A while before she sees me, anyway. A while after she's seen me, too. She doesn't seem surprised when she notices me there, looking at her. Or – and this is unusual – hostile. I've got used to being treated a certain way by this point in my Botesdale career. I'm not used to inviting smiles.

So when Maggie smiles at me for the first time I don't know what to do. Nor can I answer when she speaks.

'I've never really seen the point of cricket,' is what she says. Then: 'Would you like some of this?'

She holds out her hand, which has a Coke bottle in it full of a rich brown liquid I've not seen before. Bits of orange and strawberry float through the mixture. It looks like a cross between cough syrup and sea water, with thick dirty foam. In fact, it tastes of summer and sweetness and (as Maggie tells me when I ask, much later, much drunker) it's a cocktail called Pimms, stolen from her parents' picnic hamper.

I've never been in a situation like this before. It's heady. This girl talks just like Chieveley but her eyes don't narrow

147

when I reply and she doesn't look at me with amused anticipation. It takes me a few minutes to accept she isn't mocking me. She seems genuinely friendly, but is she?

Yes, I decide, when the Pimms is half drunk.

Weird.

She's got beautiful shoulders, this girl. They're tanned and delicate and you can see faint white marks left over from the straps of a swimming costume. She's a year younger than me but seems a lifetime older. There's something reassuring in the way she looks at me. I don't know exactly what it is, but I know it's there. Or maybe it's not there. Her eyes contain an absence. They're empty of something I've become so used to I don't notice anymore. An absence of interrogation, maybe. Of anticipated delight and confident superiority. She doesn't seem to be expecting me to say the wrong thing. It's as though she's expecting me to . . . I don't know. All I can sense is that she's prepared to like me. And that alone is enough on this day of radiant skies and sea-foam alcohol.

29

Adrienne

I guess I saw the TV version of *Brideshead Revisited* when I was a kid, because in the back of my mind I'm kind of hoping to see cute guys wandering around with teddy bears, smoking cigars and acting all louche and between-the-wars. Jerry gave me a book my last week in New York, full of photos of Oxford in technicolor summer – it looks like Disney World, only a bit dirtier and more authentic.

It's late at night when I arrive. My taxi stops on a street of tall, elegant houses and the driver points to a brass plate outside number 32. *St Botolph's College*, it says in neat letters.

As I tip him and ring the doorbell, I remind myself not to get my hopes up. Jerry's told me what to expect, and frankly, since being away from Momma's already just about the best thing that ever happened to me, I'm not too disappointed there's no big, imposing gate or anything. In any case, the jetlag and the missed sleep (added to the fact classes begin tomorrow) make me feel like this is some sort of weird dream. I'm half afraid Momma's going to wake me up and take me shopping.

But Momma doesn't wake me up. Instead, there's creaking in the passage and I hear a bolt being pulled back and a key turning, and then this guy in a white dress opens the door. He's very tall and skinny, middle-aged, with a long face and kind of greasy hair, and he looks at me like he's got no idea who I am or what I'm doing on his doorstep.

'Hi,' I say. 'I'm Adrienne Finch. I've come to enrol?'

I don't know why I'm making the statement a question, but I can't help it. Maybe I'm in the wrong place, maybe this whole thing was some set-up of Momma's, maybe I haven't been accepted, after all. Be calm, Adrienne, I tell myself, remembering Jerry saying there'd be some monks around the place – since St Botolph's is two parts university, one part monastery.

'I'm being taught by Professor Macklethwaite,' I say, hoping this information will clarify the situation for him.

But the monk just turns away, leaving the door open behind him. I hear him muttering something like 'If you'd like to come in' as he climbs the stairs, so I do, but I'm not sure if I'm meant to follow him or not, so I just stand there awkwardly, taking things in. I'm in a fairly large lobby, with black and white marble tiles on the floor. It looks a bit like Momma's bathroom in New York (and is about the same size), except for the pictures on the wall – team groups from the 1880s, a portrait or two, a whole wall full of fading, crackled boys in suits and gowns and mortar boards. All these men staring down at me, over me really, totally unconcerned by my presence, calm and confident in their sepia.

'It's rather late, as you know, and I'm afraid Professor Macklethwaite's left the college for the day. He's not a resident fellow. He is merely affiliated to us in a . . . teaching capacity.'

It's the same guy who let me in, who comes down the stairs about fifteen minutes later, looking like he's had a long walk all for nothing. When he's finished speaking he begins to turn away, like he's done all he needs to. Since there's no one else around to ask, I have to work up the courage to say something pretty quick. But I'm so nervous by this point that my throat's dry and all I can come up with is: 'Excuse me, but . . . Could you tell me where my dorm is?'

He turns round impatiently. 'I'm *taking* you there. If you wouldn't mind following me.' And then, as a barbed after-thought: 'This is all most irregular.'

He's walking quickly and I've got my bag with me, but I know I've got to keep up. So I follow him up a flight of stairs and then another one and then along a dark, winding corridor. The bag's easier to handle in the corridor because I can just drag it along and I have a moment of total gratitude for not bringing more luggage. All around us are these photos of old boys and monks. Portraits too, with thick layers of dust on the top part of their frames.

The monk guy stops outside a door, his door I'm guessing, and leaves me waiting while he fetches some keys. There's a piece of tapestry hanging on the oak, just a line of embroidered text which reads 'Conscience is not a Power, but an Act' and when the monk appears again I nod over at it, trying to make conversation and say: 'That's cute.'

' "Cute" is not an adjective I would use to describe the teachings of St Thomas Aquinas,' he says shortly. 'Or the stylistic impact of the *Summa Theologica*, for that matter.'

'No,' I say, 'okay.' But he's already far ahead in the darkness.

By the time we get to my floor, there's nothing on the walls. We're up at the top of the building now and the ceilings are lower. The plaster's cracked, too, and the paint's peeling and the whole place has this . . . mustiness about it. It smells like hundreds of damp winters and the carpet's pretty thread-bare and hasn't been replaced (or, it looks like, cleaned) since the 1950s. Even the lightbulbs in their exposed fittings look like they were bought twenty or thirty years ago and because everything's so dark the monk up ahead of me looks like a floating ghost in his white dress.

Eventually he shimmers to a stop outside a wooden door and takes out his big bunch of keys, selects one and tries it. It seems to get stuck in the lock or something, so he rattles it around for a few seconds and then the bolt grinds slowly to the side and the door swings open creakily, creepily.

'I'm afraid this room isn't used very much,' the monk says, not looking at me. 'But since the places available at the college were already full before your unorthodox application, we've had to open it especially for you.'

30

Jake

It's almost dark now and the cricket match is long since over. Maggie and I are lying on our backs in the empty courtyard. The Coke bottle's empty. We've moved to catch the last spot of sunshine while the world around us darkens. I've no idea that I'm not going to see her again for four years. I've no idea of anything, much. I'm not very used to alcohol. The sum total of my experience is a few quickly downed whiskies with Simon, stolen from the bottle his dad always keeps in his shed. They haven't prepared me for this.

We're floating in the last patch of late afternoon light. We're warm, while all around us darkness and chill spread steadily. The horizon's lurching crazily, but somehow this isn't as unpleasant as it sounds – or as it would later become, on nights without number at the Groucho Club. I'm on my back with my hands at my sides, and so is Maggie. We're not touching. For ages and *ages* we're not touching. And then . . . I don't know how it happens, but I feel the hairs on her arm tingle momentarily against the hairs on mine. It's a touch-no-touch but it ricochets through my body.

The force is too much for me. Or too much for most of me. For a horrible moment I'm sure Maggie's seen the leaping in my trousers. Then I look over and her eyes are shut. She could almost be asleep.

I don't know what I'm doing, but the Pimms has made this

much less of an obstacle than it would usually be. The dying sun has cast her face into sharp relief. A long shadow stretches across a cheek and her lips are etched in darkness. They're so close I could touch them but I don't quite dare. Instead I lie there, turning my head to look at hers.

I might have stayed like this until it got dark if she hadn't opened her eyes.

But she does open her eyes.

It's difficult to tell who moves first. All I know is that we drift towards each other. Then her lips are on mine and her tongue – her *tongue* – is feeling for mine. It's warm and wet and tastes sweet from the Pimms. Her smell washes over me, sweet but acrid also.

We stay there, tongues exploring, spines tingling, until the light's quite gone.

31

Adrienne

There's not much furniture in here – just a bed and a desk and a sink and a chair and a closet – and it's all made of dark wood. It's impossible to tell whether the stuff was once acceptable quality or whether it was always as shitty as it is now, just as it's difficult to tell how long it's been creaking around. There's a small window in one wall, looking out on a street which I'll learn the next day is called St Giles – not St Giles Avenue or Crescent or Square or anything, just plain St Giles.

'I hope you'll make yourself comfortable,' says the monk. 'Breakfast is at nine o'clock.' And then he just turns around and goes, closing the door behind him, leaving me in what's basically the dark, trying to figure out where the light switch is. Eventually I find it. Like everything else in this room, it's old and a bit fucked up and I can't help giggling to myself when I think what Momma would say if she could see me now, or how she'd threaten to sue over the light switch, which comes away from the wall when I flip it and is only attached by the wires behind it. The window's broken, too, a small pane in the lower half that sends a jet of icy air straight across my pillow.

Now it's not that I'm unequal to hardship or anything, but Jerry did give me this book full of ivy-covered walls and smooth green lawns where it was always summer and which hasn't prepared me for arriving here. Right now there's no ivy in sight and no lawns, just a brass plate and a frosty Brit in a dress and a room like a plunge pool with damp sheets and iced air and brown and orange curtains.

I tell you all this to explain the fact that what I did next, once I'd put down my bag and sat on the bed for a few minutes, wondering what to do, smiling to keep my spirits up, was burst into tears.

32

Jake

'You're late, Hitchins.' Parmesan's standing at the door of the house with a clipboard in his left hand and a pen in his right. He's ticking off names on a list as boys report to him, making sure no one's left for the long weekend before the authorized time.

'You're late,' he says again. But more softly this time. Almost gently.

To my surprise he puts an arm round my shoulder. This means his arm pit, oozing sweat, isn't far from my nose. I sway there, politely, concentrating on seeming sober. I'm having my first moment of alcohol-induced slight nausea. The run back to the house has set my insides lurching dangerously and the rows of pigeon holes in the distance are see-sawing crazily.

'I'm afraid I've some bad news for you,' Parmesan says. Apologetically, almost, as though in this case the news is the messenger's fault. His pink, glistening face stares into mine for a moment. 'It's about your mother.'

33

Julian

Whatever Maggie may have said later, and she said a great many things later, it was hardly my fault, was it? How could it have been? How can I be blamed for the fact that Jake told a stupid lie, which was bound to come out at some point?

The problem with my sister was that she refused to climb off her soap box for long enough to understand what life is *like* for most people. It's all very well talking about high-minded ideals, about meting out justice and defending the weak and so on and so forth. I suppose if you're someone like Maggie, these things are options; if you're someone like me on the other hand, and if you've read your Hobbes, you'll know that 'Experience is *Prudence.*'

The world is made up of three sorts of people: tyrants, victims and bystanders. This is the way things have always been and it's the way things continue to be, because in some obscure manner the roles of these three types complement each other. A tyrant cannot be a tyrant without a victim and bystanders are necessary for tyranny because a thirst for power invariably accompanies one for publicity. If someone is cut out for tyranny, he will almost always find a victim and an audience.

Hobbes argues that 'a perpetuall and restlesse desire of Power after Power, that ceaseth only in Death' is 'a general inclination of all mankind'. I'm not so sure. Not everyone's cut out for the kind of authority Benedict wielded at Botesdale; not everyone wants it or is capable of achieving it. Not everyone wants Maggie's kind of power, either, though that's another story.

To be a tyrant you must be able to make yourself feared. Knowing me as you do, you'll know (as my pupils know, too) that making myself feared isn't one of my talents. Maggie could do it: in subtler ways than Benedict's, she made you care deeply what she thought of you. This isn't one of my gifts, and I've known it isn't for as long as I've consciously known anything: the tyrant's role is closed to me, therefore, which leaves either that of victim or bystander.

You'll understand, I'm sure, why any hesitation on my part between the two was purely cosmetic.

34

Jake

Parmesan follows me to the dormitory, now empty of boys, as though his presence is all that will keep me going at a moment like this. Dad's coming to collect me in half an hour and I'll need more clothes than the things I've packed for the weekend. My housemaster stands awkwardly by the window, talking about the day's cricket match.

'Wasn't Chieveley bowling like an angel?' he asks, making conversation.

I ignore him. Everything seems very far away. Even the nausea has receded. There's a hushed, still quality inside my head. I find I can walk again without difficulty and there's a smoothness to my movements. I feel like a well-oiled automaton, expertly controlled.

The room's cold. The heating's been switched off. It's empty too, which makes it difficult to remember the people who usually sleep in it, the things that usually happen in it. It seems tawdry suddenly. Too drab for terror.

'I must say, you're handling this awfully well,' murmurs Parmesan.

And then I see it.

Us

I

Julian, Adrienne

Have you ever seen *When Harry Met Sally*, which came out the year I met Adrienne? Do you remember the scene in the restaurant, when Sally fakes the orgasm? You know the one – where she's moaning so loudly, so convincingly, that an old lady at a nearby table orders 'whatever she's having'.

Well I've got one question for you: what do you think a film like that does to the sexual self-confidence of the average adolescent male?

*

I don't know exactly how long I cry for, but it's long enough to make my nose swell and my mascara run, so when somebody knocks on the wall by the bed I just shut my eyes and hope they'll go away. I used to do that when I was a kid, just shut my eyes and magic the whole world right out of existence – as though, if I couldn't see it, it couldn't see me, right?

Wrong. Because the person taps again, a gentle kind of tap, not demanding anything, not really. So I open my eyes, still hopeful in a way (because childhood beliefs die hard) but I'm still in the plunge pool with the brown and orange curtains and there doesn't seem like much to do except say, but still hesitantly: 'Hello?'

'Hello,' says someone on the other side of the wall.

*

How, you're wondering, did a boy like me ever get my hands on (or into) a girl like Adrienne Finch?

It's a good question, and one I had to force myself to stop asking after a while. It used to drive me crazy with worry, the thought that somehow she'd been tricked by false pretences into falling in love with me, that somehow she'd been fooled into making a terrible mistake.

The explanation I eventually accepted, in the privacy of my own mind at least, was that I'd simply been in the right place at the right time. This seems to be the only solution that fits the facts, because by rights a girl like Adrienne should have ended up with a boy like Benedict Chieveley. She deserved the pick of the crop, the confidence, charm and physique of the indisputably alpha male. She so obviously didn't deserve a specimen as unfortunate as me, that for a long time I couldn't believe that she was prepared, apparently, to go out of her way to have a relationship with me.

As I remind my pupils whenever I can, it doesn't do to underestimate the force of the random in daily life.

*

'Hello,' says a boy's voice.
'Can I . . . *help* you?'
'Are you okay?'
'I'm fine.'
Silence for a few seconds, broken by: 'Right then.'
When the boy's voice doesn't say anything else I just sit back down on the bed and look at my feet for a while, breathing calmly, getting myself under control, reminding myself my life has just gotten a whole lot better. But it isn't that easy to feel grateful when you're sitting on a hard bed in a plunge pool, when a window pane is broken right above

you and you're being whipped in the face by a jet of cold air. It's not easy, okay? So . . . I couldn't help it, I started crying again.

Just quietly this time, though.

*

If she hadn't been given the worst room in college, right next to the second worst room in college, which was mine, I'd never have got her into bed. If the partition wall between us hadn't been so flimsy, or if she hadn't turned up so jet-lagged and exhausted, I'd never have got her into bed. If anyone more welcoming than the notoriously sour Brother Malcolm had opened the door to her, she would have been whisked off to the refectory to enjoy some supper and a good gossip with the older monks about Jerry's new life in New York and . . . I'd never have got her into bed.

Sometimes the miraculous *does* happen.

*

He taps on the wall again.

'Yes?'

'Just me.'

'Oh . . . hi.'

'Hello.'

There's this kind of awkward moment when neither of us says anything and I want to sniff really badly, but I can't while he's just . . . *listening* like that.

*

I couldn't see who was crying on the other side of the flimsy partition, of course; all I could hear were stifled sobs, but what they meant was plain enough. It was the first night of term and someone had arrived late and been put in the worst room in college. As an experienced second year, I had long since accustomed myself to St Botolph's and its strange ways; I had also had the foresight to equip myself with a highly efficient electric heater, which I had smuggled into my room against all fire regulations.

The sobs told me the person in question was a girl; nothing more. They didn't prepare me for a girl like her.

★

I just sit there, trying to think of something to say, trying to ignore the little trickle of mucus tickling my nostril. 'Sorry about the noise,' I manage eventually.

'Are you sure you're all right?'

'Yeah, thanks.'

'Hundred per cent?'

'Yeah.'

More silence. I almost sniff, but chicken out at the last minute.

'So who are you, anyway?' he asks.

'I'm, um, Adrienne,' I say.

'Hello, Adrienne. Welcome to St Botolph's.'

'Thanks.' I can't deal with this anymore, so I close my eyes (*please go away, please go away*) and sniff as hard as I can.

'Pretty impressive,' he says.

★

The girl's bawling her eyes out, so I knock on the wall again to make sure she's okay. You hear horror stories at Oxford of people killing themselves in Freshers' Week, appalled by the misery of the whole sordid ritual, and I don't want anything tragic to happen in the room next door to mine – especially if I have to listen to it.

I imagine an overweight girl with sallow skin and badly cut hair. I can almost see her huddling in a chair or lying on the bed, with a bottle of pills stolen from her parents' medicine cabinet in her hand, trying to gather the nerve to put an end to it all. From our first chat through the wall I know she is an American, and imagine a product of Hicksville, totally out of her depth, wondering what to make of the fact that all the adult men she's seen so far are wearing white dresses.

Steeling myself against the cold, I decide to leave the warmth of my electric heater and go into the icy corridor to knock on her door. I make my taps gentle, not wanting to upset her.

There are several minutes of anxious scuffling before I hear the bolt slide back.

*

'God it's cold in here.'

When Julian says 'in here' he's not speaking with strict accuracy because he's in fact standing just outside my room, in the dark corridor. It must be almost midnight, but I've washed my face in the basin by the wardrobe, so it's screeching redness all over (the water was as cold as everything else) which I'm hoping will disguise the state of my bloodshot eyes. Who am I kidding anyway? He's been listening to me sob for the last thirty minutes.

'Come on in,' I say, feeling kind of embarrassed, by which I mean *totally* embarrassed. Now everyone's going to think you're a jerk, Adrienne. You've screwed things up before they even got started.

*

Fucking hell.

The girl who's been crying, it turns out, is not only not from Hicksville and not fat with sallow skin and a bad haircut, she's the most terrifyingly beautiful creature I've ever seen in my life. She's tall, and would have been taller than me if we'd met a year before; she's got long, straight, brown-gold hair that sways off her shoulders; and instead of the expected bottle of tranquillizers in her hand, the only thing in the room which seems to belong to her is a Louis Vuitton hold-all, thrown into a corner.

There's no way I'm going to be able to act cool in front of a woman like this.

Everything about her screams worldliness: from her manicured fingernails to the cut of her designer jeans. She's not wearing anything much out of the ordinary – jeans, a roll-neck sweater – but hers are clearly extraordinary versions of ordinary clothes. The sweater is white mohair, worn off the shoulder, and the jeans are tight, emphasizing the perfection of her legs.

I can't bring myself to go into the room itself, so I just stand gawping in the corridor. Half of me wishes the earth would swallow me, the other half is glad it's not going to. After a few minutes' random chat, to my total amazement she asks me to come in.

*

But he's smiling, like he's kind of . . . amused to be in this situation. He's acting like it's kind of a funny joke, being with this weird American girl in this ice-cold room at a monastery in Oxford in the middle of the night. He's tall, taller than me, not conventionally good looking, but he has these beautiful hands which are too big for him, like he's lost his natural ones in a car crash and had them replaced by castings from a Roman statue. They're his best feature, probably. His hands and his nose, which is straight and kind of big (but not too big). An imposing nose, I guess, is what I'm trying to describe. He's also got this shyness to his manner, this slight timidity which is sort of appealing.

'D'you just arrive or something?' he asks, looking at my suitcase.

'Yeah,' I say, 'I've just come from New York.'

'You must be jet-lagged.'

'A little.'

'Er . . . making a sort of fashionably late entrance, I take it?'

'I guess you could call it that. Come on in. Welcome to my, um, humble abode.'

'It certainly is humble,' says Julian, looking round.

*

Don't ask me how I pull it off, but somehow I persuade her to come into my room, as it's warmer in there. *Thank God I bought the heater, thank God, thank God.* My room's much warmer than hers, but it's also full of unpacked books and half-open suitcases. She stops in her room for a moment to get another sweater out of her hold-all, and I take the opportunity to go on ahead, checking for dirty laundry. There's a pile of used boxer shorts and socks in the middle of my rug and I manage to stuff them behind the bookshelf before she comes in.

How am I going to entertain this vision of sophistication?

She's clearly used to something a little better than the creature comforts laid on by St Botolph's College, Oxford, and there's only one chair in my room: a scabby old armchair I picked up at a second-hand sale a few days ago for a fiver. To cover my embarrassment at its torn leather and exposed springs, I attempt to pass it off as an heirloom by telling her it belonged to my grandfather.

She sits down on the floor next to the heater and I sit down next to her, not sure where to take things from here. It's the middle of the night and I'm not used to finding myself in the company of beautiful women in the middle of the night. What's the bloke meant to do in a situation like this? What's the procedure?

Someone this gorgeous must be used to jet-set parties, but I don't have any drugs to offer her. I find myself wondering if I know anyone in Oxford who might be able to get me some, as an emergency offering, this late at night; but then I remember that Maggie asked me to look after a little package for her the week before, so that Mum and Dad wouldn't find it when they unpacked her room with her at Bridwell.

If I know my sister, there'll be something promising in that package.

*

'They're mean bastards at this college, you know. You should be grateful the heating's even on. My dad says the monks never switched on the radiators until mid November when he was here. The water used to freeze beside his bed.'

We're in Julian's room now, which is twice the size of mine and ten times as warm. It's raining outside, which makes it kind of snug to be where we are, which is: sitting on a big, square red rug, a pretty battered but still beautiful Persian, next to a tall grey electric heater belching hot air. Julian bought the heater himself – after five years at some boarding school called Bushel he's through with being cold all the time – and it's the only really modern thing I've seen since I arrived. Tall and shiny, with some kind of electronic climate control pad, it reminds me of home.

Otherwise, the room's full of piles of books, tottering dangerously, and propped up by piles of clothes which Julian's not unpacked yet, even though he's in his second year already and 'came up' a week ago. There's also a scuffed red leather armchair which used to be his grandfather's when it was new and he was at St Botolph's himself, and a ghetto blaster and a small wooden box, which Julian's in the process of opening.

'My baby sister gets it for me,' he says. 'She knows this guy in Camden who grows some pretty incredible stuff.' His long, large fingers are stroking the tobacco out of a cigarette. 'You've got to meet my sister. She's a Fresher this year, too, doing History at Briddle.'

'I'd like to,' I say, wondering whether to tell him I've never smoked a joint before.

*

Get her stoned, I'm telling myself. Get her really *stoned*.

*

It's now four in the morning, and Julian and I are still sitting on the floor, still next to the heater, only now we're next to each other, too. Not cuddling or anything, not even really touching – he just got up to get us some water a while ago and when he sat down he sat next to me. It's not like a *situation*'s developing or anything, but we're having this really cool conversation, all about where he comes from, this little village in Hampshire, and where I come from, who I come from.

'You've got to be joking,' he says when I tell him about Momma's little performance with the FBI.

And like it is some big joke, we start laughing about it. Julian can't talk when I'm done describing Momma in her Halston dress in *Vanity Fair*. He's rolled over on the floor, practically crying, and when I'm done describing Momma I just crack up too, and roll over too, and then we're both lying on the floor, looking at the ceiling, kind of enjoying the way it's spinning away from us without actually moving. And the way we've ended up, some of my hair's falling over his hand, which is stretched out on the floor, and we both just lie there like that, not moving, just talking sometimes.

*

I don't know what's in this grass of Maggie's, but it makes Adrienne totally lose the plot. She goes from being cool and aloof, elegantly in control one minute, to telling me a whole lot of rambling bullshit the next. I can't really follow everything she's saying, because I'm pretty stoned too; but I remember something about her mother and a magazine profile and an FBI man in a Halston dress.

After a few more joints, we can't talk any more we're laughing so much.

Come on, Ogilvie. It's now or never.

*

It's totally weird being in his bed, which smells strongly like *his* bed, but we're so cold and so stoned now the only way to keep warm is by getting under the covers together. Not undressed or anything, just our shoes off – but after a while Julian puts his arm round my shoulder and I put my head on his chest, which is warm and gently thudding, and then his fingers are playing with my hair and it seems the thing to do so I snuggle against him, rolling over towards him and putting one leg just a little on top of his.

'Would you think it very forward of me if I kissed you?' he asks.

*

Score!

Somehow, incredibly, I've managed to get this girl into bed. Slowly, by stages, I've succeeded in persuading her that she can't go back to her own room, or she'll die of cold. From this point the obvious solution is for us to share *my* bed, but on a strictly Platonic basis. We end up lying under my duvet, in my regulation St Botolph's single bed, fully dressed; and she seems okay with it when I start playing with her hair.

Though I'm pretty stoned, I haven't forgotten the packet of condoms, bought in a moment of wild optimism, at the bottom of my suitcase. I'm thinking about it when, without any prompting, she leans against me and puts her knee over my thigh.

2

Adrienne, Julian

It's difficult to salvage a clear memory of the last twenty-four hours from the tangle of limbs and sheets that make up my present, but it looks like I've gone from being a virgin who's never smoked a joint to being a non-virgin who has. It certainly feels that way – like something's happened in my body that's never happened before – and even though it's painful, kind of, it's exciting too. That's the first thing I think when I wake up: I'm not a virgin any more!

*

The problem with being the kind of boy who never pulls girls is that you get used to sleeping alone and to doing all the things that boys used to sleeping alone do. As my brain stirs to consciousness my hand instinctively reaches through the waistband of my boxer shorts; and quite automatically, because this is what I've done every morning since that forgotten red-letter day I first discovered the pleasures of auto-eroticism, I start stroking my morning glory, lost in a fantasy about a woman with tawny hair and long, smooth limbs.

*

Sunlight's flooding the room and the furniture's lost its midnight chic, but neither his hands nor his nose have changed. His hands, particularly, are exactly as I remember them – large, strongly gentle – and I think with a thrill where they've been as I watch them, twitching as he dreams, on the navy and maroon duvet he's obviously had since he was a kid.

Never having had sex with a stranger before, I don't know what you're meant to say the morning after sex with a stranger, so I'm pretty content just to lie there looking at him, remembering.

I'm a new person in a new place, I think. Momma and New York are far away and long ago. That's enough for the time being.

*

I'm in a forest, all green light. I'm lying on a carpet of grass, naked but warm, sunlight falling over me. It's one of those idealist fantasies, in which everything is pre-Lapsarian and chaste in its sensuality. I'm lying down. In the distance a goddess appears, composite of every advertised image of female loveliness I've ever seen; tawny hair cascading over bare, milky breasts, enticingly pert. The vibe is part Olympus, part perfume advert. The model goddess is smiling, half-innocent, half-wanton, and she's walking towards me over the grass. I hear the crackle of her feet on fallen leaves and I know she's walking towards me, and me alone.

I'm naked and she knows it, wants it; she wants *me*.

*

I don't know how long I lie there for, but long enough to drift back into sleep. There's something incredibly . . . intimate about sharing such a small bed with another person. Julian's sprawled on his back and I'm lying around him, warmed by the heat of his sleeping body. He murmurs something to himself occasionally, and I try to hear what it is but can't make out the words. In New York, Momma's probably just waking up for her 6.00 a.m. meeting with her yoga instructor, before hitting the gym (two hours) and then the spa (another two hours) which is how she fills her mornings, getting up early to pretend she has something to do.

I wonder if she did consider having an abortion when she discovered she was pregnant with me – it'd be typical of Momma to spend years wanting something and then change her mind at the last minute.

*

I keep myself for as long as I can in that half-world between sleeping and waking. I take my time opening my eyes – nothing destroys a fantasy like the harsh realities of a scabby student room, full of soiled boxer shorts and the other detritus of twenty-something life: ashtrays piled high, blue-grey and pungent; wine-soaked rugs; broken glasses. I know this from experience and I want to hold on to the possibilities of my sleep world as long as I can, so I keep my eyes shut, fighting consciousness, as the dream woman puts her hand on my hand and starts imitating its gentle, up-and-down movement.

*

Poppa was hardly ideal father material (as even she must have known, deep down) and Momma's primary allegiance has always been to her figure, so why would she have risked it without a moment's hesitation?

I'm thinking all this to myself, not upset or even angry, just thinking, when Julian starts stirring. I run my fingers through my hair and smooth my eyebrows, wanting to look good for his first sight of me, but he doesn't even open his eyes. He's clearly awake, though, because his right hand disappears under the navy and maroon duvet and he, well, he starts touching himself.

I've never seen anyone do this, except for a man in a park in Connecticut, once, when I was seven or eight. For a moment I'm a bit shocked, a bit disgusted to tell you the truth. But as he keeps on doing it, eyes still closed, the image of the man in the park fades and it seems like maybe this is the *only* thing to do if you wake up in bed with a stranger. At least he feels intimate with me, I reason. At least he clearly enjoyed himself last night – which is a relief, considering it was my first time and everything. Obviously he wouldn't be doing this if he'd really *hated* the sex and it seems like an invitation of some sort, in a way. So not really knowing what I'm doing, a little nervous, I slip my hand under the covers.

*

Aaaaaahhh . . .

*

Maybe I've got used to it over the years. As time goes by, you inevitably pick up a few bits and pieces here and there, a little technique. You learn what pace to start at, how to build up gradually, not to peak the speed too soon. Spencer's taught me a lot about giving hand jobs, but back then I was a spring chicken and didn't really know what to do with this . . . this strange, warm, rubbery *thing* in my hand.

Julian kept his eyes closed all the time, which at first kind of weirded me out, but then made me feel more comfortable.

I guess it's different if you've got a dick yourself, but if you haven't the whole idea of jerking off is basically ridiculous and I was glad I didn't have to say anything or make eye contact.

*

Orgasm comes slowly, but certainly, which is the best part of fantasy sex. It's not hampered by all the anxieties and questions of real-life sex. The point of fantasy, rather than reality, is that *you're* the focus of attention, *you're* the one people are trying to please.

*

I don't know how long I lie there, tugging patiently, trying to act like this is something I've done a million times before. Five minutes? Five hours? It feels like for ever and he doesn't even seem close to coming, so I start to go faster and faster and he moans a bit more, but my wrist's aching like you wouldn't believe.

Eventually I put myself in workout mode, counting the reps like I do when performing crunches in the gym. I can do a hundred and fifty crunches and to make the time go quicker I count them in sets of ten, so the total's only, what, fifteen sets of ten.

I do fifteen sets of ten on Julian, and then another five, by which point my right wrist is ready to drop off. But he still hasn't come, so it seems like there's only one option. At least I've given head before, so it doesn't feel like such new territory.

To tell you the truth, though, the taste (after a night of sex and general excitement) is pretty . . . intense.

*

This morning, things are more than usually satisfactory; I stretch back to let nature take its course.

*

Yes!

There's a last quiver, I pull away just in time to avoid a hot jet squirting over my hand. He opens his eyes.

*

Oh God. Oh my *God*. Oh shitting FUCK. She's *real*. In a moment I'm out of bed, apologizing furiously, face screaming embarrassment, my semi-erect member dangling foolishly in front of me.

Where the *fuck* are my boxer shorts?

Racing round the room, trying to find clean underwear in the piles of books that litter the floor, I take a moment to get my breath back without actually having to look at her. The memory of last night is slowly coming back to me, but what I remember most clearly is how stoned I was, which means that all other memories are questionable. As I rifle through a set of drawers, aware that my bum is far from being my most attractive feature and that it's on full view to the vision of loveliness I've miraculously woken up with, I have trouble establishing the precise sequence of events. Has a memory of her putting her thigh over mine sprung up because I badly want it to, or because that's really what happened? I have no idea, but it occurs to me that I can't keep scampering around like this for ever, not looking at her; so I abandon my search for underwear and put on a pair of jeans, lying stiffly on the floor, and force myself to meet her eyes.

*

The second it was over and Julian's eyes were open, he seemed to return to reality with a bump – and then he was out of bed, trying to get dressed in that messy room, looking endearingly English and moving with a serious spring in his step.

When I think of Julian now, I often think of him that first morning, of the way he moved around that little room. I'd never been naked with someone in a situation like that. My few previous experiences had been confined to the back seats of cars in East Hampton, or walk-in-closets in the city, but this was . . . real – like the movies.

*

'I'm so sorry,' I say, not knowing how to account for what, it's dawning on me, is a reaction she's probably not used to from men she's just slept with. 'I'm . . .' She's looking at me, quizzically beautiful, sitting up in bed – *my* bed – with the duvet covering her breasts and her hair tangled over her shoulders, like a Hollywood actress in a men's magazine. 'I'm . . .' But my mind's blank.

Time slows and then stops altogether. She's still looking at me, inscrutable, and I have an eternity to take stock of what a twat I am. Finally inspiration of a sort dawns and I find my tongue scraping dryly against the roof of my mouth, which feels like a small furry mammal has just made off after spending the night in it.

'Sorry to rush like this,' I hear myself saying. 'But I'm . . . I'm late for a lecture.'

3

Jake, Adrienne

In group this morning, Camilla spent two hours telling us how she first took coke during Freshers' Week at Bristol. This led to a morbid comparison of 'university experiences', which basically divided the room into two camps: the Isolated and the Manic.

When asked, I said I couldn't remember that much about it. John, therapist *extraordinaire*, deduced from this that I've 'shut myself off' from my past. Which is part and parcel of wanting to shut myself off from my present, I told him. Your future, don't you mean, he said. He seems to think I'm the joker of the group.

*

I reckon I've got an hour to kill before Julian gets back from his lecture and I really want to be here waiting for him, but I don't want him to think I'm desperate or anything. Guys don't like girls who come on too strong, right? So I sit up in his bed, trying to think, trying to plan what would seem most *natural* to him. Should he find me just where he left me? Would that be sexy? Or would it be better if I took a bath, got dressed, pretended like I was just, you know, getting on with my day, not waiting for him or anything. Maybe I should take a bath and *then* get back into bed . . . Or would that be too much?

*

Though I don't choose to share this fact with a group of recovering drug addicts, I often think of the day Maggie came back into my life. I can see myself now, as thin as ever. It's a miserable afternoon. Whipping wind, harsh prickings of rain. I'm standing in the doorway of the Radcliffe Camera, half in and half out of the library. It's Noughth Week of my second year and the city's full of bawdy Freshers on the make. I've spent the afternoon and most of the previous night with Milton. My knee's aching. My hair's long and greasy, obedient to student fashions. My face is long too, longer than it was at school but just as pale. I've got a reputation for being scary, though the few girls I've managed to sleep with describe me to their friends as 'intense'.

Predictably, privileged education in England being what it is, I'm not the only person I know at Oxford. Chieveley's here, too, in the year above. Julian Ogilvie's here. So's Simon Quintavalle, though we're not friends anymore. His dad's win changed his life, too, in ways he can't or won't tell me. We've left behind the selves who climbed up drainpipes together and can't find them again. When we met in Freshers' Week it was like seeing a ghost. We got drunk together, obviously, but there was no hiding the awkwardness. Neither of us were up to explaining the previous five years, so neither of us did, and I only see him now when I'm after some reliable skunk.

Believe it or not, I've still not made the connection between Maggie and Julian. I still don't know that the girl with the springy hair and the Pimms, who kissed me behind the Art Schools on the day my mother died, is Julian Ogilvie's sister. We didn't swap surnames at the time and haven't seen each other since. I think about her, sometimes, but only when drunk. I don't seriously think I'll ever see her again, or even seriously want to. The afternoon has its place in the moments that make up my past. That's all.

My essay on *Paradise Lost* is almost done. It's a poor paraphrase of one taken from the *Cambridge Companion Guide to Milton* and I'm smoking a cigarette on the library stairs, collecting the energy for the final page or so. It's a typical afternoon, as afternoons go. I'm expecting it to lead on to a typical night. King's Arms till closing time. Then bed, with a bad novel. Studying literature has put me off good novels, but I find I like bad ones more than ever. More than most people's company, anyway.

Pathetic fallacy weather apart, the afternoon has nothing to suggest the momentous about it – which doesn't stop Maggie from wheeling her bicycle across Radcliffe Square and back into my life.

*

I lie in bed for a while, trying to work out what to do. I'm badly in need of a second opinion, not having a copy of *Cosmopolitan* at hand for guidance, and I think wistfully of Jerry in New York. What would he advise in this situation?

Julian's room is . . . dirtier by daylight than it looked last night. The windows are streaked and I can see a pile of socks and shirts stuffed behind the bookcase. Maybe it'd be sweet if I tidied up for him a bit? I consider this option for a few minutes, biting my lip, but finally reject it – you don't want to scare men away by mothering them, and he might think it weird if I went rooting around in his things while he was out.

The room's full of books, some unpacked into the bookcase but most in piles all over the floor. There're too many books for the room's few shelves and I remember that Julian's doing English, like me, which would explain this passion. Maybe . . .

yes! When he comes back, he should find me still in bed, reading a book! Something cerebral we can talk about later, a starting point for discussion. So I get out of bed and go over to the first pile, looking for an appropriate title, which means I'm standing in the middle of the floor, totally naked, when the door opens.

*

'Maggie!'

She looks round when I call her name. She doesn't recognize my voice and can't work out where it's coming from. At least ten people are huddling on the steps smoking cigarettes and complaining about the weather. She stops a moment, then hurries on. It's definitely her. Even wet and pissed off she's so clearly the same I feel suddenly unsure.

Shouldn't memories stay memories?

*

'Christ, I'm . . .'
  'Oh my God.'
  'No, it's . . .'
  'Ohmy*God*.'

*

It takes me a moment to decide to call again, by which time Maggie's walking quickly towards the High Street, wheeling the bike. She doesn't even look round. It's raining heavily. Large, dull drops, falling monotonously. The water's collecting in her hair, which is too frizzy for sleekness. She doesn't even try to shake it out, but keeps on. Stubbornly.

Not sure what I'm doing, I go down the library steps. Down the path which leads to the gate. I don't call out again. Maggie rounds the corner on to the High Street. I speed up, not wanting to lose her in the traffic. It is her, surely? She's ahead of me now, pressing through a line of tourists getting off one of the large green buses offering guided tours of the city. I press through them too and watch her walk towards Magdalen Bridge and the traffic-filled roundabout. The bicycle has a flat tyre, which squelches in the damp. She's going quickly now, half running. The rain's beginning to bucket down.

As she turns left into Longwall Street, I'm right behind her. 'Maggie!'

She stops and turns round. Half of me wants suddenly to be wrong. Half of me wants it not to be her. As she faces me I have a flash of how her profile looked, hazy against the cool stone of the Art Schools, on that drunken summer afternoon years before.

'Do I know you?' she says.

*

There's a girl standing in the doorway, wearing jeans and a loose sweater with a clump of curly hair, tied backwards. I'm bending over, naked, and the only thing that breaks the silence is the clatter of books hitting the floor.

'I'm so sorry,' says the girl. 'I was looking for my brother, Julian Ogilvie. I thought this was his room.'

My clothes are caught between the bed and the wall and I can't get to them. What should I do? Get back into bed?

'It *is* his room,' I tell her.

*

There's something very direct about her look, which makes me nervous. I'm less tongue-tied than I used to be, but I'm hardly the bluff confident type either.

'Perhaps "know" is a bit strong,' I say eventually. 'We met once, ages ago. That's all.' It certainly doesn't seem like much of a pretext now. She's still looking at me, expecting something else. Not wary, exactly, but not friendly either. 'You probably don't remember me,' I tell her, confirming the self-evident. I feel like running away. I want to pretend this is all a big mistake, but I've gone too far for easy back-tracking. What's there to say after all this time?

'You're the first person I ever got drunk with,' is all that occurs to me.

*

'Which means my brother's a lot cooler than I thought,' she says, smiling at me, her eyes – is this real? did this happen? – running me quickly up and down before she goes over to the bed and pulls out my jeans from the gap by the wall and hands them to me. 'I'm going to look the other way and count to ten.'

While she's counting I get dressed and by the time she's at 7 I'm done, but I don't say anything, just look at her from behind, wondering what to do, as she intones: '8 . . . 9 . . . 10. Coming to get you.'

When she turns round I see she couldn't be anyone but Julian's sister – different colouring, maybe, and totally different hair, but the same jaw, the same mouth, something identical in the eyes, even though hers are dark and his aren't.

'I'm Maggie,' she says, 'and I'm desperate for a spliff. D'you fancy joining me?'

*

Maggie frowns. The rain continues.

Then she smiles. Her teeth are neat and white. Big too. She

shows them freely. Her smile brings a dash of summer liquor, sweet and frothy, to this rain-drenched autumn day.

'You're Jack,' she says. 'The boy who couldn't play cricket.'

'Jake,' I say.

We stand, looking at each other.

Maggie's on her way to a tutorial, it turns out. Her essay's on the French Wars of Religion. She's reading History at Bridwell College. We stand outside her tutor's house, both of us now soaking wet. She looks at me, weighing something, and there's a moment of awkwardness I can't fill. The thought of my Milton essay grows steadily more appealing.

I'm not prepared for any friendliness from her, so when she speaks she takes me by surprise.

'Could I suggest a cup of tea without seeming like a desperate Fresher on the pull?'

'Don't you have a tutorial?'

I sound like Julian.

Maggie smiles at me. 'I'm not sure I've got the nerve to read this essay in public,' she says, reaching into her bag and pulling out some folded sheets of paper. They're covered in jerky letters which don't keep to their lines. I catch the opening phrase of the first sentence: *In the sixteenth century, as now, God was* . . .

'God was what, in the sixteenth century as now?' I ask.

'Misrepresented,' she says, stuffing the papers through the letterbox in front of her.

*

Maggie sits down by the window and picks up the box Julian opened last night, rolling a long thin joint so expertly I'm intimidated. What time is it? Aren't you only meant to smoke pot late at night? Obviously not, because once she's rolled the joint and hunted for a lighter, found one, she hands both items to me with a friendly smile and says: 'So how do you know my brother? And why isn't he here?'

'I live next door,' I tell her. 'And he's at a lecture.'

'A lecture?'

'Yup.'

I take a hit of the joint and my shoulders relax. I can't believe I'm here – in Oxford, smoking pot in the middle of the morning with this cooler-than-cool girl, who scares me but also thrills me. Maggie takes the joint from me and our fingers touch, briefly.

'That's so Julian,' she says. 'He's the only boy I know who'd wake up with a girl as beautiful as you and even *remember* he has a morning lecture. Don't think badly of him. I can see why you might, but he's not entirely prim at heart.' She takes a deep toke and exhales slowly, blowing perfect smoke rings across the room at me. 'What was the sex like?' she asks, nodding at the Durex wrapper which I only now realize has been on the floor between us all the time we've been talking.

I don't exactly know how to deal with this question. It's not like I've got a lot of experience to rate Julian against, and there's something about Maggie which tells me she definitely has – so I try not to blush and mumble something like 'oh, great', inwardly kicking myself for being such a ditz and trying to seem nonchalant as I pick up the condom foil and put it in the bin, under some used tissues.

'That's reassuring to hear,' says Maggie.

There's a pause, which I sense is my responsibility to fill. What do you ask someone who's just asked you what sex with their brother the night before was like? It seems lame to talk about classes or where we come from after an opening like that, so I take a deep breath and tell myself I need to act cool.

'Are you having sex with anyone at the moment?' I ask, as off-hand as possible.

'Funny you should ask,' she says, 'because that's exactly what I've come to talk to Julian about.'

*

I don't know exactly when the voices started. This uncertainty emerged today, in my one-on-one slot with John, who spent forty-five minutes pulling his intrigued-concerned face.

'Would it be true to say you can't remember a time without them?' he asked me.

'No,' I said. It's become policy to avoid confirming John's opinions, whenever possible.

Silence.

John, I've discovered in the weeks since I've been here, is good at silences. He was clearly one of those annoying kids who always won the staring contests at kindergarten. He loves to out-silence the most resistant patients. Particularly, he loves to out-silence me, since silences are my speciality.

I'm surprised when he admits defeat after only a few minutes.

'What was she like?' he asks, very matter-of-fact.

'Who?'

I haven't told him much yet. I haven't even told him Maggie's name and I ignore him as one of the voices recycles an old conversation with her. I haven't heard her laugh for months but suddenly here it is. Quite clear, full of affectionate malice. 'The whole *Summa Theologica* – in a week!' she giggles.

Maggie might have been Adrienne's 'best friend', but Adrienne certainly wasn't Maggie's – whatever she chose to believe. She never saw, and Maggie was far too kind to tell her, that she was just another saddo Maggie had befriended. She thought she was special.

I smile, despite myself, despite John.

'Give me one thing about her you loved,' he says. 'Anything.'

We look at each other in silence.

'Her fearlessness,' I say eventually, almost without thinking.

*

Maggie gets up and goes over to the kettle, fills it at the basin, and switches it on. 'I've met this boy,' she tells me, 'the first boy I ever kissed, as it happens. Not that he knows that. I haven't seen him for years, but we bumped into each other the other day – it was so weird seeing him again – and then we got talking and went off to the pub, then back to my room at Briddle, and . . .'

'And?'

Maggie turns to look at me. 'You know what it's like when a boy's just, I don't know, grateful to be there? It's the enthusiasm I'm touched by.'

I swallow, hoping she doesn't hear. 'He was . . . enthusiastic?'

'I think we can safely say he went beyond enthusiasm. There was a great deal of deftness involved, considering.' The kettle gurgles, then clicks and Maggie picks up and inspects two mugs, frowning. 'Like some tea?'

'Yes please.'

'I mean, I'm not saying there's anything wrong with enthusiasm. It's sweet, if nothing else. But it's only the first step, isn't it?'

'Towards what?'

'Towards orgasm,' says Maggie. She takes two tea bags and drops them into the mugs, then adds hot water. 'He doesn't have any milk,' she says apologetically, 'or sugar.'

'That's fine.'

I'm trying not to worry about the fact I've never had an orgasm – or at least, I don't think I've ever had one. I mean, last night was great and everything, but . . . Isn't an orgasm one of those things you're never unsure about? You either have one or you don't and if you do you know all about it?

'There's only one way to describe the sex I've been getting all week,' says Maggie, settling back down in her chair and taking another hit of the joint.

'Yeah?'

'Mind . . . boggling. Absolutely mind-boggling.'

4

Julian, Adrienne

As I walk down the stairs, it occurs to me that I could very easily still be in bed with this girl, having the time of my life, but that by my own incredible mismanagement of affairs I've left myself with an hour to kill in the cold before I can return, pretending my lecture has finished.

I spend the time in a café with the newspapers before returning to St Botolph's with a romantic breakfast in a bag. As I reach the last flight I catch a sweet trail of marijuana smoke, which intensifies as I approach my room, and my heart soars to imagine Adrienne in bed, smoking a breakfast joint, waiting for me. The picture forms instantly – her fragile shoulders propped against the wall, her eyes heavy with sleep – and I feel a stirring in my dirty jeans and a soaring pride.

I stand outside the door for a moment, collecting myself, and that's when I hear Maggie's voice: high and excited, recounting something. What's she doing here?

*

For someone who's only just met me, Maggie's pretty intimate in the details she shares about her romantic life. I end up learning a lot about Jake's body and erotic tastes – he has a mole on his chest, just under his left nipple, for example, and he likes to be bitten. He also, apparently, cries out at the point of orgasm in a way Maggie finds very arousing. She sits on a cushion on Julian's floor, hair tumbling into her eyes, knees pulled up under her, and talks to me like we've known each other a long time, looking me right in the eyes, not embarrassed at all.

'I hope my brother's given you an appropriate welcome,' she says at one point, grinning.

*

I can tell they've been talking about me as soon as I open the door; I can tell from the look Maggie gives me and the way she says 'Girls' talk' abruptly, when I ask. I wonder what Adrienne's said to her but I don't want to reveal my uncertainty, so I cover it by opening a window, laying out the breakfast things. It's clear from my purchases (two coffees, two *pains au chocolat*, two small bottles of orange juice) that I've envisaged a *petit déjeuner à deux*, but typically Maggie ignores this and helps herself to half my pastry, clearly intent on settling in for the morning.

*

Things take on an easy pattern after this first day. I spend a lot of time in Julian's room, talking and working (he takes his work very seriously) and sometimes, sitting in the armchair his grandfather gave him, with a book on my lap, I have to pinch myself to underline the fact that this is my life now. It's so calming, not living with Momma, not having to spend my time doing the things Momma likes to do – shopping, the spa, bitching about other rich, bored women. Julian listens to my stories about New York like I'm describing somewhere in outer space and I love his gravity as he sits facing me, not saying much, giving me his full attention. That's one of the best things about Julian, the way he really listens to what you say and remembers it afterwards.

He's attentive in other ways, too. He often waits for me after lectures and walks me back to St Botolph's, bringing an umbrella if it happens to be raining – which it often does. He meets me after each tutorial and takes my reading list away with him, returning in a few hours with a pile of books and something gentle in his eyes.

I think Jerry'd like him.

*

Maggie does go eventually, taking her grass with her, and when she does Adrienne and I go back to bed and spend the rest of the day there. We spend the next day in bed, too, and this time I don't make the mistake of going to a lecture.

It takes me some time to stop being scared of Adrienne, to accept the fact that (for some strange reason) she seems happy to spend a lot of her time with me and to ignore the discomforts of my narrow single bed.

As the term proceeds, we grow used to sleeping beside each other in this confined space, to the careful arrangement of arms and legs that the meanness of the college furniture requires from lovers. When we sleep her long hair tickles my face and sometimes wakes me, allowing me to watch her as she dreams, eyelids twitching.

*

Maggie comes by a lot. I learn to recognize the way she leaps up the stairs, two at a time, and find myself listening out for her at the hours she most likes to visit – in mid afternoon or late at night. She tends to bring pot with her, usually quite a bit of pot, and as the days turn into weeks we smoke a lot of it. I have to be careful, though, not to try to keep up with her, or I can end up sitting zoned in a corner, watching her words wreathe round me in the smoke.

'Doesn't it annoy you, having Julian coddle you like this all the time?' she asks me one day, looking at a pile of books Julian's left on my desk with a note on top telling me which the most important ones are. We're in my room, drinking tea, and it hasn't occurred to me before that Maggie might think it lame of me to let Julian help out so much. 'I have a horrible fear he's turning into a schoolmaster,' she says, not waiting for me to reply, 'and making you into his first pupil.'

I don't know what to say to this, or how to tell her that I love Julian's studiousness, his practice of reading snippets aloud to me when he's sitting tall and straight at his desk, frowning over a book.

'Isn't it time you started doing things for yourself?' asks Maggie.

5

Jake, Adrienne

I know what Parmesan's going to say. I've had this dream before. I know something else, too, but I can't quite put my finger on it. Parmesan opens his mouth. He's clapping me on the back. 'He was bowling like an angel!' he chortles. 'Like an angel, Hitchins.'

There's something I mustn't do. Something I mustn't see.

He's leading me up a staircase, through a door, into the dormitory. I can't turn away. I try to think of an excuse, something to say. I open my mouth. It's cracked and parched. There's a sweet taste in it, nothing else. My voice won't sound. I'm screaming at the top of my lungs but he's smiling at me, laughing.

It's over there, on a shelf by the bed. I know if I see it, all's lost. Mustn't see it, mustn't see it – but I've already seen it. My hand moves out, touches it. The rough grain of paper on my finger. A mountain range of envelope, jaggedly ripped open.

*

I've been at Oxford six weeks and I'm due to attend my first 'tea party' this afternoon at Jake's house. I'm not too sure what to expect and Maggie's advice hasn't been very helpful. 'Massively relaxed,' is all she's told me. 'Just come, hang out, spend some time with him. He's shy but he gets over it. I want you two to know each other.'

Me? I'm not so sure I want us two to know each other. On the few occasions Jake and I have met, he's made me uncomfortable. There's something freaky about his eyes, the way they check you out – kind of expressionless, hard to read, but taking everything in. I don't like it. I don't like the fact Maggie's always telling me how smart he is, either. It makes me nervous, since freaky eyes and brains are not a combination I'm that used to dealing with.

What should I wear?

*

'Jake!'

The room with its long line of beds hangs hesitantly in the air. The envelope's in my hand. I can feel its weight, remember its significance.

'I didn't mean to touch it,' I say. Voice high and unsteady, like a child's. 'I shouldn't have touched it.'

'Shouldn't have touched what?'

There's a strange voice, not part of the dream. There's a strange shape, rising out of the darkness beside me. I'm in a new, uncertain place. The envelope vanishes. A hand's touching my shoulder. It's soft and holds me gently. In the distance, a vaulted window lets in moonlight. Enough to see a black tangle and large eyes whose whites reflect the light.

'Jake,' whispers Maggie, pressing me towards her. Her smell is sweet, sweaty. Slowly I remember where I am. In Maggie's room at Bridwell. We're half-lying, half-sitting in a narrow single bed. I'm wet against her warm, dry skin. She's leaning her head next to mine. She's breathing slowly, calmly, like a lullaby singer. I feel the heavy scent of her breath against my cheek. A tongue flickers over my ear lobe, sending pleasure like electricity to my toes.

For a long time we stay like this. Very still.

*

By 4.30 I've made my final decision and I'm looking *hot*.

This isn't something I admit to myself that often, but having spent three hours getting dressed I tell myself a little self-congratulation's not that inappropriate. It took me forty-five minutes just to go through the possible jeans-and-sweater options, but none of them really stood out – and anyway, Maggie sees me in those ensembles every day. What this occasion calls for is something special, yet understated, and (after much hesitation) I've finally picked out the perfect thing. It's a short, black cashmere dress, kind of fitted but not slutty or anything. Plus, the whole cashmere element makes it totally luxurious *and* sophisticated at the same time. I just wish I had a pair of reading glasses to contribute to the studious look.

*

It's streaming daylight when I wake.

Maggie's sitting, towel wrapped round her hair, in a puddle of light by the fireplace. She's holding a cup of steaming tea, staring into its depths. She doesn't see me.

She brought Adrienne to my house yesterday. Overdressed and desperate to impress. Mostly, though, we've spent our time alone in the six weeks since we met. She hasn't forced me to be a part of the rest of her life. She hasn't included me in her doings, or reintroduced me to her brother. I'm grateful for all this. I've got my own life, my own few people to see. I don't want someone else's.

We've steered clear of involved emotional conversations. Maggie's sensed that they make me uncomfortable. She seems willing to take her time, which means we haven't strayed far from the standard fare of earnest undergraduates. Class A drug consumption. Sixteenth-century poetry. Third World debt.

'Rough night?' asks Maggie, handing me a cup of tea.

This is *not* something I feel like talking about.

'Look, I . . .'

But she raises her hand, almost impatiently. 'I've got the perfect remedy for bad dreams.'

'I, honestly, I . . .'

She looks at me, cheerfully. Steadily. There's something soothing in those big, dark eyes. There's no mockery in them, or embarrassment. She waits a moment, waiting for silence. Then she says, matter-of-factly, companionably: 'What would you say to a mid-week weekend in the country?'

*

It's 4.30 and I'm going to be late if I don't get myself together and leave now, so I stand in front of the mirror for a minute, checking out my hair (pinned back in a chignon, totally cerebral-sexy) and my legs, which look kind of good too, and I think to myself I'm not such a bad person. I've spent the morning reading *The Economist*, the *Spectator* and *Private Eye* and the last three weeks ploughing through George Eliot's *Middlemarch*, so I've even got something to talk about.

A *lot* to talk about, I tell myself as I pick up my bag and head out.

*

Maggie and I leave the wood. It's a bright day, but chilly. The trees are evergreen and thick with foliage. Ahead of us is blue sky and sloping ground. A green field, dotted with sheep. Telephone poles surge ahead of us. Down the valley, up the other side, to the house she's pointing to.

We've walked all the way from the station. We've left an ugly provincial town behind us, skirting its chain fast food stores and video shops. The houses we've seen on the road have been square and drab. A post-1950s development, cheaply made, insulting its view.

We left the road half an hour ago and climbed through fields to the top of this hill and its wood. It's cold, but walking has warmed us. Maggie's cheeks are flushed. Her hair's pinned back, haphazardly. She's wearing a thick, old houndstooth coat. Bought at a charity shop, she told me when she put it on. It's a little too big round the shoulders. A man's coat. She seems half lost inside it.

'Last one there rolls the spliff!'

The incline's steep and Maggie goes quickly. I'm behind her, a little out of breath. The sheep ahead scatter, bleating. A dog barks. Ahead of us, above us, on the other side of a small stream, is a long, low house. It stands on a flattened piece of turf, planted with rose bushes. They're bare and jagged now, but orderly. A child's swing hangs from an old wych-elm, by a pond which reflects scudding clouds in a cold blue sky.

The day has gone oddly. Calmly. Maggie hasn't mentioned the events of the night before. I'd think she'd forgotten them, if it wasn't for the secret half-looks of concern I catch her giving me. One thing I don't yet know about Maggie, though I'm beginning to learn, is her capacity for nurture. That's the quality you can't buy, however well-trained your therapist. That's the quality that ripped from my life when I lost her.

*

In the window of the newsagent's at the corner of Jake's road, I check my hair. Still looking good. This is kind of exciting, I whisper at my reflection, in an attempt to convince myself *I'm* kind of exciting.

Let them like me. Let them like me.

*

She's waiting for me when I arrive. Panting steam in the cold air. I catch a trail of her coat's smell, rich with age and dust. Underneath it is *her* smell. So young it makes you wonder if she could ever have grown old.

'This is where I grew up,' she says, turning to me. 'But you won't have to worry about meeting grown-ups. My parents are on holiday in Brittany. We've got it all to ourselves.' As she speaks, she's fitting a key into a glass-panelled kitchen door. It turns with well-oiled ease. 'Come in.'

The first thing I notice is the smell. It's part dank, part sweet, heavily smoky. Flagstones, thatch, dogs, fires burned low night after night. It's a lived-in, homey, country smell. Very different from the aerosol freshness of the house I grew up in or the sanitized clash of disinfectant and sweat in the corridors of Botesdale.

Except for one or two things in the kitchen, everything's old. Appliances aside, there's not a single piece of modern furniture, not a single strip of plastic or shining chrome. The colours are muted. Once rich, now faded, invitingly sensuous. Long, narrow rooms lead into and out of one another. The floor's highly polished, dark wood, spotted with rugs. Silver-framed photographs of people in expensive clothes clutter heavy mantelpieces of polished stone.

As Maggie leads me through the house I remember the Quintavalles' sitting room and the veneer table Mr Quintavalle wrote my cheque out on. I see our lounge in Fareham, with its three-piece suite and the Staffordshire figurine my parents were given as a wedding present. I think of the betting slip, rusted with blood, that took me away from rooms like those and brought me here to a room like this.

*

I find Jake's house okay. It's a typical Oxford house, a small Victorian terrace off of St Clements, one of a long row of others just like it. Outside are the bikes and overflowing trash cans that tell me it's a student house, the one I'm looking for.

It's got a big bay window on the ground floor and I can hear people laughing and talking inside, as the frame shakes to the regular pulse of a bass guitar. I take a moment trying to recognize the music they're playing and decide it's the Cure – though as I leave the sidewalk I reason that it's probably better not to mention it, in case I'm wrong. The curtains are drawn, giving the place a look of secrecy. The only thing to do is ring the doorbell, which I do – once, then again, then again.

Several minutes go by before I hear someone in the passage and the door creaks open. A girl's standing in front of me, wearing overalls and a T-shirt and no shoes. Her hair's in dreadlocks, which look kind of weird given her pink and white complexion.

She doesn't say anything.

'Hi,' I say. 'I'm Adrienne.'

I don't know if I should put out my hand, or kiss her European-style, or just do nothing. The girl pulls back into the passage, making space for me.

'I'm Maggie's friend,' I tell her.

The girl turns and walks down the passage, into the room with the big bay window. The smell of pot is pretty overpowering and there's not very much light, so it takes my eyes a moment or two to get accustomed to the dark.

I'm *way* overdressed.

*

It snows in the night. Maggie and I go to sleep in a bed with a pink and blue eiderdown, under a pile of stuffed animals and dolls.

'I won't hear a word against my dolls,' she says, pushing them to one side and making space for us.

'I didn't say anything.'

'No, but I could tell you were on the verge of being disrespectful – and I couldn't allow that.'

They're a ragged collection, these childhood relics. They stare at us through wide eyes as Maggie takes her clothes off, pulls my boxer shorts to my knees. The sheets are icy when we get into them. Maggie pulls me to her, for warmth, and I bury my face in her neck. Her curls tickle my cheeks. 'Thank you,' she says softly.

'For what?'

'For calling out to me that day in the rain.' She pulls away from me, holding my head in her hands. Moonlight sparks in her pupils.

'Thank you for missing your tutorial.'

She looks at me gravely. I can just make out the outline of her jaw in the darkness. Behind her, through the open curtains, snow flakes fall, hushed and heavy. 'I'm excited by this,' she says.

'By what?'

'By us.' I feel her breath on my cheek. She pulls me towards her again and for the first time we sleep together without making love, bodies pressed close in the cold.

*

The fact hits me, kind of sickeningly, in the pit of the stomach. For a moment, until Maggie notices me and comes over, giving me a hug, telling me how great I look (which only makes things worse), I seriously consider just leaving, as if I never came. Surely no one would notice?

Maggie's wearing flared seventies jeans and an almost see-through black lace shawl, pinned with clips. Her hair's frizzy and wild, there's a frenzy in her eyes and when she pulls me to her and kisses me on my right cheek, wetly, I know she's been drinking.

Some 'tea party' this turns out to be.

*

Maggie isn't there when I wake up. The room's full of dazzling light, bouncing off unblemished snow. The clouds have cleared and the ground's like a wedding cake – smooth and white, reflecting brightly. There's music coming from somewhere, piano music. I get up and pull on my boxer shorts and walk downstairs. The air's tinged with fire smoke.

I see her from the drawing room door. She's sitting at the piano, naked except for a blanket pulled over her shoulders. The instrument's by the window and she's facing away from me, into the garden, sitting very straight. Her wrists are strong and supple, bending gracefully. She seems unaware of me, lost in the music which runs happily like water in a stream. The piece ends with a flourish which resolves in two gentle chords and she stays still as the vibrations die in the instrument.

'Good morning.'

She turns towards me and the blanket slips off her shoulders. Her nipples are hard in the chilly room, though there's a fire crackling in the grate.

*

There are about ten people here, sitting on the sofa, lying on the floor, on a beanbag by the radiator. A TV set is on in the corner but only one guy, with a belly and round glasses, lazy-clever-looking, is paying it any attention. *Disbelieving crowds watched mesmerized as the Berlin Wall, symbol of what Winston Churchill called the 'iron curtain', was opened today by East German police who* . . .

One of the guys is wearing his boxer shorts and a T-shirt, like he's just got out of bed or something, and there's this smell of unwashed people and ganja. None of the girls are wearing any make-up and I see Jake, locked in some kind of intense discussion, sitting on the floor in front of the window. He's wearing old black cords and a Support the Miners T-shirt, which looks like it hasn't been washed since it was made.

Maggie takes my hand and leads me across to the window, where Jake finally notices my arrival. He looks at me for a moment. As usual, his eyes don't give anything away, but it looks to me like his lips twitch.

'Hey,' he says, not getting up or anything, not offering any other gesture of greeting. *Thousands of ordinary people on both sides of the divide climbed the wall, embracing on the top.*

'Hey,' I say. And then, to fill the silence: 'Cool party.'

*

Maggie hands me what's left of the joint. It's dark outside now and we've made a fire. The room's lit by its orange chuckling, as we are. We're naked, lying on cushions, covered with a blanket. Maggie's skin is darker than mine, but firelight makes me look less pasty than usual. Several days have gone by. I don't know how many. The freezer's so full of food we could live here a month. Every day or two we go to the garage and get something out. There's no point in getting dressed just for this, so we usually wrap ourselves in blankets and brave the cold. There's nothing like five minutes in a sub-zero garage, I've discovered, to wake you up for sex.

We've had a lot of sex.

Maggie lifts herself from the cushions and sits with her knees pulled up under her chin. Her back's arched to the flames. Vertebrae picked out in shadow. We haven't spoken for an hour or so. We've been watching the fire and each other. We're both very stoned. We've both been very stoned for days.

'What was it you shouldn't have touched?' she asks quietly.

'What?'

'The night before we left Oxford you had a nightmare, remember?'

'Yes.'

'I woke up before you did. I lay watching you, half asleep, wondering whether to wake you.' She smiles at me. 'You were twitching and turning, then you went still. I could see you were still dreaming, but your whole body was frozen. You started saying something, I couldn't hear what. I'd finally decided to wake you when you woke yourself, screaming about something you shouldn't have touched.'

She looks at me soothingly. But firmly also, now.

'What was it?' she asks quietly.

'You can see it if you like.'

She watches as I walk across the room to where our clothes are still lying from the day before, maybe two days before. I reach down and pick up my trousers. From their back pocket I remove my wallet. From it I take my mother's last letter to me, something I've kept there for five years. Slowly, almost cautiously, I take it out of the envelope. I've never shown it to anyone.

My mother's handwriting is round and regular, unchanged

since she was thirteen. She didn't have occasion to write many letters. I scan the phrases.

> . . . *you will find your birthday money inside don't spend it all at once.*

Benedict Chieveley has added a semicolon after 'inside', in neat red pen.

> *I was talking to Dorothy from next door (I know she does me head in usually, but she's good for news!) and she told me the Quintavalles have moved house, somewhere really posh Sally from Bishopsfield Rd told her.*

He's crossed out 'me' and written *my* above it, and underlined the parenthesis. Added neatly in the margin: *colloquial usage.* I scan to the end of the page.

> *Well Jakey Dad and I think your great we're really proud of you.*
> *Happy 16th – lets hope its sweet!*
>   *Big hug,*
>   *Mum*

She's circled the *i* of 'Big'. By an arrow pointing to the circle, Chieveley has written *unfortunate.* He's added a full stop after 'great' and capitalized the *w* of 'we're'. 'Your' now reads 'you're'. Apostrophes have been added to the final sentence. He's underlined 'sweet' and written *touching* beside it, in neat letters.

At the bottom, underneath my mum's looping, careful signature, in neat red pen: *6/10. Not bad for a beautician.*

'I found this the day she died,' I say, giving it to Maggie. 'The day I met you.'

6

Julian, Adrienne

'Where's Jake?'

I haven't seen my sister for the better part of ten days, time I know she's spent at home, in our house, alone, with Jake 'Itchins.

'He left by train,' she tells me, getting into the car. 'He wanted to spend a night with his dad in Fareham.'

'Right.'

We drive in silence. Maggie doesn't seem inclined to tell me anything, and if she doesn't want to say then I don't want to ask.

*

About two hours have gone past and the only good thing is that Maggie's stopped trying to include me in the conversation. Everyone's talking way over my head, which is doubly embarrassing given how stoned these people are. The room's full of words and sweat and smoke and all I do is all I can do: try to shrink back into the wall so I won't be noticed, listening hard to see if there's a suitable opening for anything I might be able to say.

No one's discussing George Eliot or even nineteenth-century fiction and I get the feeling none of these people have read a newspaper for months – except the boy watching the news, who's definitely the geek of the group. So much for all my preparation. I try not to look at Maggie and when other people laugh I join in as hard as I can, just to give the impression I'm having a really good time.

The girl with the overalls is sitting on the edge of the sofa, with her feet in the lap of a scraggly boy with long hair wearing, it looks like, a pair of pyjamas. He's holding a long joint and periodically takes a deep toke on it, holding the smoke in for longer than most Olympic swimmers can hold their breath.

'That's just patriarchal bullshit,' overalls-girl is saying. 'Augustine didn't come up with the concept of self-knowledge. He nicked it off St Jerome, who nicked it off the Delphic oracle. *She* was the one who first said "Know thyself".'

'Yeah, but it was Apollo speaking through her, wasn't it? We're back to a male god.' The guy she's arguing with is sitting on an armchair across the room, with a six pack of beer in his lap and a smirk on his face.

'It's not relevant,' says Maggie, pacifically, 'precisely who said what first. Concepts exist; people find them, express them, at different times in different ways. Thoughts ebb and flow.'

'It's the motion of the notion,' says the scraggly boy, very slowly.

*

It's not, by the way, that I mind about my sister and Jake 'Itchins, not exactly; not initially. At least that's what I've been telling myself: you can't impose your own standards on other people and I've never been one for protective, older brother antics. If my sister wants to go out with Jake 'Itchins, school joke, then that's her choice to make.

It's spattering rain and Maggie's hair is wet from it; it looks like she's been standing in the garden, slowly drenching herself in the drizzle.

'How've you been?' I ask. 'Did you enjoy yourselves?'

She turns and considers me. Her movements are slow and calm; I'd think she were stoned if she didn't look at me so directly, so forthrightly. 'Enjoyment doesn't begin to describe it,' she tells me.

'Righto.'

We drive on in silence for a few minutes.

'Anybody home?'

Maggie looks away from the window abruptly, as if I've caught her in the act of doing something she shouldn't. Her brow wrinkles and I see that she's irritated by the question. My sister's not someone I associate with irritation: she can rage and storm with the best of them, but she's very rarely irritated – or rather she's very rarely irritated with me.

When she smiles, I can see it takes some effort. 'Just daydreaming,' she says.

'About what?'

'Oh, you know. This and that.' She stretches languidly in her seat.

*

It's been such a long time since I've recognized a single name in the conversation, that when the girl mentions Thomas Aquinas, his leaps out at me. I think of the embroidery on Brother Malcolm's door and feel this moment of nausea, like I used to in school plays when I was younger.

Say something, Adrienne.

So I do.

'I've always thought there's a lot of wisdom in what Aquinas says about conscience,' I say, forcing myself to speak clearly.

Everyone turns to look at me, like they've forgotten I'm there and there's an almost tangible sense of surprise. Maybe because overalls-girl has broken off, mid-sentence, just to look amazed I've *spoken*, I feel a bit more confident. 'You know,' I go on, trying to copy their off-hand style, 'it's that bit in the *Summa Theologica*, when he says conscience is "not a power, but an act". That's a pretty original formulation.'

I'm sure I've got the quotation right. Overalls-girl looks like someone's spiked her drink. For the first time in two hours, Jake looks at me. He actually seems *interested*. It's too early to know for sure.

*

'Have you fallen hopelessly in love wiv 'Itchins in the last ten days?' For some reason, my irritation is audible in this question and when Maggie notices it I smile, pretending it away. She looks at me sharply and raises an eyebrow, one of her favourite tactics.

'Would it please you if I had?'

I consider this for a moment. Though I know that what I should be saying, indeed that what I am about to say with great enthusiasm, is 'absolutely', I've always found white lies difficult in front of my sister. She has an irritating habit of knowing, fairly accurately, what I am going to say in advance of my actually saying it; and the way her eyebrow sits, jauntily accusatory, in the middle of her forehead makes me uncomfortable – as it has always done.

'Absolutely,' I say.

'Well then . . . I think I have.'

'Righto.'

'*What* did you say?'

I'm not prepared for the violence of Maggie's reaction. She's

looking straight at me, eyes sharp, gaze pointed; it's an effort
to keep my eyes on the road.

'I said "righto", I think.'

There's silence. Maggie looks out of the window.

'What?'

'Nothing.'

Silence again.

*

'Have you read the *Summa Theologica*?' It's the stoned boy on
the sofa, who lets out a lungful of smoke as he speaks. There's
something in his voice. I'm expecting suspicion, but instead it
sounds like he's . . . *impressed*.

'Yeah,' I say.

'All of it?'

'Yeah.' I don't want them thinking I'm some dumb
American who doesn't read books through to the end. 'It's
very thought-provoking.'

'How long did it take you?' Overalls-girl bites her lip, clearly
pissed off he's talking to me.

'Oh, you know . . . A while.' I'm getting kind of high on
the fact everyone's paying attention to me. Even Maggie's
looking at me like she's pretty surprised to find me giving such
a good account of myself. 'Almost a week in fact' – which is
how long *Middlemarch* would've taken me, if I'd really tried to
get through it quick, and *Middlemarch* is pretty much the
longest book there is, right?

There's silence. Everyone's totally impressed.

'Hmmm,' says Jake. 'The Berlin Wall comes down and
someone reads the *Summa Theologica* in a week. We live in
miraculous times.'

*

This isn't like my sister. Maggie, usually so full of words, seems to have no use for them now; or, it occurs to me as we drive on through the rain, she is perhaps afraid of what she might say. She looks like a woman doing her best to keep a grip on herself – though why it should be such an effort to be civil to me, since I've driven all the way from Oxford just to do her a favour, is beyond my powers of deduction.

'What a blissful day for a silent journey,' I remark.

It's starting to rain heavily now, sheets of rain lashing the windscreen wipers, making driving difficult on an icy road. The task at hand requires all my concentration and ahead I see a bank of fog rolling towards us; cars are disappearing into the mist, remembered only by gleaming tail lights which glow a moment before fading to nothing. In the two or three minutes of silence that follow, I prepare a relatively promising piece of sarcasm; I don't usually take my sister on, but this time I'm not going to put up with . . .

I'm interrupted in my train of thought by the realization that Maggie is now staring at me intently, giving off what seem to be fumes of silent rage. This is too much: my careful speech evaporates, faced with the necessity of immediate articulation, and all I can find to say (again, but with more venom this time) is 'What?'

'You are such a pompous fuck.'

She turns in her seat to face me and all I can see from the corner of my vision are her eyes – which are blazing.

'For God's sake, can't you come up with something a little more fervent than "Righto"? I've just told you I've fallen head over heels in love with someone, someone you *know*, someone you'd care about if you had any sense, if you could get over your public school snobbery and stop calling him "'Itchins".

And all you can find to say, when told the burning news, is "Righto". Jesus Christ.'

*

It's later, much later. I'm just letting myself into St Botolph's, a bit unsteady on my feet, totally *psyched* with myself. It's not like I said much, I grant you, but it's not like I was a total mouse all evening, either. As I'm walking across the hall, I see Brother Malcolm walking up the stairs. I'm overcome with gratitude.

'Brother Malcolm,' I say, following him. I'm not sure how I'm going to thank him, given how little I can tell him of how I've spent my afternoon, but I want to let him know I owe him one.

'Miss Finch?' He turns around to face me, very stern as usual. He needs to lighten up, I'm thinking, though obviously I don't tell him this. 'What may I do for you, at this late hour?'

'Well . . .' I don't know what to say, but I want to say something. 'The quote from St Thomas Aquinas on your door is really, you know, inspirational.' This seems as close to the truth as he's likely to be comfortable with, but I'm not prepared for the reaction. Brother Malcolm actually . . . *smiles*. He looks like someone's just told him he's great in bed, or something – though obviously, being a monk, that's not the most appropriate comparison.

'The wisdom of the church fathers, Miss Finch, is a potent force even today.'

He's looking down at me – 'pleased as punch,' Julian would call him – and it occurs to me what would *really* please him.

'Could I borrow the *Summa Theologica* some time?' I ask.

He pauses for a moment, almost overcome. 'What a *very* responsible challenge to set yourself in your early twenties,' he tells me. 'Frankly, Miss Finch, I'd put you down as quite another type of undergraduate altogether. I'd happily lend you the first volume, and you can take the others as and when you're ready for them.'

He's leading me along to his study now, very jaunty, kind of skipping along.

'And how many volumes would there be, in total?' I ask him.

'Twenty-two,' says Brother Malcolm brightly, holding the door open for me, 'but don't let that daunt you.'

7

Julian, Adrienne

We've just left the dual carriageway. Despite the weather, being in this car with Maggie is suddenly so unpleasant that I've decided to take a short cut, threading my way on tiny roads through the Oxfordshire countryside. The absence of decent lighting makes it all the more dangerous to take my eyes off the road for an instant; weighing all this, I decide to say nothing and instead peer intently ahead at the darkness.

'You can't start something like this and then wimp out halfway through.' Maggie's on a roll now. 'That's also typical of you. At the first sign of anything approaching conflict, what do you do? You put your tail between your legs and scamper away. Is there *anything* you care enough about to actually take some sort of stand over? Anything at all? Or are you going to spend your whole life looking on from the sidelines, just like you watched Jake being tormented for years and years without doing *anything*. It makes me sick.'

This is too much. For a moment I turn towards her. I'm so full of indignation I could scream, but instead, remembering I'm the older one, I—

'*Careful!*'

A Triumph Spitfire, 1972 I'm guessing, a beautiful French blue, roars past us on the narrow, winding road and ducks in front almost at once to avoid a sharp corner. It's over in a second. The car's swerving, out of control, slipping on the wet tarmac. Up ahead, beyond the bend, there's a squeal of brakes and a churning of undergrowth as it disappears through the hedge.

It takes me a moment to remember I know the car.

'Christ,' says Maggie again, in a different tone of voice.

*

I'm kind of relieved when I don't see Maggie or Jake the next day. I'm kind of relieved when I don't see them the day after that, either, but by the third day, and then the fourth, I'm beginning to wonder whether maybe they're avoiding me.

On day ten, it becomes clear they're avoiding me.

I haven't told Julian about Jake's party or about my record-breaking sprint through the *Summa Theologica*. I don't know if Maggie's told him, but if she has I *do* know I don't want to know about it, so I haven't even mentioned her name in his presence.

He's in the Radcliffe Camera when I get there one morning. I see him as soon as I enter the circular room, with its cheap brown carpet and painted stone columns, but he doesn't see me and so I just watch him, just check him out for a moment. He's sitting at a desk by the window, kind of dishevelled, totally cute, wearing his reading glasses and chewing on the knuckle of his right index finger.

When I take a seat next to him I see he's kind of preoccupied. He's reading a volume called *Middle English Romances*, which doesn't look like it's about love affairs in the middle ages, and he's taking notes in a scrawny notebook, almost absent-mindedly. He lets me sit next to him, but he doesn't push his knee against mine or take my hand, so I don't do the same to him, either. Needy women never get what they need, right?

I'm trying to remember this, trying to concentrate on my

own book, but I can't stop myself from looking at him every now and then. He doesn't seem to be reading that much and after a while he gives up on the project altogether and concentrates on his doodling.

*

We pull over on the verge. The Triumph has left a gaping hole in the hedge and come to a stop in a thicket dividing two fields. Maggie's silent now; it doesn't seem the time or the place for our argument.

'You wait here,' I say, opening my door.

I'm halfway to the car when I realize that Maggie is following me, running after me. I hurry on, wanting to find out the worst before she does: she's my baby sister, after all, and I want to protect her from what I dread to find, if I can. My heart's in my mouth; I'm almost oblivious to the rain, or to the mangled fox I step over gingerly. This, possibly, is what the car has swerved to avoid, though not quickly enough to save the fox. Its head has been wrenched from its body, which has been thrown clear of the road by the impact, and it's lying at my feet, oozing blood from its neck.

Time slows as I approach: I've never seen death before, only talked about it, written about it; mangled bodies have never been a part of my reality and I find myself unwilling to make them one. But there's no going back now, not after the altercation which Maggie and I have just had – which means that it's pride, rather than courage, which makes me continue, and pride rather than courage that dissolves into nervous laughter when I find him.

Benedict Chieveley is in the driver's seat, seat belt on, head back, snoring loudly. He reeks of whisky.

*

Trying to look like I'm not looking, I glance over his shoulder to see what Julian's drawing. There are a few lines of text, copied down from the book, a few squiggles and random patterns and in the middle of the page the horizontal rectangle he's working on now. I watch him as he draws, thinking how sexily he grips his pen, while he adds a few more squares, half way up the rectangle, and then starts tracing squirls between them.

It takes me a little while to realize he's drawing a house, a long, low house set into a hillside, with ivy clambering over it. He takes his time over the sketch and adds details like a smoking chimney and a rose garden meticulously planted in the foreground. On one of the hills he draws two figures, though who they are is difficult to tell because they're on top of each other, their stick arms and legs crazily intertwined. By the time he's done with them they look like some kind of spider – and I'm about to ask him what he's doing when he frowns, pauses a moment like he's thinking something over, and then rips the page from the notebook and crumples it in his hand.

*

The discovery of Benedict Chieveley, fast asleep but otherwise unharmed, in the driver's seat of his scratched but basically undamaged Triumph Spitfire has had the oddest effect on Maggie. I don't quite know what I expected from her: relief, maybe, or nervous laughter. These, certainly, have been my reactions, in precisely that order: I'm delighted, of course, that Chieveley hasn't died; delighted, too, that I haven't been obliged to find him dead; but the whole scene does have an air of the ridiculous about it. Besides which there's something in me, some small corner of my soul that will be forever thirteen, that can find happiness in the fact that Benedict Chieveley, golden boy of Botesdale, effortless, popular, feared Benedict Chieveley, has just done several hundred pounds' worth of damage to the paintwork of his most prized possession.

Maggie, on the other hand, has hardly reacted at all. She has looked, with me, at the snoring body on the front seat; she has watched me feel for Chieveley's pulse and heard him mutter, eyes twitching, as I first move, then hold, his wrist. She has assured herself that he is, essentially, unharmed; and now she's standing, quite silent, a few feet from the car, staring away from me, across the field. The rain has eased and finally stopped; a moon has appeared from behind dark clouds and is bathing the scene in a tranquil, if eerie, glow. If I didn't know my sister better I'd think she was lost in thought. Maybe she's praying, giving thanks of some sort. I move around her to see her face, which is blank and expressionless; the only indication of mental activity is in the twitching of the very same eyebrow that has, until so recently, been facing me provocatively from the middle of her forehead.

8

Adrienne, Julian

'Adrienne!'

I'm dreaming of Maggie, far away across a river, calling to me. She calls and calls but I can't reach her and then I'm awake and I realize she *is* calling my name, she's right outside my door in fact. It's the middle of the night and there's something in her voice, a strange high note I don't understand, so I get up and go to the door, unlock it, and she's standing in the corridor, cheeks flushed, eyes urgent, and she looks at me and says, 'God, I'm glad to see you,' and I almost think I'm still asleep.

*

'Maggie? Are you okay?'

She doesn't turn round; she gives no indication of having heard me at all.

'He's all right,' I offer, explaining the obvious. 'He's not dead or anything.'

'Quiet, Julian,' she says. 'Just be quiet a moment.' There's a note of dismissal in her voice which fans an ember of my old anger. I'm about to open my mouth to speak when she turns round and walks straight towards me. Her eyes have narrowed and her strides speak purpose. 'Get out of the way,' she says; and I can tell that her subsequent 'please' is only an afterthought.

*

Maggie's sitting on the end of my bed now, talking quickly, with Julian hovering in the background. Her sweater looks like it's got . . . blood on it, and Julian's staring alternately at the blood and then at me and he's pale, with something in his eyes that looks like a plea. Maggie's talking so fast, and I'm so dazed from sleep, the dream's still so vivid, it's all I can do to remember that this is reality.

When I ask her where she's been she tells me she's been at home, with Jake, all alone for ten days – and she shoots this look at Julian, who looks sheepish and a little defiant and says, 'I thought I told her. Sorry,' like he's too exhausted to argue.

*

'What on earth are you doing?'

'I'll explain everything in the car. Just leave me be a minute.'

'But you're . . . That fox . . .'

'Shut up about the fox, Ju. It's dead.'

'But . . .'

'I'll explain everything in the car. Trust me.'

*

'So you see,' Maggie's saying, 'it's going to be simple. We invent a crime he hasn't committed to punish him for one he has.'

'But that's crazy,' Julian interrupts, the first thing he's said in half an hour. 'The whole idea's crazy, there's no . . .'

Before he can finish his sentence Maggie's turned round to look at him, and there's something in her eyes that stops him in mid-phrase – but he's angry, I see, exasperated really, and he says again, but less assertively this time, 'The whole thing's crazy, Maggie.'

She takes a deep breath, slowing herself down. She's looking at him squarely, calmly, and when she speaks her voice is very measured, quiet almost.

'Just. Fuck. Off,' she says. 'Adrienne and I have a lot to talk about.'

*

The last storm cloud rolls away, leaving the field drenched in light. This adds a further element of surreality to what is, already, one of the more surreal moments of my life so far. My sister is kneeling over the fox, picking it up; its neck is gurgling blood, the head is nowhere to be seen.

'What on earth are you *doing*?'

Even as I speak, I register the fact that my voice has betrayed me. I sound like a child whining, which is precisely what I am: a child, unable to do or say anything to influence a sequence of actions I can't begin to understand. Maggie doesn't even bother to reply, but picks up the dead animal and walks grimly towards the car.

'Maggie . . . *please*.'

*

When Julian turns around and leaves, without another word, I feel like I should go after him, but there's something about the way Maggie's sitting, back rigid, eyes scorching, that makes me think twice about moving. I'm trying to concentrate on what she's saying but all I can think about, apart from whether I should go after Julian, is the fact she's *here*, in my room in the middle of the night, talking to me like I'm the only person in the whole world she wants to be with right now. She's obviously decided she doesn't care about the *Summa Theologica* and this fact alone fills me with a gratitude that almost brings tears to my eyes. I want to hug her, let her know how grateful I am to her for not giving up on me, but she's lost on the trail of her own thoughts.

'So that's what we'll do,' she finishes. 'We won't keep it up for ever or anything. Just for long enough to make him feel what he should feel.'

'Which is?'

'Uncomfortable.' And then, after a moment, with a smile of large white teeth: 'Very, very uncomfortable.'

*

Maggie's standing in front of the Triumph, in front and a little to one side. Slowly, deliberately, she places the fox on the centre of the windshield and watches as its blood trickles down the glass. She is careful to expose only the fox's severed neck to the glass and fastidiously removes stray bits of hair and bone, which she flings impatiently aside, into the hedge. When she is satisfied with the windshield, she bends down and begins to decorate the bumper in a similar manner.

All this takes a matter of minutes. Finding myself unable to speak, I consider beating a retreat to my car, still parked at the top of the bank, and waiting for her there. I know enough of Maggie to know that there's no point in attempting to dissuade her from whatever it is she has in mind; she is utterly absorbed in her task and executes it with meticulous precision, standing back now and again to take in the effect of the whole.

When she's done she walks slowly to the edge of the field and flings the fox's body over the hedge and out of sight. Then she leans down once more and wipes her hands on the wet grass. There's blood on her sweater, not much but enough to notice; she pays no attention to it. Instead she comes back towards me, over the grass, and for the first time in several minutes she looks at me.

'Come on, Ju,' she says gently. 'Let's go.'

9

Jake, Julian

Maggie's talking quickly, full of energy. She's walking briskly, frog-marching me away from the station, where she's met my train from Fareham. She washed her hair this morning. A sweet, fresh smell of apple blossom trails her. The streets are full of cars and taxis. She walks us swiftly past their stalled lines. Someone on a bicycle waves at her and calls something, but she doesn't notice. Possibly she doesn't choose to.

'Predictably,' she's saying, 'Julian's being a real wet blanket about everything. All the way home in the car last night he couldn't shut up – once he'd got going, that is, which took him about half an hour. We were almost in Oxford before he actually *said* something, and then he made me sit and listen to him, freezing cold, at one in the morning, until he was finished ranting. He gets so worked up, you've no idea. He always has.'

*

I wake up with a dull ache behind my eyes. Naturally I ignored Adrienne's pacifying knock at three o'clock this morning, though that doesn't mean I don't approve of its sentiment. The bed's cold and lonely without her in it and I can't sleep. Getting up and switching on the heater, I see from the window that the pristine snow of yesterday and the day before has been cleared from the streets and is churning to a black sludge in the gutters, which chimes with my mood.

It's clear now that Maggie's apparent reasonableness in the car last night was a ruse; it disappeared the instant I let her into St Botolph's with my night key and she didn't listen to a word I said about Adrienne definitely being asleep by now. The fact that Adrienne clearly *was* asleep when we got to her room didn't influence her either; she just kept on banging on her door until she woke up. And then, and this is the infuriating thing about Maggie, Adrienne was *delighted* to have been woken up, at two in the morning, by my sister pounding on her door.

Maggie certainly owes me an apology, though I know just as certainly that I won't get one: she's embarked on a new crusade and I dread to think what lunacy she dreamed up last night under the intoxicating influence of Adrienne's rapt attention. The thought of them together is . . . wounding, I suppose, as is the fact that Adrienne chose to stay up with Maggie rather than come after me.

*

'And what did Julian have to say?'

'What do you think?' Maggie looks up at me, quizzically, and slips her arm through mine. 'I'm going to let you take a wild guess.'

We're on Broad Street now, walking to Bridwell. Neither of us has said anything about it, but we both know we're heading for Maggie's college and Maggie's bed.

'Let me see. Obviously the police are going to find everything out, arrest you at once, me too probably (not that Julian cares much about me) and the next thing you know, you'll be on death row. We'll both be on death row.'

*

I lie in bed, trying to ignore this nasty little fact. After several minutes of unsuccessful effort I decide that since I can't sleep I may as well do some work, so I get up and dress. Gathering a few things from my room – a pen, a pad of paper, enough money for a cup of coffee – I make my way through the empty corridors of St Botolph's and down the stairs.

The world outside is full of bustle, but I'm in no mood for morning cheeriness and keep my head down, thinking that if anyone greets me I can pretend not to have seen them. I suppose I'm not the only person in Oxford to look at the pavement while walking, because some bright spark from the Dramatic Society has cottoned on to an excellent free advertising space for a play called *We Know It Was You*; the title's written on the paving stones, at regular intervals, the whole way down Broad Street.

*

'Julian's scenario runs like this,' says Maggie as she lets us through the side gate of Bridwell. 'Benedict Chieveley takes himself off to the police station, admits vehicular homicide and is told that, in fact, no one has died. It's all a big mistake. Could we make you a cup of tea? Would you like a lift home? You get the picture. The young Chieveley, being a sharp fellow, works out instantly that someone's been playing a nasty trick on him. Of all the people who might wish him ill, he picks you. In the time it takes to say *Semper Botesdale* he's got Inspector Knacker of the Yard on the case, who gets to me through you.'

'How does death row come in?'

'Julian didn't actually mention death row. I did point out you can't be sentenced to life imprisonment for playing a joke on someone. Even he had to admit that. But he seems to think the proctors are going to find everything out and that we'll all get sent down – as if the proctors have time to care about stupid undergraduate antics. It's not like cheating in Finals or anything. I told Julian they wouldn't give a shit. I *guaranteed* to him that no one's going to give a shit apart from Benedict Chieveley, but he kept me in his freezing car anyway, talking about how he was my big brother, how he had to take care of me, etc. etc. Like it hasn't been the other way round since he was four and I was two and a half.'

*

I'm looking left and right to cross the road when I see my sister and 'Itchins, arm-in-arm and laughing, at the traffic lights. He has a rucksack slung over a shoulder, which suggests that she's gone to meet him at the station, and already I can see the transformation Maggie's wrought in him: he moves differently, less furtively than usual; his head's held high and his strides are longer, more decisive, than they ever were when we were at school. He has his arm around her waist and there's something about their physical easiness together which confirms what I've tried not to think about – that they've been fucking like rabbits all term.

Worse than that: they've been fucking like rabbits for ten days in *my house*, in the place Maggie and I spent our childhoods.

*

It's later. Maggie and I are lying on her duvet, by the electric fire. My socks are off.

'Time for your present,' she says. 'Something I think you'll find quite special.'

She gets up and goes to the bookshelf. There's a large folder leaning on a second-hand copy of *The Adventures of Tom Sawyer*, her favourite novel. She takes a sheaf of photocopied pages from it. They're pages of newspaper, reduced.

**OXFORDSHIRE GIRL VICTIM OF HIT AND RUN DRIVER.
POLICE APPEAL FOR WITNESSES TO FATAL ACCIDENT**

reads the headline.

'I wrote it,' said Maggie proudly, 'and took it round to the *Cherwell*'s offices early this morning, after leaving Adrienne. They were having a deadline crisis, so it wasn't too hard to get it in. Someone on the news team hadn't sent in their copy.' She grins at me. 'I've taken the trouble of having it sent round to all colleges in official post.'

IO

Adrienne, Julian

It's late the next afternoon. I've overslept. Julian's not in his room when I knock on his door and he doesn't come back in the hour or two I spend sitting in mine, waiting for him, during which time it gets dark and I get more than a little frantic. Not having had a proper boyfriend before I don't have a lot of experience in dealing with romantic fights, and I'm finding it less and less easy to remember all the persuasive things Maggie said to me last night, this morning, as she sat on my bed in the dark.

*

I spend the day productively (though not very enjoyably) attempting a piece of Middle English translation, and by four o'clock I'm slightly irked by the fact that Adrienne hasn't come to find me: the least she could have done, given her lack of loyalty last night. I've chosen the Radcliffe Camera to sulk in because it's the first place that anyone looking for me would look, which means that Adrienne can only have failed to find me if she also failed to try.

Hmmm.

I decide to get a cup of tea to cheer myself up. The *Cherwell* reps are handing out free copies of the newspaper and since I don't have anyone to talk to I take one, thinking that gossipy student journalism will entertain me quite adequately.

I'm sitting in a coffee shop on Broad Street, cup of Earl Grey in hand, when I see what Maggie's done.

*

Julian's in the Radcliffe Camera.

I see him from the steps, hunched over his books, frowning, with the scrawny little notebook beside him. He looks more dishevelled than usual and I worry that he hasn't slept properly. He doesn't see me until I'm right beside him and when I say 'Hi' and touch his arm, whispering, he looks at me with this vacant expression on his face that makes me anxious. I'm expecting anger, maybe, or hurt, but what I get seems calmer than either of these.

'Hello,' he says, and turns back to his book.

There's no talking allowed in the library and I see one or two people look up at me and then down at their work, frowning, and I can tell from the way they sigh through their noses that this isn't the place to say whatever it is Ju and I need to say to each other.

'Do you want to get a coffee?' I ask, trying to make it sound casual.

'No thanks.' He carries on copying out from his book. 'I had a cup of tea two hours ago.'

'Come on, Ju . . .' There's silence and I just stand by his desk, hoping he'll change his mind. When he doesn't look up again but keeps on copying out his notes from *Middle English Romances*, no doodling now, his writing regular and neat, just as usual, maybe *more* so than usual, I touch his arm again.

This time he does look up, but instead of saying anything he reaches into his rucksack and pulls out a copy of today's edition of the *Cherwell*, Oxford's student paper. He hands it to me and turns away and when I touch his arm again he makes an impatient movement and shakes me off.

*

It's dark by the time Adrienne deigns to come looking for me; I've done two translations and read as much of *Middle English Romances* as I'm ever going to read. I see her the moment she enters the library (I've been watching for her all day, after all) and for the first time what I've always understood as fawn-like grace seems more like rabbit nervousness. Her uncertainty – eyes twitching, limbs tensed for flight – irritates me, as does the fact that her wide-eyed enthusiasm has spurred my sister into converting rash words into even rasher action.

I'm expecting an apology and am ready (despite the day's fuming) to accept one; instead of offering anything of the sort, however, she sits down next to me, looking into my eyes with nothing more meaningful than an anxious desire to please – which suddenly tires me.

II

Julian, Jake

They're everywhere.

Reduced photocopies of the page from the *Cherwell* are flapping uselessly in the wind, attached to every available noticeboard in Oxford; and Oxford is a city of notice boards. I see the first in the lodge of Hertford College, on my way home from the library. Adrienne's long since left, having failed to get me outside for a 'coffee'. I know that what she's really after is for me to spend an hour telling her everything's going to be back to normal by tomorrow – which I'm beginning to see is an optimistic prognosis.

A small group is clustered by the Hertford notice board, killing time; one of them is reading the page from the *Cherwell* and I watch her nudge her friend, who looks over at it too. They move on and I take my chance, idling over to the board and removing the poster with as much nonchalance as I can muster.

'Oi, what you doing?'

It's the Hertford porter. He's striding out of the lodge, red face redder than usual, bent on the protection of college property.

'There's an error on the page,' I tell him, putting on my best look of winsome innocence. 'We need to recall all these copies.'

He looks at me, threateningly suspicious. Fortunately

one of the girls who was reading the poster earlier taps at the lodge window, breaking the silence. She has a note to leave and with a gruff 'You wait here', the porter shuffles off to attend to her.

I make good my escape, photocopy stuffed under my coat.

*

Maggie's kneeling on the carpet, about to roll a joint, holding up an empty packet of rolling papers. She's looking at me mock-pleadingly. We've been indoors all day while the rain lashes the window panes. We've been laughing about Benedict Chieveley, wondering when he's going to see the piece in the *Cherwell*. Now we're sitting in front of her gas fire. Maggie's wearing an old silk dressing gown with her hair tied back. I'm sitting in my boxer shorts.

Since neither of us want to face the hike down a hundred stairs and the cold trip up the street to the corner shop, we hunt through her room. A rolling paper is the kind of thing you can usually find if you look hard enough. I watch her going through her drawers. I love the attentiveness on her face. I sit on the sofa, feeling behind the cushions for a spare packet.

Ten minutes of searching yields nothing.

'Never mind,' I say, getting up and kissing her neck, reaching for my clothes. 'I'll go.'

*

I never knew there were so many colleges in Oxford, or so many savage porters mounting Cerberus-like guard over their noticeboards. It takes me over two hours to remove only those posters stuck up in the colleges between the Rad. Cam. and Bridwell. It's a time-consuming business since each enterprise requires a lot of loitering and forced carelessness – which, given how generally pissed off I am, and how little sleep I've had, isn't easy to muster in large quantities.

There's nothing I can do about the poster in Trinity, whose porter has just asked to see my *Cherwell* ID card. 'These were sent round in official post,' he says with that look of belligerent officialdom so beloved of porters and the staff of station ticket offices, 'and you'll have to show me your card if you want to take 'em down.'

Unable, of course, to produce such a card, and having attempted to fob him off with a briskly waved driving licence and failed, there's nothing for it but to retreat into the rain-drenched street. In search of an early evening whisky I stop off at the King's Arms, which is bustling with people whose cheeriness only emphasizes the storminess of my mood. It's getting colder and later and I'm getting hungrier; but if I don't take the posters down now, I'll only have to waste more time tomorrow removing them.

Four whiskies in quick succession restore my resolve. I walk down Bridwell Lane towards the college, full of determination: I'm bloody well going to get the *Cherwell* piece off the Bridwell noticeboard if it kills me.

*

The staircase outside Maggie's room is cold and gusty. Some-one's left the bottom door open. The quad's empty. I stand in the lodge for a minute, looking at the photocopy of the *Cherwell* page. A few bored students, mainly rowers, are standing around. They read the notice and move on to others. I imagine Chieveley standing here, checking the times of a rugby prac-tice, seeing it.

Maggie's impetuosity makes me smile. I think of her, many

stairs away, waiting for me. I'm full of something I've not experienced before. Not gratitude, exactly, though there's some of that in it. Not just excitement, either. It's a realization, perhaps, of past loneliness. An understanding that it's over. It's optimism, maybe. Hope for the future.

After the heat of her room it's good to be outside again. I'm halfway down the street, filling my lungs with damp air, when I see Julian. He's hurrying towards Bridwell, clutching a batch of photocopied sheets, wild-eyed. It takes me a minute to work out what he's doing.

Stupid fuck. He's obviously spent all afternoon running around Oxford in the wet – and what's he got to show for it? A bundle of damp newsprint, staining his hands. Doesn't he realize Maggie's article will be read in the newspaper itself?

*

Nothing the Bridwell porter can say or do will stop me: that poster's *mine*. I'm halfway down the street when I see 'Itchins walk out of the front gate of the college, looking nauseatingly pleased with himself.

Chin squared, head raised, ignoring the drip-drip of rain down the back of my sweater, I remind myself that I don't even need to acknowledge him; I'm quite happy to walk right past, keeping my distance.

*

I know Julian's seen me. It's clear from the way he glances back over his shoulder. I see him wondering whether or not to retreat. He doesn't want to talk to me, but he doesn't want me to think he's running away, either. He doesn't like me very much. Maybe this explains why he got so uptight about

Maggie's plan for Chieveley. For anyone else he wouldn't object – but because *I'm* involved in this, and sleeping with his sister on a regular basis, Julian feels his hegemony is threatened.

Which perhaps it is.

I'm not having any of this avoidance bullshit, though. We're not at school any more. So I keep on walking up the street, enjoying the panic signals he thinks he's disguising so well. He tries to hide the papers under his coat. He pauses by a doorway, obviously planning to take refuge in it. I walk more quickly. He moves away from the doorway and reluctantly sets himself on a collision course with me.

When we're a few yards away from each other, I call out to him.

*

'How's it going, Julian?'

Jake's smiling at me, leering really, and I can see one of Maggie's long, frizzy hairs on the yellow sheepskin of his coat's collar.

I nod a greeting and keep on going, but he looks at me appraisingly and takes in the photocopied pages under my arm – which, though wet, remain readable. 'Wouldn't touch those, if I were you,' he says.

'Oh, wouldn't you?'

It's not meant to be a question, but being Jake he can't resist pretending to take me seriously. 'Uh uh.' He shakes his head slowly from side to side, grinning at me, giving me a look that reminds me of Maggie's expression as she sat in the car outside St Botolph's last night, patently ignoring my advice. It's a *Poor Julian* look of dismissal and pity in equal measure; and there's something so provocative in this behaviour, something so infuriating in the way he's implying that he knows my sister better than I do, that I suddenly want to hit him.

*

Julian and I talk for a minute or so. I let him know I've seen what he's carrying. He seems flustered and awkward. A little defiant too, maybe. Like a child caught out of bed when he shouldn't be.

In fact, he's more old man than child. An obsessive compulsive old man. Even his coat is an old man's coat. I watch him trying not to shiver. 'You should put those back,' I tell him, 'and get yourself inside. You'll catch your death of cold.'

*

As I contemplate the line of Jake's nose and visualize how satisfying it would be to break it, I think to myself with a kind of exhilaration that this is the first time in my life, my post-kindergarten life anyway, that I've actually wanted to cause another human being some kind of physical pain.

He leans over towards me. 'We wouldn't want Maggie finding out, would we?' His voice has the high, sing-song quality of an adult talking to the child of an acquaintance he doesn't particularly like.

The voice decides me.

12

Adrienne, Jake

I hear Julian shuffle heavily up the stairs and into his room, closing the door firmly behind him – a probable slam, but I can't tell for sure. Ever since I left him at the library I've been sitting on my bed, doing my best to keep recent events in perspective. At first I tried some yoga breathing exercises and they worked for a while, but I couldn't really concentrate so for the last hour I've been reading *Ulysses* – which has just made me feel totally incapable, on top of everything else.

I don't know whether Julian's mad at me, or at Maggie, or at both of us. I guess I should've gone after him when he went, not waited until Maggie left. Okay, I know I should've done that – it's hard, in fact, to remember why I didn't, which is what I'm trying to do in case he gives me the chance to explain.

I've never been that good at stating my case in front of angry people.

*

Julian's still in the streaming gutter, staring up at me. I make a feint with my foot, like I'm going to kick him again. He flinches and when I chuckle quietly to myself he yells 'You can't' at me.

'I can,' I say. I'm leaning down to pick up his papers. Our

fight has sent some into the street, which I don't bother about. I pick up the ones lying nearest to hand. When I've got a few I stand up again and look at him.

'You can't!' he squeals again.

'Cunt's a strong word,' I tell him as I walk away.

*

Julian's standing in front of the mirror with his back to the door and all I can tell is that his shirt's soaking wet. It looks like he's been swimming in it – in a pool that hasn't seen a poolman in a while. He's got dirt and leaves sticking to him and this is so far from what I expected to find that I forget everything I'd planned to say and just ask him, kind of lamely, if he's okay. Which, when he turns to look at me, I see he isn't.

'Oh, my God.'

Blood's dripping from Julian's nose and his shoulders are hunched, like it's hard for him to breathe or something. Everything he's wearing is soaked in the same muddy, leafy water, and his coat (which he's dropped in a puddle on the floor) is belching sludge across the brown carpet. One of his eyes has a scratch under the lid, which is already starting to bruise nastily, and the swelling on his top lip makes him look permanently enthusiastic, like he's leaning forward to hear what I've got to say.

'Are you all right?' I whisper.

*

This is typical of bloody Julian. It's almost endearing the way he's spent hours traipsing around Oxford, taking down these posters. The whole thing must have killed him. As I stand in line at the corner shop, waiting for Rizlas, the image of Julian trying to get chummy with a variety of college porters makes me smile. Then laugh.

What a twat.

*

Julian doesn't say anything for a moment. He turns back towards the mirror and carries on dabbing at his gushing nose with a Kleenex, taken from a box on the shelf. I see the waste bin's full of bloodied tissues, crumpled and drying.

'Are you okay?' I ask again, walking slowly into the room.

No response.

Taking care to step over the coat, which is smelling of where it's been, I go across to him. I've seen enough movies to know what my role should be in this situation, which makes me feel better than I've been feeling all day. Julian needs to be nursed and comforted, that much is clear, and who better to nurse and comfort him than me?

When I'm standing behind him, right up close so I can smell the drain water, I swallow and put my hand on his shoulder.

'Are you all—?'

'No, I am *not* all right.'

He's still standing with his back to me, looking into the mirror, and our eyes meet in the reflection as I catch a strong trail of . . . it smells like bourbon, on his breath. He's *drunk*. He's also seriously pissed off. In fact, he's shaking with anger, though this could also be shivering from the water plus the fact he's trying to dry off in an ice-cold room. I see he hasn't even switched on his heater and lean over to do it for him.

*

As I come out of the shop I hear a roar in the King's Arms and turn to look. A rowdy group is spilling on to the pavement.

Rugby players. From the noise they're making I'd estimate they've got four or five hours' solid drinking behind them. I recognize one of them. He's short and squat, almost square. His name's Tom Baird and he does English with me. The group's coming towards me, swaying and singing.

Benedict Chieveley is at its centre, his arm in a cast and sling.

'Oi, 'Itchins! Been playing in the mud again?'

Even when pissed Chieveley doesn't slur his words. His eyes are swaying in and out of focus, but when they get me in perspective I recognize the same narrow look in them. He stops. Because he stops, the group stops. Their beer-heavy breath wafts over me, mingled with sweat and fag smoke.

'What happened to you?' I ask, nodding at his arm.

'Rugby practice,' he says gruffly.

*

'Don't touch that.'

I leap back from the heater, like it's electrically charged. I've never heard this tone in Julian's voice before. It's quietly serrated and doesn't leave any room for disagreement and the way his jaw's set, under blue eyes looking at me like I've just produced a dildo at the Met, makes me take a step or two away from him.

'I'm . . . sorry, Ju,' I tell him.

He carries on swabbing his nose, and when the blood's stopped completely he touches it gently and winces and I can tell from where I'm standing (though I don't say this, of course) that it's broken, pretty badly bashed up right across the bridge.

*

Chieveley roars with laughter as he leads the group up the street, away from Bridwell. He won't be back in college anytime soon. Looking down at the folded sheets in my hand I feel a jolt of exuberance. For the first time in my life I know something Chieveley doesn't. This fact brings a thought with it. I re-enter the corner shop and buy a pen, a blue highlighter.

'You're looking perky tonight,' says the woman behind the counter.

*

I make myself wait in silence, giving Ju some time to cool down. Never confront a man when he's angry, says Momma – but I don't feel like I can leave him in this state so I just wait, trying to project a sense of calm, and when he goes over to the closet and starts taking off his shirt, towelling himself dry, I speak.

'Who did this to you?'

'Good of you to be so concerned,' is all he says, talking carefully. His lip's split open and it's difficult for him to sound the words clearly.

'Of *course* I'm concerned.' I can sense he doesn't want to be touched, but I put out my hand anyway and try to stroke his hair – which I realize is a mistake because he opens his mouth and starts shouting at me.

*

I walk through the gates of Bridwell, humming to myself.

There are more people in the front quad now, milling around after dinner in hall. It must be a guest night of some sort, because everyone's wearing gowns. Cheap synthetic reminders of a time when learning was fashionable. The rain has stopped but the ground is wet enough to explain my drain damp. A few people look at me sympathetically.

Chieveley's room is in the garden quad. I walk through Queen's quad and across the grass-scented garden. There are two people crouching in a recess of the wall, smoking something. They don't see me.

When I find his staircase I let myself into it with the college code. It's the date of the college's foundation, the same for all staircases. I punch 1380 into the brass plate. It opens. I'm inside. From the hand-painted list of the staircase's inhabitants, I see that Chieveley, B. C. H. lives on the third floor, in Room No. 5. I don't meet anyone as I go up. The place smells dank and dusty. Typically for Chieveley, he's got himself one of the best rooms in college. Most sets facing the garden quad are reserved for tutors. Only a few undergraduates live here and none of them are around now. As I stand in front of his oak, I imagine the splendours within.

*

'Sore assault!'
'What?'
I'm backing away from Ju because he's screaming at me, 'Sore assault! Sore assault!' He looks like he's either going to burst into tears or hit me and it takes me a while to work out that what he's trying to say is that it's all my fault. I stand there, speechless, while he tells me I should've left Maggie alone and come with him when he asked me to.

'But you didn't ask me to,' I say pleadingly, hoping he'll remember what seems to me to be a crucial detail. Obviously this is the wrong thing to say, because Julian pushes past me, quite roughly, and goes over to the chest of drawers and while he gets out a T-shirt he doesn't stop yelling, not once, telling me 'You're a character' again and again and when I tell him I don't understand he gets really mad and picks up a photocopy of the piece Maggie put in the *Cherwell*.

YOU ENCOURAGED HER he writes on it, in big square letters. And then: GET OUT.

*

I try the handle, telling myself not to get my hopes up. It turns easily. The door, as they say, 'swings open'. I'm surprised. Most people lock their rooms. Not Chieveley, obviously. He's retained from school a sense of his own inviolability. I walk in. There's a light switch next to the door and I flick it, closing the oak behind me.

The room I'm standing in is the sitting room of a set. It's panelled in dark wood and there are two worn-out leather sofas, facing each other, in front of the fireplace. It looks like a rather mouldy version of a London club. There are books scattered messily about and a pile of dirty games clothes. It seems that when Chieveley gets undressed he leaves each item exactly where he took it off. I follow a trail. Socks, rugby shorts, rugby shirt, jock strap. It leads to a small door on the opposite wall. This gives onto a tiny bedroom, which smells.

Opening the page in my pocket on the desk in the sitting room, I highlight certain key passages in blue.

. . . a typical evening for Mary McCorbett, 11, out walking her dog Jasper . . . much-missed member of the North Oxford Pony Club . . . Police are appealing urgently for any witnesses . . . blue Triumph Spitfire seen leaving the scene at speed.

What else should I do? I stand in Chieveley's sitting room, thinking of how Maggie spent the morning before meeting my train. Then I write WE KNOW IT WAS YOU at the top of the page, in careful capitals. We may as well go for consistency.

I leave the paper in the middle of the floor, next to the jock strap.

13

Adrienne, Julian

I spend two days in bed, wondering if Julian will knock on my door, wondering if I should knock on his, the decision see-sawing in my head – yes I should, no I shouldn't – as I listen to him through the wall, moving around, the total *ordinariness* of the sounds he makes underlining how pointedly he's ignoring me.

For forty-eight hours or so I can just about live with the fact he's pretending I don't exist, but after that I get . . . upset, and then kind of pissed off. This seems like a lousy way to spend the last few days of term, and I'm not going back to New York miserable.

I won't give Momma that satisfaction.

*

It's worse the next morning. I look like a creature from the pages of a science fiction novel: hook-lipped, leering, half human. I don't know whether or not Jake has broken one of my ribs, but breathing is painful; my nose has gone an attractive shade of puce and though I don't have the conventional black eye, I do have a deep gash under my right eyelid – how did this come about? a nail? a stone lodged in the sole of his boot? – and a protruding top lip of terrifying proportions.

*

On the morning of day three I get out of bed and open the brown and orange curtains, which are glowing like lava lamps. Outside there's a bright sun and the snow's almost gone and people are striding briskly around, responding to the weather, looking forward to their vacations.

I'm just picking up my robe when I catch sight of Maggie in the street. She's on her bicycle, huge houndstooth coat sailing out behind her, dodging neatly through the traffic, and when she slows down by the entrance to St Botolph's she looks up at my window, like she can sense I'm there, and holds up her hand to her eyes, shielding them from the light. I pull up the sash and am about to call but she raises her finger to her lips and points upwards, before disappearing into the building.

*

Adrienne's next door; I can hear her pacing about her room and once or twice in the night I thought I heard her crying. If I didn't look as hideous as I do, I'd go in and comfort her, tell her I'm sorry for shouting at her last night; but I'm hardly in her league at the best of times and at this moment I wouldn't blame her for running from me, screaming. Besides, she has her pride. As I sit on my bed, listening to her, I realize I haven't got the courage to face her now: my physical humiliation is too complete.

*

All I hear before Maggie opens my door is a single creak as she turns the handle, tip-toeing into the room with a basket in her left hand.

'I thought we'd have a little working breakfast,' she whispers, taking two cups of coffee, a bag of pastries, and a pretty beaten-up old tape recorder from the basket and putting her arms around my shoulders. I'm suddenly conscious I haven't bathed, that I'm not looking my best, but Maggie doesn't seem to notice (or if she does, she doesn't let on) and as she lays things out on the desk it seems like a good moment to ask how Julian is.

'I've got a suspicion he's avoiding me,' she says, taking a box out of her coat pocket and picking up a copy of the *Female Eunuch* (hers, she lent it to me weeks ago) to roll a joint on. 'I was going to ask you.'

'I don't know.'

'What do you mean you don't know?'

'I think he's avoiding me too.'

*

For two days I stay in my room, nerving myself for my encounter with Adrienne and reading Elizabethan revenge tragedy. When I think of 'Itchins – which I do continually, especially when a character meets a particularly nasty end – I can't help wishing I'd been a little . . . not braver, no; more effective.

I never took the boxing lessons offered at school; the exercise of self-defence seemed trivial and useless. If anyone's going to attack me, I thought, they'll do it with a gun or a knife and no amount of neat boxing tricks will help me.

Not so, as things turned out.

Sitting at my desk, trying to concentrate, I imagine Jake and Maggie, laughing about me; I hear him telling her how easy it was to kick the shit out of me. Easy if you're a psycho, mate.

*

'Do I detect a fight?'

Maggie looks at me gently and I realize, mortifyingly, that I've got tears in my eyes. Soon they're spilling out and I'm trying to wipe them away, all the time crying more and more until eventually I'm sitting shaking, sobbing. She leaves her chair and stands over me, holding me in her arms which feel firm and strong and smell like rain. My head's heaving against her breasts and in the middle of everything I think how bizarre it feels to be hugged like this by someone who's not Momma. Maggie feels so *different* from Momma, she smells so different.

It takes me a long time to calm down. I'm tempted to tell Maggie about her brother's bruises, but if he hasn't told her maybe he wouldn't appreciate me telling her, either. Guys have their pride, right?

'What you need is some distraction,' she says. 'A bit of news from the outside world.'

*

The sun comes out on the third day and the air fills with end-of-term jollity which only accentuates the ugliness of my mood. I'm standing at the window, looking at the street full of carefree strollers, when Maggie turns the corner on her bicycle and stops with a squeal of brakes. She's carrying a basket, which gives her a vaguely Florence Nightingale air, and I duck out of sight to avoid being seen.

*

Maggie finishes the joint, rolling it crisply as she fills me in on the last few days, and hands it to me. I take it and her fingers graze mine as she holds a lighter to the tip.

'Does Benedict Chieveley really think he's killed someone?' I ask, leaning towards the flame.

'It's hard to say for sure. He definitely knows someone's trying to make him think he has, which is probably enough for our purposes. I was with him in the post room this morning, watching him go through his mail – and when he got to the card he went white, looked over his shoulder and left quickly. Not the action of an untroubled man, if you ask me.'

'What did it say?'

'What we've decided we'll always say. I got an old friend from school to send it – just a bland tourist postcard with an anonymous postmark and one line of text. Just to warm him up, nothing too serious. I've come to you to discuss the first round of stage two.'

*

Maybe Jake's violence has reminded Maggie where her loyalties lie. This thought lifts my spirits and I sit on the bed, waiting for her tread on the stairs. There's no sound of my sister's usual bounding, however; all I hear to indicate that there's someone on my floor is the creak of a board in the passage. I ready myself for Maggie's knock, composing my features grimly – I may be prepared to forgive and forget, though I won't make it easy for her – but all I hear is a soft click as . . . *Adrienne*'s door opens.

*

Maggie's standing beside me, fiddling with the tape player. Of course she's right: just because I'm going out with Julian, just because we're in love and everything, doesn't mean I have to agree with everything he thinks or says. Why should I let him decide what I can and can't do? It's not like it's really any of his business, what goes on between Maggie and me. At least, of course it's *partly* his business, in the sense that she's his sister and everything, but . . . She's also my best friend. Doesn't our relationship have a right to privacy?

Next door I hear Julian's chair creak heavily and before I can stop myself I've seen him at his desk, reading, with his bruised face aching, and suddenly I'm feeling tender towards him, anxious to get things back to normal between us.

'Don't be put off by what Mr Wet Blanket might say,' says Maggie gently, reading my thoughts.

'But . . .'

'Julian's never going to know.'

'He thinks I'm encouraging you too much already.'

'Oh come on. I'm not *that* corruptible.' She grins at me and squeezes my hand.

'What if he heard you in here? What if he asks what we were talking about?'

'He's not going to. But if he does, invent something. For now, just make sure you speak quietly.' She looks right into my eyes as she presses Record.

*

What the fuck? I put my ear to the wall, a partition so flimsy you can almost see through it, and the fact I can't hear anything from the other side confirms my worst suspicions: Adrienne and Maggie must be whispering.

Are they whispering about me?

14

Jake, Julian

Getting prescription medication out of the college doctor at short notice requires convincing histrionics. I make the appointment on the phone, in a voice of breathless bleakness. The fact that Maggie and I spent last night, as so many past nights, screwing instead of sleeping works in my favour. Standing in front of the mirror I see a text book case of student depression. Bad, greasy skin. Eyes so darkly under-ringed it's difficult to imagine I've ever slept well. Turning the shower control to *hot* and standing naked while the icy bathroom fills with steam soon works up an impressively realistic sweat. A clamminess, suggestive of restless sleep and anguished perspiration.

Obviously I don't look anything like as impressively self-destructive as I will, years later. But for a nineteen-year-old, at his physical peak, the effect isn't bad.

*

Maggie spends so long in Adrienne's room I almost go in and confront them. What eventually dissuades me from this course is Maggie's unpredictability in front of an audience: at home next week, one on one, I'm fairly confident of being able to convince her of the dangers of going out with a council-house thug; with Adrienne dancing attendance, however, there's no saying what might happen.

I think of my sister the night of Chieveley's car crash, of her wild eyes and impassioned plans, as I sit with my ear against the partition wall. Every so often I hear rustling and murmurs, so muted they shriek deception.

*

To be honest, I thought Julian would've come squealing to Maggie by now. I've been expecting him every time someone's knocked on her door. I've made sure I've been around, too. I don't want his account passing as gospel truth. I've an idea he does a pretty good line in bleating and I'm worried that Maggie will have reservations about sleeping with someone who's caused her brother as much cosmetic damage as I have.

I focus on this worry as I wave her off on her bicycle in the sunshine. I need all the anxiety I can muster this morning.

The offices of the college doctor are in the basement of a staircase on the front quad. They smell of damp and underuse. Their walls are decorated with fading seventies posters that equate healthy living with bad dress sense. A bearded man in brown flares plays the guitar to a girl in floral print above instructions for *Safer Loving*. On the table in the waiting room are piles of neatly stacked leaflets that haven't been touched for years. A set of cartoons explicating proper condom technique. Pastel-illustrated advice on syphilis, gonorrhoea, Hepatitis C, genital warts, herpes, HIV. *For When You Need a Friend*, re-assures a poster for the university counselling service, above a number with an out-of-date dialling code.

*

When I open her door several hours later, Adrienne's wide eyes attempt an innocence which her tense shoulders contradict, and two empty coffee cups arranged in cosy intimacy on the desk offer all the proof I need. As she jumps up and comes over to me, I clock my reflection in a cheap wall mirror: my skin has gone a very pale, rather shiny yellow, undershot with hints of purple that give me a more than passing resemblance to a prune and custard pudding, well beyond its sell-by date.

'I hope you've enjoyed yourself with my sister.'

The words sound colder than I'd intended – it's Maggie, after all, who's responsible for this mess; Adrienne doesn't belong in our crossfire – but when she tells me, quite calmly, that she's been alone all day, my throat goes dry with rage.

'I saw her come into college,' I say icily, watching the colour rise in Adrienne's cheeks.

*

Dr Monroe, Dr Lydia Monroe, is a young GP fresh from med. school. I know this because I've checked her biographical details in the college magazine. I know that she's heading the research committee on student stress and that she has strong views on the unhealthiness of the exam system. I'm not expecting her to be beautiful, so when I see that she is I do my best not to notice. She has sharp, bird-like features, high cheekbones and thin wrists and perches on the consulting bed with a clip board and a look of erotically vigilant concern.

'Take a seat,' she says. 'Please.'

I walk unsteadily forwards and lower myself on to a plastic chair.

'What seems to be the matter?'

I turn to her numbly, striving for words. It seems I cannot find the means to express the enormity of my pain. 'Could I . . . have a glass of water?' I ask, throatily, warming up.

*

'The least you can do is tell me.'

'Tell you what?'

'What Maggie's planning to do.'

Adrienne moves over to the window, looking down at the street, and when she turns to face me I see that she's in tears.

'It's not funny any more,' I say, ignoring this fact. 'If she does anything illegal she could get thrown out of university. Is that what you want?'

'Of course not.'

'Well tell me, then.'

There's an agonized silence before Adrienne sinks wearily into an armchair. 'She's going to . . . graffiti his car,' she says quietly, avoiding my eyes.

*

Half an hour later, I emerge with a prescription for a week's supply of Diazepam – just something to get me sleeping normally again.

Dr Monroe has offered to 'have a word' with my tutor. 'I know it can seem like the stress is so bad, your only option is to keep on going,' she has said. 'But I promise you, all you'll do is run yourself into the ground. What you need now is complete rest. No work. Plenty of exercise. Plenty of sleep. Plenty of healthy food. Stay away from McDonald's.' I've done my best to seem doubtful but enthusiastic. I've kept my eyes focused firmly in the middle distance. I've not looked at Dr Monroe's small sharp breasts.

'You should take one tablet at night, before you go to sleep. If you're still not asleep two or three hours later, you can take one more. That should do the trick.'

'Thank you, doctor.' I've been resisting the urge to blink for several long, dry minutes. This means that when I finally do so my eyes water. Oddly, I almost *feel* close to tears. Dr Monroe looks at me sympathetically. 'Look,' she says. 'I know college can be tough. I know they put far too much pressure on students. I was a student myself, not so long ago.'

She smiles. I nod, wanly.

'And no alcohol while you're on those,' she calls after me as I leave.

*

Ever since we were children it's been like this: Maggie conceiving the grand ideas, lost in her own invincibility, drawing others to her like flies to an electric grid; me running round after her, tidying things up, keeping her out of trouble. I leave Adrienne in her room – she wants to have a bath, she tells me, and I suspect we both need some time to cool down – and for a while I pace around mine, deciding what to do.

It will take me years to admit this to myself, but I spend the last twelve hours of my sister's life extremely, *acutely* angry with her.

*

Benedict Chieveley is in the King's Arms. It hasn't taken me long to find him. He's sitting where he usually sits. On the green leather sofa in the back parlour. Under the black-and-white framed photograph of W. G. Grace. Beside the gas fire whose fake coals do not glow. His arm, in a near-pristine cast, hangs from a sling round his neck. A small group of fellow drinkers crowds round him. His face wears the look of bored condescension it was born with, though I'm pleased to see blue rings under his eyes.

Dr Monroe has advised one tablet per evening. She has allowed the possibility of two. I have four in my pocket, already free of their foil blisters. I don't want to leave any room for error, but then again I don't want to kill him either. Maybe three would be a safer bet. At any rate, the immediate difficulty is getting them down Chieveley's throat.

What to do?

*

The best way of thwarting Maggie, I decide, is to keep watch on the Bridwell garage and threaten to raise the alarm if I see her doing anything to Benedict Chieveley's car – an activity that starts pleasantly enough, in brisk winter sunshine, but soon degenerates as clouds roll over and misty drizzle descends. Fooled by the temporary cheeriness of the weather I didn't bring an umbrella, so I pull up the collar of my coat and stand in the doorway of a small, late Tudor house across the street.

The college's garage was built in the sixties and looks out of place in central Oxford: a squat, low building of dirty bricks and sliding metal doors. With adequate sidling and loitering, I'm able to discover its entrance code as people start filling their car boots: 1380, the date of the Bridwell's foundation.

Only I would not have tried it already.

As I stand in the wet, waiting for my sister, Bridwell Lane fills with cries, wishes for a happy holiday, and I begin feeling like the incompetent detective in a mob movie.

Who do you think you're fooling? whispers a malicious wind as it glazes my neck.

*

I buy a pint of Guinness, suitably dark. I take this with me to the gents and place it behind the cistern. The place stinks of piss and breaths are best taken shallow. I take the pills from my pocket. They're oval and off-white. A clutch of flattened eggs laid by a bird of the future, a techno-avian. I put the first on the top of the cistern and grind it with the spoon I've brought for the purpose. I could've done the grinding in my room, but the thought of the dirt on the cistern in the men's loo of the King's Arms has been appealing. It makes me smile to think of Benedict Chieveley drinking traces of other people's urine.

When the first capsule is fine dust, I grind the second. Then the third. I stand looking at the fourth for maybe five minutes, thinking hard. Weighing outcomes, possible consequences. Eventually it's the stench of piss I can't stand any longer. Chieveley's six foot two, a strong, fit male at his physical peak. He can take it. So I grind it similarly and brush the resulting powder into the black stout, which I stir gently.

Holding the glass carefully, attentive to the dangers of spillage, I leave the bathroom.

*

By early evening, when Maggie still hasn't appeared, I become conscious of the fact that my legs are so sore, they're unlikely to work again. I've tried sitting on a step, but that only makes my bum cold; and already I can feel a rawness at the back of my throat, the onset of a nasty bout of flu. My patience snaps when the street lights come on: the only way to end such an unpleasant day is drunkenly.

As I enter the parlour of the King's Arms, it strikes me as an unpleasant irony that I should've spent my entire afternoon protecting Benedict Chieveley's property while he's been in here getting pissed. He's ensconced in a corner and looks as though he has several hours' hard drinking behind him. As I move towards the bar he tries to stand up, but appears to have some difficulty with the established procedure: his eyes scan the room, blankly; it looks like he's trying to recognize something, to remind himself where he is.

*

Chieveley's where I left him. I'm just in time to hear him shout, 'Get me a packet of cheese and onion crisps while you're at it.'

At the bar is the familiar hairy frame of Tom Baird. He's waving to the barman, attracting his attention. 'A pint of Guinness and a bottle of Delirium Tremens, please. And a packet of crisps. Cheese and onion.' He's in the first stage of drunkenness, merry and talkative. I sidle up next to him, facing the opposite way down the bar, and put the pint of Guinness I'm holding on the gleaming mahogany surface.

'You don't see tits like that in Oxford every day,' I murmur, looking at the far end of the room. Tom looks too. The barman finishes pulling the pint of Guinness Tom's ordered for Chieveley and places it in front of us. Keeping the movement gentle, I slide my Guinness and Diazepam cocktail towards it. 'Over there,' I say, turning round and pointing towards the door. With a quick look behind me to make sure I select the correct one, I pick up the fresh pint of Guinness and take a long draught. 'You've missed her now.'

'Typical.' Tom grins at me and reaches to accept a packet of cheese and onion crisps from the barman. Putting it between his teeth, he picks up the Delirium Tremens and the Guinness waiting innocently for him.

'Ta ra, mate,' he says, moving off.

*

It takes Chieveley several attempts to get to his feet, but he won't let his friend help him, a great square oaf who's laughing and clapping him on the back. I move away as he approaches but he lurches by without seeing me, and when he turns left out of the pub it becomes clear he's heading for Bridwell.

Watching him stagger down the street, oblivious to anyone behind him, it occurs to me that though experience may be *prudence*, this moment is better suited to Machiavelli than Hobbes: the time has come to act decisively, to subdue Fortune to my will.

15

Jake, Julian

I watch Maggie flirting with the porter. Eyes wide and self-deprecating. 'I'm so stupid,' she says. 'I suppose I'll be paying the fine off until I'm middle-aged.' She's lost her room key, she explains. And the spare. The porter, well beyond middle age himself, with a belly to prove it, isn't used to so much flattering attention from female undergraduates.

'You'll have to bribe me,' he says jokingly, but he's already unlocking his drawer.

'Consider yourself bribed.' Maggie leans across his desk and kisses his cheek. The old sod actually blushes.

'Here you go,' he says shyly, giving her the college's master key. 'I'll need it back tonight, mind.'

*

Benedict's so drunk he can barely walk: he lurches down the street, weaving across the pavement, stopping occasionally to shake his head. I follow him, keeping well back in the shadows, trying to still a rising elation – the illicit thrill that accompanies any uncharacteristic decision, taken quickly, hotly, in the rush of the moment. He has trouble navigating the heavy gates of Bridwell; for several minutes he sways outside them, attempting to type in the correct code, before they open and he nearly falls through them. A girl is letting herself out and looks at him with undisguised distaste, before wrinkling her nose and disappearing into the night.

I give him a few minutes before letting myself through the gate, in time to see him disappear through the archway to the garden quad, clearly on his way to the sanctuary of his bed. At the foot of his staircase he sits down, heavily, as though in need of a rest; and when he finally stands up he shakes his head again, violently, leaning with his hand on the arch of the door, before gathering the energy for the final leg of his journey.

*

Maggie and I give Chieveley two hours for the Diazepam to take effect before crossing the quad of Bridwell. From the college bar come sounds of revelry, the last 'bop' of term. *Heaven is a place on earth!* Belinda Carlisle assures the crowd. As if to prove her right, a girl in fancy dress, white angel wings and suspenders, clatters past us on high heels.

Maggie's hair, bunched behind her, catches the moonlight. 'Come on,' she says, ducking into the shadows, leading me on. The staircase creaks under our weight. We go slowly, moving cautiously. Outside Chieveley's room we pause to listen: nothing.

The master key fits snugly in the lock. It pleases me that Chieveley locks his room now. Inside, things are more chaotic than last time. Suitcases open and half-filled. Books face down and dog-eared. The smell's got worse. A dusty, fetid smell of old furniture and sweat that creeps deep into your nose.

Maggie tiptoes towards the half open bedroom door, skirting a coat reeking of pub chatter and drowned sorrows. I hold my breath as she pokes her head round it. She looks in and turns to me, grinning. I'm about to cross to her when we hear someone on the stairs. A soft, surreptitious tread which makes us freeze.

*

I spend twenty minutes pacing the icy garden, giving Benedict plenty of time to pass out in his room. The clouds are clearing, revealing gleaming stars as the temperature plummets, but I'm warmed by the thought of impending triumph.

This is not to say I'm wholly calm; my pulse races as I return to Benedict's staircase and move slowly up it, treading carefully to avoid creaking boards. If anyone asks, I've come to visit Hansen, J. F., whose name I've memorized from the hand-painted list on the ground floor; it's as well to have an explanation ready, in case I'm challenged, but I don't meet anyone as I climb two floors.

I pause outside Benedict's door, collecting my courage; then I try the handle and find, as I expected, that he was in no state to lock the door behind him. Inside, the sitting room is lit by long shards of moonlight and seems quite empty, but I stand quietly just in case, listening for Benedict's breathing – which emanates, loud and regular, from the open door to his bedroom. His coat is lying a foot or two from me, in a puddle on the floor, and a quick examination of its outside pockets yields a wallet, a lighter, a crumpled lecture list, but no keys.

*

Maggie nods swiftly at the sofa and I squeeze myself between its dusty leather and the wall. She slips behind me, pressing her back against mine. She's breathing quickly and holds down her mass of springy hair with one hand. The door opens with an ominous creak of hinges.

Silence.

264

The person stands, quite still, for over a minute. Then there's a sound of ruffling and a loud tinkle, followed by a sharp intake of breath. I edge forwards, away from Maggie, and poke my head round the sofa's edge. I don't know exactly what I'm expecting to see – but it certainly isn't Julian, kneeling on the floor.

Shit, shit, *shit*. Even in the dark his face looks impressively fucked up.

*

Yes!

I find Benedict's keys after a moment's sifting in the dark: they're in an inside pocket, on a large chain, and make a dangerous clinking as I hold them up. I wait, holding my breath, but there's no sound from the bedroom, and I'm about to leave when a black shape rises from behind the sofa, sending adrenalin sluicing through me.

I crouch over Benedict's coat, blood pounding through my head, as the shadow straightens itself, turning my fear to astonishment, because there's no mistaking that frizzy silhouette.

'What happened to you?' asks Maggie.

*

'Why don't you ask your boyfriend?' I hear Julian hiss, and it seems childish to spend further time behind the sofa at this point. He's half standing, half crouching over Chieveley's coat. I get some satisfaction in the fright I give him as I stand up. He's not expecting two of us.

Maggie moves into the centre of the room. Now she's standing between us, uncertain. 'Okay,' she says, 'what happened to Julian?'

This doesn't seem the moment for frank confession.

'Beats me.' I speak loudly, staring Julian straight in the eye, daring him to contradict me. It's pleasing the way he flinches at the sound of my voice.

'Sssh! You'll wake him.' He points in the direction of Chieveley's open bedroom door – but with forty megs of Diazepam in his gut, Chieveley won't be stirring any-time soon.

*

I've given a great deal of thought to how I'm going to handle the moment Maggie discovers what a violent oaf her boyfriend is, but none of the many scenarios I've imagined has taken place in Benedict Chieveley's rooms while he sleeps next door. Caught off my guard, I redirect Maggie's question to the man who should answer it, but there's an evil glint in 'Itchins' eyes which suggests that he's not to be trusted in a situation as delicate as this one – a suspicion confirmed by the volume at which he answers me. He's quite crazy enough to wake Benedict, which would complicate matters unduly.

*

Maggie goes over to her brother, who takes several steps away from her. 'Want these, do you?' he whispers, holding up a set of car keys. 'Well you're not going to get them.' He's smiling now, smugly.

'What are they?'

'What you came here for. The keys to Benedict's car.' I'm pleased to see that this information distracts Maggie from her brother's bruises. So does the fact that there's something resembling triumph in his eyes. He's edging away from her, towards the door. 'Adrienne told me all about your idiotic plan.' He stands up straight as he says this, chest puffed out.

'What?'

Julian's eyes narrow. 'You didn't expect her to, did you? It never occurred to you she'd choose me over you, did it?'

'What are you talking about?'

'I know all about your little "discussion" this afternoon. She told me you were going to vandalize Benedict's car.' He pauses, as though savouring a moment. 'Life doesn't always go smoothly, you know, Maggie. Not even for you.'

*

Maggie's looking at me, incredulously. 'You mean you're going to steal Chieveley's car?'

'If that's what it takes to stop you from doing anything to it. Term's over tomorrow, he'll have it back by then – and it'll be too late for you.'

'Don't be ridiculous, Julian.'

She's trying to regain the advantage, but she's forgetting that I'm the one with the keys. 'I don't think you're in a position to lecture me about being ridiculous.'

'What are you going to do with it?' Jake's voice rings out from the shadows, startling both of us. I look at him witheringly.

'You don't honestly expect me to tell you.'

'As a matter of fact,' he says, moving away from the sofa towards Benedict's desk and picking up a large glass paperweight, shining coldly in the moonlight, 'I do.' He smiles dangerously, giving me his *Poor Julian* look. 'Because if you don't tell me where you're going to hide the car, I'm going to throw this as hard as I can at Chieveley's bedroom door.'

*

I weigh the paperweight in my hand as Julian starts fidgeting. Stepping neatly between him and the door to the staircase, I toss it in the air and catch it. Maggie's watching us. 'I'm going to count to, let's see . . . two,' I tell him. 'One . . . one and a half . . .' My voice rises dangerously. 'One and three-quarters . . .' I hold the paperweight delicately between my thumb and index finger, taking aim.

'The St Botolph punt shed.' This emerges as a strangled squeak and I start to laugh. Julian takes his chance and darts past me, out to the landing and down the stairs. I turn to Maggie, expecting her to share the joke, but she's looking at me coldly.

'There was no need to humiliate him,' she says.

*

I emerge into the icy night in soaring spirits, congratulating myself on having kept my head so coolly. At the Bridwell garage I punch in the code and watch the door slide smoothly upwards, though I'm careful to keep my back to the CCTV camera: there's no point in slipping up on a technicality at this stage.

Benedict's Triumph Spitfire is in a far corner, covered in a dust sheet. The car's been cleaned and is gleaming; all traces of blood and bone have been removed, though its paintwork remains heavily scratched. Inside, all is immaculate; and as I slide into the driver's seat I pretend for a moment (to myself; I'm quite alone) that it's mine, that all its nonchalant glamour belongs by rights to me.

For one night at least, I'm King of the Road.

*

'Maggie, I . . .'

But she raises her hand to stop me. 'Let's just finish what we came to do.'

I try to take her hand, but she brushes mine aside and leads the way into Chieveley's bedroom. The place is gaudy with adolescent trophies. Group shots on a beach. Chieveley with three, no four, awkwardly tall beauties. Smiles. Bronzed faces. Sporting awards. I'm trying to see the look on Maggie's face, to read her expression, but she doesn't look at me. Her features are inscrutable in the darkness.

Chieveley's spreadeagled on his back. On the shelf by his bed is a bewildering display of medals and cheap plastic figurines, set in *faux* marble. On the mantelpiece are invitation cards. *Mrs Harry Slade, at home for Harry's 50th, Charlotte's 21st and Hugo's 18th birthday. Dinner and Dancing. Carriages at 2.00 a.m.* It's out of date by six months, I notice, as Maggie goes over to the tape player on the bedside table.

Chieveley looks childish in slumber. Golden hair tousled on the pillow, a thin rope of spittle trailing from his mouth. I feel a momentary urge to hurt him. To set about his arm with a lamp. Instead, I take a permanent marker pen from my pocket. Its tip makes a rough scratching on the plaster of his cast. There's a click as Maggie slips a tape into the machine and presses Continuous Play. Then a hiss and whirring, as Adrienne's voice fills the room, echoing the words I've just written: *We . . . know . . . it . . . was . . . you.*

16

Adrienne, Jake, Julian

The thought of spending the vacation with Momma asking me snidely about my 'boyfriend' – who I'm not sure even *wants* to be my boyfriend – makes me jittery, as does the fact that Julian doesn't come back all afternoon. I take a long hot bath and then go out and walk around Oxford as the sun goes down, kind of hoping I'll run into him – but he's not in the library or in Blackwell's and as it starts to get dark and cold I get bored of this wandering and decide to be practical.

*

Maggie closes Chieveley's door gently behind her. She doesn't say a word to me. She doesn't even look at me as we walk to the lodge together. Her face lights up for the porter as she returns the master key, but her lips tighten as soon as his back's turned. I follow her up winding stairs to her tower room. Her landing's dark. She stops outside her door and turns to face me.

'For the second time,' she says quietly, 'what happened to Julian?'

She won't be put off with another denial. There's no point, anyway, since Julian has the whole vacation at his disposal to feed her his side of the story. I try distraction instead.

'D'you fancy a celebratory joint?'

'No, I do not fancy a "celebratory joint".' She unlocks her

door and walks into her room. 'I want you to explain to me why my brother has bruises all over his face.'

*

I leave the car, lock it carefully, check again that it's quite locked, that I haven't forgotten anything inside it, and begin the long walk home. The streets are littered with plastic cups and vomit and various other mementoes of seasonal good will; groups of students sway down them, hands draped round each other, cameras swinging from wrists.

The thought of Maggie's fury only heightens the thrill of being me at this moment, as does the knowledge that 'Itchins won't ever be able to favour me with another *Poor Julian* look. Even my bruises feel less tender; certainly my pride heals as I consider how the events of today will sound when narrated to Adrienne. I intend to give her the edited highlights – cut the waiting-in-the-drizzle sequence, home in on the drama in Benedict's room and my successful escape with the Triumph Spitfire.

She'll love it!

*

It's later. I rolled the joint and smoked it, but Maggie wasn't tempted. She's pacing the room like an angry cat. I've pretty much told her the truth, omitting the fact that Julian missed when he struck the first blow.

'Why didn't you tell me before?'

'Probably for the same reason he didn't.'

She looks at me searchingly. 'You must have provoked him.'

This isn't how I've imagined this night at all. 'I don't think he likes me very much,' I tell her, quietly.

'Come off it. He doesn't go round hitting people just because he doesn't like them.'

I think of Julian lying in the drain, screaming at me. 'Do you want my honest opinion?'

'Of course.'

'I think it has more to do with you than with me.'

*

Adrienne's in her room, packing. Her Louis Vuitton hold-all's on the bed, burping quantities of clothes, and she squeals with laughter as I push her down among them and kiss her deeply. She gives no sign of being put off by my bruises; in fact, she holds me so tightly, so joyfully, that I'm reminded of a time before Maggie's meddling. We lie together between toppled piles of sweaters and shirts and her smell washes over me, sweetly arousing.

'What made you so happy, all of a sudden?' she asks.

'You,' I say, simply.

*

Julian's all over me, hugging and kissing me, throwing me down on the bed, bursting with news. He doesn't exactly say he's sorry for ignoring me these past three days, but he does thank me for telling him what Maggie was planning. He has everything 'sorted out', he says proudly, and although I guess I should feel duplicitous and bad about deceiving him what I really feel is just . . . relief.

He goes next door to get us something to drink, a bottle of port his godfather gave him for Christmas, and when he comes back he starts his story, running his hands through his hair like a clever schoolboy waiting for his progress report. I sit back and watch him talk, constructing the account I intend to give

Momma: 'He's very bright, one of those educated English guys . . . Tall and blond and slender. He's got his great-grandfather's chair in his room, the one his great-grandfather had when he was at Bushel . . .'

*

Maggie's calmer now, but still restless. Seeing the state of Julian's face has inspired some sibling tenderness I could do without. I go up to her and put my arms round her shoulders. She doesn't shake me away this time, but she doesn't press against me, either.

'I'm going to have to go and find him. I can't leave things like this.'

'Of course you can.'

'Don't tell me what I can and can't do.'

She turns and faces me. Her cheeks are flushed under wide, bright eyes. Slowly, delicately, she takes my left hand in hers and brings it to her lips. 'I'm not a pushover like my big brother,' she says, sinking her teeth savagely into it.

*

'So where did you really put the car?'

Something about the way Adrienne asks this – she's stretching her arms, looking down at her side, not quite meeting my eyes – gives me my first moment of doubt all evening. It intrudes uninvited, bringing with it the memory of her and my sister next door, the silence of their scheming.

'I told them the truth,' I say smoothly. 'It's in the punt shed, but you needn't worry – the structure's quite secure.'

*

I don't know why Julian told Maggie where he'd put the car – she's not the kind of girl to ignore a challenge or be put off by a rusty padlock and a set of college rules. I'm guessing that his stealing the keys is likely to have pissed her off, or at the very least given her an idea, but he looks so proud of himself and he's so clearly not in the mood for scepticism, that all I do is look at him enthusiastically and say 'cool'.

*

'How're you going to get into St Botolph's at this time of night, Maggie?'

She turns and looks at me, shaking her head. 'You don't understand, do you Jake? Julian's not at St Botolph's.'

'Where is he then?'

'In the St Botolph punt shed, with Chieveley's car.'

I look at her to see if she's joking, but she isn't. 'You honestly think he told you the truth about where he was going to put it? You should have more respect for your own flesh and blood.'

*

I don't know what time it is when I wake up the next morning, but outside it's dark. Julian's asleep on his back, mouth open, body sprawled across the bed. He's like a little boy when he sleeps – one arm thrown behind his head, his legs twisted in the duvet – and when I disentangle myself from him and sit up he stirs and pats his hand on the pillow where my head's just been.

I don't know if it's the fact that the first thing I see are his keys, lying bunched on the desk, but almost immediately I'm thinking of Maggie. Has she done something to Benedict Chieveley's car?

I sit there, trying to be responsible. Today's the last day of term, everything's almost over. All I have to do is . . . nothing, but doing nothing is often the hardest thing to do and anyway there's not that much risk. If Julian wakes up I can explain I went to check on the car, to make sure it was safe – which is basically what I *am* doing, I think, as I slip out of bed and pick up his keys, taking care not to let them jingle.

*

Maggie goes over to the cupboard and takes something red and knitted from a drawer. 'Julian's Admiral of the St Botolph Punts, or whatever they call it, so he'll have the keys to the shed. He told me where the car was because he *wants* me to come looking for him. I guarantee you he's in the front seat right now with a Thermos of hot chocolate, waiting for me, planning his lecture and building up grievances to spend the whole of Christmas moaning about. He thinks he's set me a challenge I won't be able to resist.'

She slips the jumper over her head.

'I can't leave him there all night, can I?'

*

The street lights stop at the gates which lead to the St Botolph playing fields and up ahead there's darkness. The ground's wet from the night before and my feet sink into it, coating them in mud, but there's a lighter in my jeans pocket which shows me the gravel path that snakes down to the river and the punt shed. It's a large wooden structure, kind of decrepit and imposing at the same time, and it takes me a while to get its rusty padlock open.

Inside, everything's black as an ink stain and the small flame only clutters the darkness with the shapes of punts stacked end to end, punt poles, oars. I navigate my way carefully around a rubble of paint tins. There's definitely not a car in here, which means either that Maggie's stolen it and hidden her traces pretty well, or Julian was lying to me and it was never here in the first place.

I'm standing by the door, about to go, when I see her – lying against a boat stack, facing away from me, with her hand at an unnatural angle to her wrist.

Now

I

Julian, Adrienne, Jake

I watched Adrienne get up that morning. She slipped out of bed slowly – *too* slowly, perhaps – and I kept my eyes shut, feigning sleep, fighting the rising knowledge that she'd chosen Maggie over me after all, that once again my sister's radiance had relegated me to the shadows. I'd left the keys to the punt shed in full view on my desk: a mean-spirited test, perhaps, though I wasn't to know what would happen that day, or that greater events would rob my suspicion of all importance.

She kept on looking at me as I lay there, whether to check I was asleep or because her heart was genuinely torn, I couldn't say; but in the end she took the keys and left – intending, presumably, either to give them to my sister or to do her dirty work for her.

I never found out.

By the time she woke me an hour later, sobbing, whispering that Maggie was dead, that she'd broken her neck on the metal support of a boat stack, that her hair was matted with blood, there was no way I could ask her; there was no longer any point in asking her. She stood, burying her face in my neck, tears tickling my chest. 'I can't believe it,' she said again and again, as if repetition might bring her back; and I held her, dazed, as she shook against me, thinking that I could believe it.

I thought of my sister congratulating Jake on how he'd

forced me to tell them where the car was. I could hear them screaming with laughter, deciding to prove me a fool; I could see their red eyes and their unchecked, unrepented hilarity. The vision was incontrovertible, each detail – the heaving of his spindly shoulders, the note of Maggie's laugh – brightly vivid, harrowingly possible.

Of course the car wasn't in the punt shed. I'd parked it in a public car park on the outskirts of the city; a place visited only by tourists, shoppers in from the country and the security men who guard it. It had amused me at the time, the thought of Maggie trudging over wet fields to graffiti a car she wouldn't find; I'd looked forward to her fury, to showing her that for once she'd underestimated me.

It seemed impossible that something as serious as death had intruded on us like this.

*

I kept saying her name that morning – even though I knew she couldn't hear me, wouldn't answer me, as though if only I could get the pitch right, tune the frequency, everything would be okay. The truth is . . . I didn't want to touch her body and find it cold and stiff. Does that make me a bad person?

I stayed in England for her funeral, which was the week before Christmas. I didn't tell Momma why I was staying, worrying that, being Momma, she'd fly over and 'comfort' me. I just told her what I was doing, not giving a reason, and I thought as I put down the phone that I'd never have done something like that before meeting Maggie.

'You just make sure you have a great time,' said Momma, crisply.

The service was held in a small church near where Julian's

parents live, the kind of church where angels spy at you from the tops of shadowy pillars. It was cold inside, full of old people looking at their feet, not totally sure what to say.

What *do* you say at the funeral of an eighteen-year-old girl?

Jake said: 'I should have tried to stop her.'

Julian said: 'Don't blame yourself.'

I didn't say anything – but I knew that the person responsible was really me. If I hadn't invented that bullshit about the car, Maggie would never have thought of it. It seemed weird that neither of them said this, but the way they were with me I could tell they thought it. I used to think it was generous of Julian to forgive me like that – but I learned later it wasn't forgiveness he showed me that day, it was politeness.

*

Maggie's death seems to exercise a morbid fascination on people like John. He spent the whole of our one-on-one session yesterday prodding me for details. Did I see the body? Did I dream of it afterwards? How did it make me feel?

'How would it have made you feel?' I asked him.

'This isn't about me,' he said.

We looked at each other in silence till my time was up. Neither of us mentioned the word 'guilt'.

To be fair to Julian – and I said this on the cold, dull day of her funeral, in a church full of dust and lilies – it wasn't his fault. It wasn't anybody's fault. He looked at me blankly, as though he hadn't heard. His eyes were ringed, his mouth tighter than usual. That was all. Grief, it seems, can't conquer youth – at least not in a week. He was standing with Adrienne, fingers locked in hers without enthusiasm. Did they blame me? Perhaps.

'I don't blame you,' said Julian, extending a hand.

It was clammy. He was fidgety. Like a toddler promised a sweet if he'll *just sit still* for twenty minutes longer.

Adrienne had been crying. She looked like she'd been crying for days. Her skin was see-through, her body like a package carefully wrapped in cling film. Without saying anything she hugged me, for what I realized was the first time.

'You're right,' said Julian, 'Maggie wouldn't have wanted us to blame ourselves.' His pale eyes met mine. 'Any of us,' he added meaningfully, handing me a service card.

*

As Adrienne shook against me that morning, I found myself calmed by her paroxysms, my thinking alert but distanced, as though I was watching events unfold through the wrong end of a telescope. The car had to be returned, of course, that much was clear: if Benedict woke to find it missing and called the police, awkward questions would inevitably ensue. Adrienne had already called an ambulance and had come to my room to fetch me to the scene; further officials would not be far behind and he couldn't be expected to sleep all day.

'I can't face it,' I told her slowly, blankly, in a voice that didn't feel my own. 'Not now. I can't, I don't . . .' I looked at her, and when the tears failed to come, not tempted by the contagious sympathy of the shared cry, I turned away. 'I need some time alone.'

'Really?'

I nodded. 'Could you – could you possibly go down there and deal with the ambulance men? Just give me half an hour.'

She pressed her hand into mine. 'Sure,' she said, with guilty eyes.

It was still quite dark outside; I walked quickly to the car park with the wind hissing in my ears, wondering whether I could cry – but the tears wouldn't come. I found the car where I had parked it and returned it to the Bridwell garage. As I left the building I glanced up and saw Maggie's window at the top of the tower, half convinced she'd draw back the curtain and wave.

Adrienne was waiting for me in the porter's lodge at St Botolph's, urgent and tear-stained. The police had been called and were examining the scene; I was to come as soon as I could; she had been sent to fetch me. Not saying a word, not touching, we made our way down St Giles, through the traffic, into the university parks and through them. A group of men stood self-importantly on a muddy bank in the distance, and they clapped me on the back with stern gravity when she told them who I was.

It had become a beautiful morning. As I stood at the open door of the punt shed, a burst of sharp winter light pricking my neck, I noticed the freshness of the air; it seemed strange that the weather had not taken notice of this momentous event. If anyone's death should have provoked gnashing winds and anguished hail storms, it was Maggie's.

The only light drifted sluggishly through dirty windows set high up in the wall. The police established later that Maggie had climbed the drainpipe outside one of them and got in that way, but they weren't sure how or why she'd fallen. The paint tins eventually made everything clear: the college groundsman confirmed that they'd been stacked, in piles, under the window, and suggested that Maggie must have put her weight on a stack, thinking it would support her, not knowing what it was.

I saw the police photographs later. Maggie's head was tilted, almost jauntily, against the metal boat rack and although you couldn't see the deep sharp cut in her neck, you could see the blood that had oozed from it during the night. It wasn't red any more, but a worrying purple: a velvet cushion supporting her head, lifting it off the dry earth floor. Her eyes were wide open, staring at the photographer's lens, as though she wanted to ask whether she was really dead – and if so, why?

*

Later, in my pew, I looked at the bruise left by Maggie's teeth on my left hand and thought how strange it was to have abolished her like that. To have done something to her memory we'd never have dreamed of doing to her face. When had she ever let anyone speak for her when she was alive? Now we had both spoken for her. Julian and I, brother and lover. Only Adrienne had stayed silent, and for the first time I felt a twinge of respect for her. She hadn't sullied herself. She knew how things were.

Adrienne and Julian sat together, up front with Maggie's parents. I wasn't asked to join them or the other Ogilvies. We'd never met. Maggie hadn't, apparently, spoken of me to her family. ('You shouldn't see this as a reflection of how she felt about you,' said Julian, briskly.) Neither of her parents looked remotely like Maggie. They were both bland, like Julian, and blond and carefully dressed. Her mother cried throughout the service, soundlessly, shoulders shaking. Her father sobbed once. A harsh dry bark.

I imagined them in the rooms I knew so well. I put them on their drawing room sofa, side by side, reading the Sunday papers, while Maggie and I screwed under a blanket by the fire. *My semen's on your Persian rug*, I thought. *I've had sex in your bath.*

I tried not to think of Maggie's cat-like pacing and angry eyes on her last night with us.

*

I couldn't stop Jake from coming to the funeral, but I could make damn sure he didn't receive the sympathy usually accorded the partner of the deceased. I told him that Maggie hadn't mentioned him to our parents and that this would be an awkward time for them to share a pew with a stranger. I stressed the word stranger and looked to see how he would react.

'I understand,' he said.

We were in church, half an hour before the service started, watching the witnesses of Maggie's life accept service sheets from the ushers and rustle their ways into their pews. People were greeting each other, acknowledging acquaintances not seen for years; it felt almost like a wedding.

As if to break the silence, Jake said, keeping his voice down so Adrienne wouldn't overhear: 'It isn't your fault, Julian.'

He looked embarrassed and shifted on his feet, his fist clenching and unclenching in his pocket.

'What isn't my fault?'

'Maggie dying like this,' he said. 'It isn't your fault, any of it. I just wanted to say that.'

This was almost too much. If we had been anywhere else, anywhere but in a filling church, minutes before my sister's funeral, with my mother whimpering – I could hear her, all the way from the front pew – and my father sitting, thin-lipped, pale-faced, beside her, I think I would have broken something in him. The knowledge spread through me, like a flame across paper, that this time I had nothing to fear, that this time I would hurt him.

'I don't think it's any of our faults,' I said instead, and turned away.

The simple fact, which hung heavy between us in the incensed air of that sad day, is that if Maggie had never met

Jake 'Itchins she would still be alive, none of this would have happened, none of it would have occurred to any of us – or, crucially, to her.

He sat behind me during the service and I could feel his eyes boring into my head. I wondered what he was feeling. Certainly nothing as decent as grief or culpability; he had neither of these in him. Did he feel sorry, even? Would he miss her?

*

The funeral was beautiful, full of people and flowers. A bishop who had gone to Bushel with Julian's dad preached the sermon, but so quietly no one heard a word of it. Later there was a big English tea and everyone was crying and hugging each other – it's amazing how many people Maggie knew. Jake seemed kind of distant and left early, without saying goodbye.

When Maggie's parents came over to greet me and her mother took my hand, I wanted to . . . I was going to say I wanted to die, which in the circumstances isn't respectful. I wanted, I guess, to apologize.

'I'm sorry,' I said. 'I'm so, so sorry.'

'Thank you, Adrienne.' Maggie's mother smiled at me kindly, pulling me towards her and kissing my cheek. She smelt of rosewater.

*

I didn't cry for Maggie in the beginning. For months I couldn't quite accept this wasn't an elaborate, Mark Twain-inspired joke. Her funeral was so phoney. A ritual for someone much older, much more pompous than she was. I half expected her to turn up at it, like Tom Sawyer at his.

I kept on seeing people in the street who looked like her,

too. Once or twice I knew positively I'd seen her. Something about the flick of a head, a deft swift leap onto a moving bus. I'd follow, heart beating.

*

It was raining the day Julian dumped me. In spite of this we sat at one of the outside tables of a café, by a burning gas heater which scorched my left side while my right one froze. Julian wasn't looking at me but his lips were moving, he was speaking steadily, with emphasis, like he was trying to recite a long speech in front of a casting director.

The last thing he said was: 'So I hope you understand.'

What could I say?

When he stood up to go I wondered if he was going to hug me, but he didn't. He just looked at me, almost curiously, like he was seeing me for the first time and watched calmly as I shrivelled up and desiccated inside. He stood there in the rain, not saying anything, not even looking like he was trying to say something, just watching. With a black umbrella in his hands, not bothering to open it, just standing in the rain.

'Can I call you sometimes?' I asked.

'Of course.' He nodded, then coughed – like the favour embarrassed him.

He took care to leave the money for our two cappuccinos and didn't wait for the waitress to come back with the change. I watched him go. When he was at the corner of the street he turned and looked back and did something that seemed cruel at the time, almost purposefully hurtful.

He smiled.

2

Adrienne

There was no way I could go back to Oxford after that, no way I could deal with living next door to Julian for the rest of the year. Momma arranged my college transfer like a personal victory – and because this time she was in control, not Jerry, she went full throttle into 'supportive' mode. She chose Vassar because Jackie Kennedy Onassis went to Vassar and because the chairwoman of the Vassar Alumni Society was also the treasurer of the MOMA Fund, to which she's a big donor. Poppa provided the cash without asking questions, Vassar gave me credits for the semester I'd spent in Oxford and I went back to America and to college, this time to a college close enough to New York to satisfy Momma's need for 'togetherness time'.

I never went back to my Oxford room or climbed past the embroidery on Brother Malcolm's door. I never saw Julian's red armchair again or the view from Maggie's window. I never went back to any of these places and I never called Julian (or hardly ever) and in time, roughly four therapists later, I started finding it easier to get up in the mornings.

Three years to the week after Maggie's funeral, in Los Angeles to attend my Vassar roommate's wedding shower, I met Spencer in the elevator at the Four Seasons. He looked so familiar I smiled at him, thinking he was someone I knew, a friend of Poppa's perhaps – and it was only when he smiled back and raised an eyebrow that I realized I *didn't* know him, I'd just seen him in a magazine, read a piece on him somewhere. He was wearing a grey suit and dark glasses and he came and stood right by me, right behind me in fact, so close I could smell him – this sweet, soaped smell of moisturized skin undercut by tangy citrus aftershave. I could feel him breathing down my neck, very gently, very softly, just enough to tickle the skin on my shoulders, and although this could've been creepy it was . . . exciting, somehow.

He didn't say a word, though, and when the elevator doors opened he walked off towards the hotel exit, turning around just once by the bowl of lilies and nodding at me.

I guess he asked the concierge for my name, because a note arrived from him that evening which said *My room number's 2217. What's yours?* and was signed *The guy in the elevator*. It was . . . thrilling, I suppose, to be summonsed like this, but I didn't really see myself as the kind of girl who shows up outside a guy's room in the middle of the night, so I took it as a compliment and left it at that. He told me afterwards that it was when I didn't reply that he got interested. I guess he wasn't used to being refused by people – and when Spencer's interested in something or someone he's better than most at getting hold of it or them.

Two days later I was out by the pool, in one of the private cabins. The phone by my lounger started ringing and when I answered a man's voice said quietly: 'You're very aloof.' He was sitting on the other side of the pool, also in a cabin, and when I looked up he took his glasses off and our eyes met.

'No, I'm not,' I said.

'Prove it.'

'What?'

'Come have lunch with me.'

'I can't. I'm flying to New York in three hours.'

'Then let's have lunch in New York. Tomorrow.'

Lunch seemed better than an invitation scribbled on a hotel message pad.

'Okay,' I said.

We did have lunch. We had lunch every day for a week before he asked me to dinner for the first time, in Rome. He was just under twice my age, at forty to my twenty-two, and although he'd spent twenty years making a living by generating high-octane drama he made a brief detour into romantic comedy with me – weekends in Europe, sunset drives in the Hollywood hills, late dinners, energetic sex. He had an eye for seductive details, like looking into my eyes when we clinked glasses, or sounding troubled on the phone when we were apart, and I was too young to know that what works in movies doesn't last in real life.

He proposed to me six months later, in the courtyard of the Louvre in Paris, at one o'clock in the morning, and when I said yes the fountains sprang to life and I wondered whether he had orchestrated them, too.

Spencer's big on orchestration. I think that's what drew him to me – he could sense I was malleable, knew perhaps that something had broken in me in the time before we met. I don't know when it stopped being fun, playing my part in the drama of Spencer's life. For the first year or two it certainly was fun. It was a relief to be with such an opinionated person, someone who made things happen around him, but once I'd lived through every scene in his romantic repertoire it became more and more difficult to fill the gaps between them – the silences at the breakfast table, the missed moments for romantic confidences late at night.

We carried on having regular sex long after we'd got bored

of playing lovers. As Spencer got older, it became a matter of honour with him – the fight against age, the maintenance of virility. He went into exercise overdrive in his mid forties, turning a toned body into a powerhouse, but as the years passed there was something about the way he no longer looked into my eyes when he moved on top of me that told me he was doing this with other women, too.

After a while, I stopped minding about that. Spencer never talked about it and was usually careful not to leave any blatant traces, like store receipts for gifts or something else I couldn't pretend not to have noticed. For my part, I ignored it when he came home smelling of someone else, and didn't mention occasional bite and scratch marks that appeared in some surprising places on his body.

What I valued most about Spencer when we met was the way he lived his life in the present, in technicolor, because to keep up with him I had to live like that too – which made it easier to forget that other life I'd almost had, but hadn't.

3

Jake

The rest of Oxford passed in analgesic routine. I spent approximately thirty hours conscious in any given week. The rest of my time I spent drinking myself to sleep, into sleeps which lasted for days. Most of my thirty conscious hours were spent in bed, masturbating flaccidly and reading. I felt closest to Maggie at moments of orgasm. Otherwise I lost myself in violent dramas and catty satire. After reading *Titus Andronicus* I dreamed about serving Chieveley Maggie's head in a pie and couldn't go back to Shakespeare for months. The arrogance of the Restoration Wits was a better distraction. Dryden and Rochester, with their withering asides, suited my mood. I liked their scraps – and when Rochester said of Dryden that 'when he would be sharp, he still was blunt: / To frisk, his frolic fancy, he'd cry, "Cunt!"' I thought of the self-conscious way Julian smoked cigarettes and occasionally said, 'Fuck.'

All this reading inoculated me from the general frenzy when Finals came round, but my liver never really recovered. I sometimes think I should've become a stoner instead of a drunk. Alcohol's a drug of diminishing returns, if ever there was one – but the last joint I ever smoked was in Maggie's bed, as I waited for her to come back.

It's my Miss Havisham's wedding feast, that spliff.

The voices began about this time. They came and went in the early years. Sometimes they'd be silent for weeks. Other times they'd never shut up. During the ten days I spent in a panelled room at the top of a pink marble staircase, in a tatty black gown, writing Finals, they were often so loud I couldn't hear anything else. They made concentration during the exams difficult – especially once, in the Restoration paper, when they all started reciting Rochester in unison. I wrote for three hours with one phrase ringing in my head and when I clipped the sheets together at the end, I found I'd copied it out twenty times, all over one page: 'the false Judgment of an Audience / Of clapping fools'. Again and again, angrily haphazard.

I didn't do anything with my degree. For five years I didn't do anything much at all, as the first half of the nineties limped by. I got a job in a café, cooking breakfasts. Then one in an office, typing letters. I stopped going home. I couldn't bear my dad's disappointed silences. I wondered what would happen to my life.

I found out on a clammy June day in 1995 while walking down Oxford Street.

'May I take your photograph?' asked a slim woman with expensive hair.

'If you want,' I said.

She was a producer, developing a show called *Who's The Real Artist?* She took my picture against a backdrop of shoppers and Selfridge's. She took my number too, and said she'd call – which she did, a week later.

The show's aim was to puncture the myth of modern art, to rip the new clothes from the old emperor by giving the people its voice. Add a little live action drama, a few tense phone-ins, and you've got a wildly successful piece of infotainment. I was asked to attend an open audition, then a closed one, then a screen test. At which point I became Contestant C.

Contestant A was Mona, a graduate of Central St Martin's College of Art. She was the 'real' artist of the group – a harshly dressed twenty-two-year-old with straight black hair who used words like 'fluid' and 'labial' and smoked only French cigarettes.

Contestant B was a semi-professional footballer from the Midlands called Turkish. He was far from being Turkish, in fact his real name was Chris, but 'Turkish' was what he chose to be called – and what magazines aimed at the teen market were happy to call him. He could, at a pinch, have been Spanish. Dark hair, dark eyes, faintly jaundiced complexion. With make-up to give him colour, he became the heart-throb of the group. Ratings soared when, through a whole week of hot summer weather, he worked shirtless on his installation.

Contestant D was a blonde-haired hairdresser from Glasgow called Claire, who was chosen because she was good at 'engaging'. This talent for 'engaging' took the form of long, candid, confessional monologues, directed at the camera and through it at the viewing public. Claire liked to get 'up close and personal' with her work. She'd never tried art before, but she found it 'really helped' in dealing with relationship difficulties.

On the first day of filming she asked me if I was in a relationship. I said no.

The show's premise was: Let the public decide. The prize was £50,000 and an exhibition at a top London gallery. Hank's gallery, in fact.

We were each given photogenic studio space in the same building and two months to work on an 'installation', plus unlimited materials. The show was aired twice a week and made up of tapes recorded over the previous three or four days. We were encouraged to 'interact' with each other, as well as to concentrate on making the art. A TV crew captured all this and an editor picked the highlights and spun it into a workable narrative.

At the end of each week, the public was invited to vote for the piece of art they happened to like best at that moment. Once the pieces were finished, a Phone-In Final would take place, with starting points awarded to the contestant who'd scored most votes in previous weekly polls.

Viewers loved it. Reviewers were initially sceptical, but soon succumbed to the tide of public opinion. Hatreds blazed. Loyalties flared. *Who's The Real Artist?* became the one thing in Britain everyone could talk about. A small-talk staple in a country obsessed by small talk.

Highlights of the show . . . The night Mona snogged Claire. The afternoon Turkish broke one of Mona's resin cast breasts in a fit of jealousy. The screaming match between Mona, Turkish and Claire that followed. I kept out of these antics. I hadn't bargained for this much drama, but I found it strangely relaxing. To be watched by thousands of people you don't know while you watch three people you don't like behave strangely is useful therapy.

As the Phone-In Final approached, a second series was commissioned due to unforeseen ratings. Hundreds of young hopefuls auditioned to be the new contestants. Words like 'controversy', 'furore' and 'event' were bandied about in the press. Broadsheet columnists had their own axes to grind and Mona and I provided the perfect pretext for professional injury. Reputations were staked on the value of our work and defended tooth and nail. They were not staked on the value of the work of Turkish or Claire. This led to a certain amount of bitterness at the studio, which was great for the ratings.

'It's as if you were famous,' said my dad one evening, flipping through a double page spread on me in the *Daily Mail*.

He said this as if being 'famous' was a quality some people are born with. As if a whole industry isn't dedicated to the manufacture of spurious celebrity.

'And what do you think of your work?' purred Tina, the show's svelte young presenter, the night before the Phone-In Final. Mona and I were neck-and-neck. Turkish and Claire, who had found love with each other in a last-minute attempt to recapture the limelight, were trailing by 107 and 124 points respectively.

'It's a piss-take, frankly,' I said.

'You mean . . .' Conscious that this was going out live, Tina smiled threateningly, then laughed.

'I mean it's a piss-take. It's not meant to be taken seriously. It's a piece of crap.'

Contestant Admits Piece Is C*** ran a headline on the front page – the *front page* – of the next morning's *Daily Telegraph*. *Crap the cash and run!* quipped the *Daily Mirror*. The resultant phone-in was the largest non-charitable event of its kind in television history. All four of us were wheeled out in front of a live studio audience to hear the results. Claire and Turkish stood hand-in-hand and announced their engagement, to be featured in the September issue of *Hello!* No one paid much attention. Mona eyed me frostily from the depths of a skin-tight Issey Miyake cat suit. A group of teenage girls in the crowd waved banners with my name on it, in red.

'And the winner is . . .' Tina's manicured hand fumbled with the envelope.

4

Julian

It has been galling, over the years since Maggie died, to watch how Jake has capitalized on his student glamour to turn himself into a famous-for-being-famous figure (aka 'conceptual artist'). Not that I pretend to be any authority on art, but as Jake himself frequently admits – publicly, drunkenly, exhibitionism in full flow – his work itself is crap. Apparently that's the point: he's *ironizing* the void of aesthetic judgement at our culture's heart by . . . exploiting it; that's at least what the critical book on him my mother gave me last Christmas argued. So he's become the emperor's tailor, but makes the whole process 'original' by informing his client in advance that he is naked.

How does this happen? How is it *allowed* to happen?

It all began with a television show on a Thursday evening, seven or eight years ago. I'd had a long day and was beginning to suspect that I wasn't the kind of person who would ever be able to command the respect of thirteen-year-old boys. To comfort myself I'd bought a bottle of good Chablis and intended to spend the evening in front of the television, sitting on the armchair I'd brought from Oxford, in the tiny flat next to the sports annexe where I lived.

You can imagine how it felt, after a minute or two's channel surfing, to be confronted by Jake 'Itchins, fashionably emaciated, puffing inscrutably on a cigarette and examining a large pile of what seemed to be fluff in the corner of a large, over-lit, white room. A girl with straight black hair and large breasts, wearing tight black trousers, walked in and said: 'Claire's just told me she and Turkish are engaged,' whereupon she burst into tears.

It was surreal; I sat transfixed, staring at the screen. I couldn't believe it was him and yet I knew it was.

'They deserve each other,' he said, and the sound of his voice eliminated any lingering doubts.

Had he mourned my sister by becoming a soap star?

At the first ad. break I ran down five flights of narrow stairs and across three blocks to buy a newspaper, all the newspapers, and while flipping through to find the TV listings I saw a photograph of Jake and the large-breasted woman, captioned *Clash of the Titans*. For one horrifying moment I thought that 'titan' might refer to Jake himself, but a closer reading showed that the titans in question were in fact the respective arts editors of the *Guardian* and *The Times*, and that the 'battle' was theirs.

I almost called Adrienne, in New York. I needed someone who'd understand the horror of what he'd done, its inconceivable enormity. I imagined us united, however momentarily, in our revulsion; but I knew it wasn't possible, not really.

Adrienne and I couldn't continue after Maggie's death. There was no form our relationship could take and far too much that couldn't be said. She stayed in England for Maggie's funeral and when our parting came I thought it best not to dwell on specifics. Adrienne had made her preference perfectly plain; she had chosen Maggie over me and with Maggie dead it seemed tasteless to bring this up. I think she felt this too – at least she seemed to – though for years after she went back to the States she used to call me at odd hours, sometimes months apart, in tears, crying as though she'd lost the most valuable thing in her life.

'I'm marrying Spencer Crawley,' she said during one of these telephone calls.

'As in the producer?'

'As in the producer.'

I could hear her breathing on the other end of the phone and imagined her in her mother's apartment on Park Avenue, all white upholstery and grey carpets. I'd seen it, a few months before, in *The World's Most Desired Pieds-à-Terre*, a large coffee-table book which someone who didn't know my father very well had given him for Christmas. Only Adrienne's mother could refer to a 6,500 sq. ft apartment as a 'pied-à-terre', and only someone like her daughter could live in it with her.

'It's kind of sudden, I know,' she offered. 'We haven't known each other that long, but it feels like the right thing. I thought you should know.'

'Thank you for telling me,' I said, head reeling. How else could I have responded? 'I hope you'll be very happy.'

It seemed a suitably insincere thing to say. When I sent her a wedding gift, an ugly Lalique vase chosen from the list at Asprey's, I made sure to repeat it.

I didn't go to the wedding.

In the same spirit, I resisted the temptation to phone her that Thursday night and turned instead to the television and the secrets it held. Jake was now slouching in a doorway, heavily stubbled, watching a spat between a bluff Glaswegian blonde and the girl with black hair; he was smoking a cigarette, borrowing the aesthetic entirely from middle-brow French cinema.

What Jake claimed later not to know, with what sincerity I

leave you to judge, was the fact that, by comparison with the other morons on the show, he seemed like the genuine article. By episode three, his perennially ringed eyes and silent pouts were being noticed – and, predictably, misinterpreted. So too was his general suggestion of 'unkempt fanaticism'. That's what Barbara Gordon, in the *Guardian*, called the basis of his 'tantalizing allure', leading Sally Goodall in the *Mail on Sunday's You Magazine* to argue that 'if not washing and forgetting to shave is the foundation of "tantalizing allure", then half the buskers on my street should get modelling contracts'. According to Simon Ledger, arts editor of the *Telegraph*, the views of both these women were 'typical' and indicative of 'an obsession with superficial beauty which is, unfortunately, all too common among so-called "cultural commentators" today'.

The cultural commentators in question, united for an instant, a passing column, rounded on Simon Ledger. By the screening of episode four, tempers in the brasserie of Soho House were frayed and friends were taking sides: allies were being reminded of past favours owed; artists, real artists, were jostling to give interviews in which they either deplored or celebrated the extension of the cultural franchise to the general public. Jake began to get fan mail.

By episode eleven the only serious contenders for the prize were Jake and Mona. Her Self for Sale installation – which took the 'age-old notion of woman as commodity to its postmodern extreme', according to Alicia Stein of the *Independent* – was almost finished; and whatever your views, you couldn't deny it was arresting. On a set of glossy shelves that could have been taken (indeed probably was taken) from the perfume department of a large store, Mona had laid out resin casts of her body parts: hands, legs, head, wrists, ankles, breasts. These were tagged and labelled, displayed for sale, a 'glittering dis-assemblage of a woman', said Stein, 'and a searing interrogation of beauty as consumption'.

Jake, would you believe it, was collecting dust. Ordinary dust; dust from the studio itself, from pavements, railway tracks, leisure centre gyms. Cameras followed him through the city as he carefully swept the interiors of taxis, the kitchen floor of the Ivy, an out-of-order lift in a council estate in Tower Hamlets, a slide in a rather grimy Fareham park. 'In this unexpected *tour de force,*' wrote Barbara Gordon, 'all of London finds a voice.' He took the dust with him each day to the studio and deposited it on the dust heap in the corner; occasionally he would tend the pile, sweep and smooth its edges. More often, when not actually out collecting, he would sit as far away from it as possible, listening to Mona and Turkish scream at each other.

There was a time when Jake was on television twice a week, when his name was known to every cab driver in London and his image, sullenly pouting, polluting, adorned the billboard on the Hammersmith flyover, a sign I was compelled to pass each morning on my way to work unless I was prepared to take a long detour.

Publicly, with people who knew me, and who knew I knew Jake, I pretended not to know anything about the show, not to be interested in this piece of clumsy voyeurism. I told my friends and my pupils that this kind of meaningless pap was a threat to the culture.

Privately, I spent hours each day calling the premium rate telephone line and registering my vote for Mona. Once I'd discovered that no measure was in place to prevent this, I called the line continually, registering hundreds of votes in Mona's favour. I spent the last two weeks of the series with my finger seldom far from the repeat button on my telephone, the recorded voice of the acknowledging operator ('Thank you for your interest in *Who's The Real Artist?* Your vote has been registered') a constant soundtrack in my dreams.

The night the winner was announced, as families gathered round their sets, I sat round mine, biting my nails and pressing redial. I had a double vodka on the rocks to fortify me and when it was finished and they still hadn't made the final announcement, I switched up the volume of the TV so that I could go into the kitchen to fetch another without missing anything. The neighbours didn't even notice the noise; they were watching the show too.

'I'm in a position to tell you that the winning margin is only . . . 347 votes!' cooed the generic presenter from beneath fluorescent curls while the audience went wild.

I closed my eyes in a moment of silent prayer.

'And the winner is . . .'

Oh God, let it be Mona.

'. . . Mona Streubel!'

Bliss! Rapture!

For a brief twenty-four hours I was content – more than content; but the day after the grand adjudication, unable to resist the temptation to gloat, Alicia Stein unwittingly reignited a now-dormant row by declaring that her own support of Mona had allowed the public to recognize the dawning of a new era in British art.

'British tart, more like,' sneered Sally Goodall in the next week's *Mail on Sunday*, prompting Barbara Gordon to bemoan at length the fact that the viewing public, yet again, had proved itself incapable of recognizing true genius when it saw it. That genius, apparently, was Jake's. His pile of dust had allegedly 'fulfilled the crucial function of a work of art, that of reminding us of our shared humanity'. He had 'no need of gaudy game show trophies'. According to the breathless Ms Gordon at least, 'Hitchins' work stands alone, an arresting demonstration of a powerful truth so often forgotten: that we are all beings of clay, that we have all come from dust, that to dust we shall all return.'

Despite *Private Eye*'s best efforts to pour scorn on the protagonists of this banal drama, Mona's resin cast body parts were quite forgotten in the resulting scrap, which raged throughout the second, less successful, series of *Who's The Real Artist?* and had the effect of confirming Jake Hitchins as a household name.

I was in the bath one morning, wishing there was more hot water in my flat's ageing cistern, when I heard on the radio that Valentine Serle, media mogul turned art collector, had bought *Dust to Dirt* for an unspecified sum and intended to display it prominently in his privately run museum.

This was outrageous, and though others shared my outrage, the controversy that surrounded Jake only served to make him seem 'avant garde'. Supporters of reason asked how someone who had never even been to art school could call himself an artist, provoking angry assertions that the point of Hitchins' work was the concept, not the execution.

Jake's first show only emphasized this point. He filled a London gallery with items of melted garden furniture, finding plastic emblems of suburban culture (deck chairs, garden gnomes, children's dolls' houses) and torching them in his studio, before offering the glutinous ruins for sale at prices that were as obscene as the installations themselves. He called it *Apocalypse* and positioned himself as the art world's favourite angry young man – a pose which worrying numbers of people now began to accept. When I made the point that anyone could have made this 'art', the cry would rise up that though anyone could, only one person had.

Over the next three years, Jake secured his market niche as prophet of exorbitantly priced doom. Valentine Serle, wishing no doubt to exploit the market's gullibility and add value to his collection, spent a widely publicized £150,000 on *Golden Wedding*, an installation involving a 1970s three-piece suite which looked like Jake had set about it with an axe. Other high-profile buyers followed in his footsteps and Jake catered to them: once you've hacked one sofa to pieces, it's not hard to apply the treatment to other objects, and this trite savagery made his work instantly recognizable.

When the Tate bought a video installation of a bonfire of melting mannequins called *Summer Sale (2012)* I stopped admitting to knowing Jake; I found the interest such an admission provoked too infuriating. I stopped debating his work, too; I felt it lent his charade credibility and instead of participating I'd change the subject or leave the room when his name came up.

5

Jake, Adrienne

'I think we'd all like to give Jake a big round of applause and lots of support and good wishes for his sobriety,' said John this morning. My month in the loony bin is up. Today was my last session of group therapy and I endured the braying smiles and clammy hugs of my fellow patients with a relatively good grace.

We all left our plastic chairs for one last 'togetherness embrace'. That over, I was allowed to spend the next few hours in my room, getting my stuff together, waiting for Hank. Camilla Boardman came in to say goodbye.

'Are you really going to do it?' she asked, coyly.

'I'm really going to do it,' I told her.

'*Naughty* boy.'

*

'You've got to be joking, Adrienne. There's no way I can fit in a trip to London this month. Have you seen my schedule?'

It's 6.30 a.m. and Spencer's standing by the bed, in jogging shorts, smelling of sweat. He runs five miles every day before breakfast, except for every second Sunday, when he lies in until 8.30.

'I've got to be in LA for two weeks. Then I'm back here for two days, then to Riyadh for a week.' He's in pre-production for the second series of *Heroes*, provisionally subtitled *Mayhem in the Middle East,* and when Spencer's in the middle of a project he doesn't like distraction – a fact I think I can use to my advantage.

'I was planning to go by myself,' I say.

*

It's the day before the opening. Hank's frantic. He's stomping round the gallery, mobile phone in one hand, clip board in the other. 'I'm gonna get your fuckin' *balls* blown apart,' he's screaming into the mouthpiece attached to his lapel.

I raise my eyebrows.

'Fucking caterers,' he mouths back.

It has taken two months of non-stop work to assemble enough pieces for a full-blown exhibition. I haven't touched any alcohol. My body's full of lithium and the gallery's heaped with broken objects and with large white screens displaying the breaking of objects in slow motion. My two assistants, who have done most of the manual work required, are currently hauling large canisters of pigs' blood through the gallery and into the tiny office, behind the scenes, where they will be opened and decanted into the large vat I have designed for the purpose.

The show's centrepiece has not been exhibited in the press previews. In a dry run, the only one I've had, the device worked perfectly. My assistant Tim has been assigned the task of manual pumping, with precise orders as to the speed of the filling process. The tank itself has been thoroughly cleansed and is now unblemished perspex once more. The outer wooden case, painted black, is ready to be fitted. The interior lights work. Deborah has her cue for twenty minutes after Chieveley arrives, whenever that is.

*

Spencer looks at me sharply. 'Why do you want to go to London by *yourself*?'

Spencer's never understood the concept of doing things alone. He spends his life surrounded by people, moving at the centre of a swarm of assistants and publicists, co-ordinating and managing, keeping them on their toes. He doesn't even jog alone – his personal trainer does that with him, checking his pulse, carrying the water bottle.

He moves over to the dressing room and takes his shirt off. For a few seconds he stands in front of the full-length mirror, looking critically at his abdominals, then lays a towel out on the bedroom floor and starts doing crunches. 'In fact,' he says, between repetitions, 'why do you want to go to London at all? The weather's lousy, the rush hour lasts from six in the morning until midnight. Food's crap.'

*

My house is very quiet after the bustle of the gallery. I'm not used to it. I'm not used to what I have to *do* in it now, either, which is nothing. No booze, no sex. 'You've got to work on yourself,' John's told me. 'You've got a long journey to travel before you're ready for a relationship.'

'I don't want a relationship,' I told him.

I don't, either. Definitely not. I want vodka.

I go into the kitchen and open the fridge. The motion sends a wave of longing through me. I remember that the vodka's still in the freezer compartment, perfectly chilled, waiting for me. I stand where I am, considering. Weighing the fact that I promised Hank I wouldn't touch any alcohol against the fact that he'd never know if I did or not.

The fridge is full of healthy food I don't like. Broccoli, green beans, cartons of organic soup. There's a packet of Parma ham which I open. A lot of packaging to get through for six gossamer-thin slices. I stand chewing the first one, thinking or trying to, unable to close the fridge.

Eventually I move across to the sink and fill the kettle. This is a foolish move, because I've never liked tea. I've never even liked the thought of tea. I return to the fridge. Taking the lever of the freezer compartment in my hand, I close my eyes and pull.

The vodka's gone. There's nothing there. Tears catch in my throat.

*

Spencer freezes in the crunch position, holding it, looking at me over his knees.

'Has your mother been on your case again?'

'No.'

His jaw's tense with the effort. 'So . . . ?'

'A friend of mine's having an art exhibition.'

'You want to spend six hours in a plane just to go to some art show?'

'I thought I'd spend a few days in the city, maybe look up an old friend or two. I need some time alone.'

He looks at me shrewdly. 'Doesn't that old boyfriend of yours live in London? That Julian guy?'

*

'I confirmed all three of them yesterday,' says Deborah, the six-foot gallery PR director with ebony skin and daunting bone structure. 'I spoke with Mrs Crawley's secretary Martha, who says that Mr Crawley has decided to join her on the trip. They're staying at Claridge's.'

'Mrs Crawley's mother?'

'Not coming. This is strictly a couple only thing. A romantic weekend break in London.'

'Excellent.'

'Mr Ogilvie is coming with his mum. She's quite a fan of yours.'

'He didn't give you any problems?'

'No. He even RSVP'd the invitation. No one does that.'

'What about—'

'There *was* a problem with Mr Chieveley,' Deborah cuts me off. 'I thought we had him. I confirmed last week, arranged the car and everything. But his secretary tells me this morning that he's had to give a speech to OPEC ministers in Paris and he's . . .'

'Do not tell me that Benedict Chieveley is going to be in Paris.'

Deborah looks at me gravely. 'It's a possibility.'

*

Standing in line at passport control at Heathrow, *alone*, I give thanks for my husband's crammed schedule. In fact, I feel almost dizzy with delight, like a kid cutting class the day of a biology exam. The airport itself, with its repetitive carpet patterns and identical chairs, is beautiful to me at this moment and the thought of four days by myself, free from Spencer and Momma and Martha, makes me almost delirious.

Somewhere at the back of my mind, on a shelf I don't look at very often, is the thought that maybe, just maybe, I'll see Julian again. If Jake's asked me, he'll have asked Julian too, right? This doesn't mean that Julian will come, it doesn't mean anything solid – but it *does* mean he might.

Even the official who stamps my passport seems unusually friendly.

*

'If they're not here in five minutes, I'll get you *castrated.*' Hank's at the door, bawling into his mobile phone. The words streaming from his mouth are purple, stinging like gentian violet. The voices round on Hank. One of them won't shut up about the odd stink of aftershave and coconut milk that drifts from his too-tanned skin. Another one's wondering whether he's making a move on the thickly built caterer currently carrying a tray of glasses into the gallery.

'Go away,' I whimper. I'm not in the mood for him.

He waves at me and walks over to the filing cabinet where he keeps his coke.

The thought of Hank on any more coke than he's already had is too much for me. The lithium has calmed the voices but there's no sense in provoking them. I need to be outside, somewhere calm where I can think.

*

The bell hop pauses for a moment outside my door, smiling at me. 'If you'll excuse me a minute, Madam,' he says, handing me the key to the room and disappearing down the corridor. I slip the key into the slot and hear the electronic lock click. I stand still for a couple of seconds, savouring the solitude of this moment, the thought that for the next four days this room will be *mine* – mine and mine alone.

*

Deborah's at her desk at the back of the gallery, smiling into her cordless headset. 'Do you know what?' she's saying. 'Oil is *so* chic right now.' Though from south London, Deborah doesn't speak English. She speaks American with an English accent. She might be a distraction from the voices. There's something soothing about the way she works. Her purpose-fulness. Her total trust in her own capacities.

She's doing her high, cooing voice. This means she's speaking to a woman she wants something from. Her purr's low and sensual when the object in question is a man. Playful and coquettish when it's a gay man.

'And there's no one better for the story,' she confides, 'than the glamour couple of international petroleum.'

With a self-satisfied click of the tongue, she puts down the phone and looks at me seductively. Breasts thrust out. Cheekbones on show. Pout: ON. 'I've got a surprise for you,' she tells me, 'but first you have to tell me I'm the most fabulous PR person you've ever had the pleasure of working with.'

*

I push the door open and find myself in a lushly carpeted hallway. It looks like Martha's reserved me a suite. I take off my shoes and go into the bathroom – which is larger, even, than Momma's though otherwise pretty similar, all art deco marble and his 'n' hers sinks. Humming to myself, feeling more truly alive than I've felt in months, I wander into the bedroom.

*

'You're the most fabulous PR person I've ever had the pleasure of working with,' I tell her.

'That's right. And you'll be glad to know that I've got confirmation on Benedict Chieveley. I just spoke with his wife. She's dying to be in *Tatler* and I've told her their editor-at-large is interested in doing a feature on petrol's power people and that she'll be here tonight. I said it would be great if she and her husband could meet her, so she's promised to move heaven and earth to get him here. I can't do better than that.'

*

Lying on the bed, in jeans and a sweat shirt, biceps bulging, is . . . Spencer.

6

Julian, Adrienne

It's possible, I remind myself, emerging from the shower for the third time today, brushing my teeth for the second, that Adrienne won't be there tonight. Jake may have invited her – he told me he'd invited her in his letter – but that doesn't mean she'll come. In fact the likelihood is, if we're talking probability, that she won't come.

Why should she?

It's not that I'm trying to impress anybody – certainly not. What I *am* intent on doing is avoiding the possibility of any *Poor Julian* looks tonight, to which end I've spent a week's salary on a wildly expensive haircut, something which Fabrice at Nicky Clark's assured me was *très à la mode*. He couldn't disguise his horror at my existing arrangement, the standard longish fringe with short back-and-sides, and in a move to regain some credibility in his eyes I told him I was going to the private view of Jake Hitchins' new show.

This changed everything.

Cups of coffee appeared magically before me, Fabrice disappeared into anxious consultation with his manager and I emerged two hours later looking quite unlike I've ever looked before. 'But zees is perfect, very "A-List"', Fabrice assured me; and I remind myself of this as I stand in front of the mirror, applying some wax from one of the many bottles and tubs of unguents Fabrice sold me, trying to remember his instructions: 'Pull forward on zee top, mess eet up at zee front . . .'

*

It didn't occur to me Spencer would be this territorial. He's cancelled seven meetings in LA to fly over to London and 'surprise' me, which is the kind of stunt he hasn't pulled in six or seven years, and ever since he got here he's been in romance mode – dragging me to the theatre and kissing me in the back of taxis, ordering room service and discussing babies' names. He hasn't even gone jogging for three days.

I sit on the edge of the bed, listening to him singing 'You're the Tops' in the shower, wondering if he'd find me if I left by myself, just ran out right now. I consider the practicalities. Leave the hotel, grab a cab, give an address – eluding a husband's hardly international espionage.

'You're the smile on the Mona Lisa . . .' sings Spencer.

I don't want him at this party, but he's already seen the invitation. He actually *asked* to see it last night, like he knew I'd try something like this. I guess he's worked out that if Jake's having the exhibition and I'm invited, Julian's probably invited too – which is why he's in London, keeping an eye on me.

How can I tell him he doesn't belong to that part of my life?

*

'I feel terribly glamorous,' says my mother, stepping gingerly out of the taxi. She's not used to taking taxis, or even to being in London very much; the simple combination of smog, sullied pavement and the extravagance of spending £12.50 on being driven from Paddington has gone to her head.

'You look very handsome,' she tells me approvingly as I pay the driver.

This remark sets alarm bells ringing, since mothers only tell their sons they look handsome when they obviously don't. Maybe I should have gone to the hairdresser's a week ago, to allow time for any short-term errors to stabilize; maybe the experiment with asymmetry was ill-advised. Maybe . . . I catch sight of myself in the reflection of a shop window and am suddenly horrified. The dwindling cluster of hairs on my crown has been decimated with shears and the sides, lauded by Fabrice as 'cool' and 'ragged', now seem to be shaved all but bald, emphasizing the length of my face and consequently my more than passing resemblance to a horse. I'm overcome by a desire to back out, to return to the party once my hair's had a chance to grow back.

'Cheers Mum,' I say.

7

Us

My mother and I are so early there's not a single person in Urban Life. Fortunately I can see this from the end of the road, because the gallery is lit and fronted with glass, an advertisement for emptiness, and this means I can steer her down a side street and into a pub. 'On time', for my mother, means the precise hour stated on the invitation, in this case eight o'clock. 'Do you think it's been cancelled?' she asks anxiously, as I set a gin and tonic in front of her. 'I had been looking forward to seeing Jake again.'

'What do you mean, "seeing Jake again"? You've never met him.'

She looks at me, affronted. 'Nonsense, Julian. I met him several times when you were at Botesdale. I've known him since he was a boy.'

She takes a sip of her gin and tonic and I can see I've offended her, which is exactly what I promised myself I wouldn't do. I'm here tonight as a treat for her; what does it matter if 'Jake Hitchins' has become a name to drop?

'You have a very successful career too, darling,' she coos, vengefully reading my thoughts.

*

Mustn't drink. *Mustn't* drink. Mustn't *drink*.

*

I'm standing by myself at the window of the gallery, watching people arrive. My mother is murmuring analysis of the 'art' somewhere to my left and I'm watching cars line up and disgorge their occupants on to a red carpet (how naff!). The whole scene screeches kitsch and its vulgarity almost succeeds in silencing the insistent voice that blames my mother for making us turn up before the photographers had gathered.

Not that I care about celebrity trappings; but the fact remains that I had one chance in my life to be photographed walking up a red carpet and thanks to my mum I've blown it.

*

I watched Julian and his mother arrive on the security video. I've spent the half hour since they came sheltering in the back office. I don't want to see them until enough people are here. I don't want to have to fill silences with them.

Julian's done something disastrous to what's left of his hair. He's wearing a mangy grey suit. With, my God, a tie. It satisfies me, obscurely, that Julian's already beginning to bald. I'm amused to see that he's used so much wax his scalp looks like the scene of an environmental disaster. Via the video monitor in the office, I watch him standing by the window.

I didn't know he bit his nails.

*

Spencer loiters expectantly in front of the photographers and he so expects to be recognized that they snap him frenziedly, just in case he's as famous as he acts. There's a line forming behind the obligatory red velvet ropes and a beautiful six-foot-two black woman – no a transvestite, no a woman, I can't tell – is ticking off people's names on a list. This is hipper than your average exhibition launch and I struggle to imagine Jake, I mean we're talking *Jake*, at the centre of all this drama.

*

Another blandly beautiful woman gets out of another long black car. Holding the large hand of another wealthy, powerful man, she smiles daintily into the eyes of a million gossip column readers enjoying their morning coffees.

*

I note with satisfaction that when Julian sees Adrienne arrive, he drops his drink.

*

'Look what a mess you've made,' my mother hisses into my ear. I've spilt some wine on the grey wool trousers of my suit and the glass has broken on the unpolished cream marble of the gallery's floor. A waiter hurries over and begins to mop up the mess. He doesn't mop me because the wine stain is right on my crotch and I watch with horror as Adrienne advances up the red carpet, thinking that the first thing she'll think when she sees me is that I've wet myself.

*

Julian's here.

I scope him the second I'm through the door, even though he's facing away from me – and suddenly I'm light with adrenalin. Turning to Spencer, I compliment him on how great he looks, forcing myself to make eye contact and squeeze his hand. Ever since we left the hotel, Spencer's mood has been worrying me – I can tell when he's out to prove himself and the signs at this stage in the evening aren't good.

'So where's your boyfriend, Adrienne?' he asks casually, as though to find this out isn't the entire reason he cancelled four days of meetings and crossed the Atlantic.

'I don't have a boyfriend,' I tell him wistfully. 'Just a husband.'

*

Shit, shit, *shit*. Adrienne's just walked in, putting herself directly between me and the bathroom, so there's no way I can deal with the crotch splotch. I search the room for alternative exits, taking care not to look directly at her, hoping that Fabrice's handiwork will serve as a temporary disguise.

*

I touch the button on the CCTV display, shifting between Julian (standing petrified in a corner, talking to himself) and Adrienne, who's just arrived with an older man whom I recognize from various magazine spreads as her husband. She's looking tense, as usual.

For the first time all day, I feel calm. Even enthusiastic. Watching Julian begin to sidle towards the fire escape, it occurs to me that the moment's come to play host.

*

I stand as long as I dare staring intently at another of Jake's fatuous 'artworks'. It's a large wooden box, painted black, with a Perspex lining visible through cutaways in the wood. It's filling slowly with dark red fluid and *already* has a red sticker on the label; other people examine it curiously and I hear various faux-intelligent *Aaahs* murmured over it. The injustice of Jake's fame, of his fortune and success, rises like indigestion to the back of my throat; I feel a momentary urge to break this shoddy contraption, to kick it in with all my strength and spill its fluid all over the floor.

But now is not the time for violence or bitterness. Quite apart from the fact that I would be charged ten years' salary for the pleasure of destroying it, I've got to get out of here before Adrienne sees me – specifically, before she sees my trousers.

Speaking frankly, I only ever imagined the *possibility* that she'd be here tonight; it was a pleasant fantasy, a daydream. I have no plan for how to negotiate an actual encounter; no idea of what I could possibly say to her, or even of what I want to say. I remember the day I saw her last, sitting in the rain, trying not to cry; I remember the sense of freedom that washed over me as I turned the corner in the drizzle. We have no place in each other's lives, I remind myself, scanning for a possible exit; and I've just located a promising exterior door when I hear the sound of purposeful footsteps behind me.

*

'Julian's over there,' I say pointedly. Pointing him out. Looking at Spencer. Gauging his reaction. His hand's positioned possessively on his wife's toned arse. I wonder if he knows Adrienne and Julian were lovers? 'I know Julian will be very excited to see you,' I tell her, looking at him. He makes tough guy eye contact above the glistening smile.

As I'm about to leave them, hoping Spencer will see to it that Julian's cut off before he reaches the safety of the fire escape, a small woman in black accosts me with trembling enthusiasm. It takes me a moment to register that she's Maggie's mother.

*

When I tap Julian on the shoulder to say hi, he jumps like I've, I don't know, *scalded* him or something. With typical Englishness, he greets me with a kiss on the cheek, like we last saw each other last week, like running into each other again is a run-of-the-mill social event, and now he's standing in front of Spencer like a naughty schoolboy, hands folded in front of him.

'Great to meet you,' says Spencer dangerously, with a hyper-manly chuckle, clapping Julian on the back so violently he stumbles forward, almost stepping on a pile of broken willow pattern china and bones, laminated and priced at £155,000. It's called *Afternoon Tea in Kabul*.

I don't know what I'm expecting from Julian. Excitement? Surprise? Something to suggest he's clocked the fact that the last time we saw each other he was dumping me, leaving me alone with my cappuccino in the rain. It would be nice to think he's missed me, even a little, in the years since we last saw each other.

'You make good money teaching?' asks Spencer.

*

I swallow tightly, unnerved by her unchanging smell – of freshly washed hair, expensive moisturizer, soft skin. As Spencer talks ('Greatchameetcha,' he begins, moving quickly on to job, salary, car, in that order) I try to look at her, to see if she is as I remember, to see if *she* remembers. She's not looking at me; she's almost, but not quite, as memory has her. She's still young, still fresh-faced, but there's something older in the set of her mouth, something tougher; I find myself sidling an inch or two to my right and I steady myself against the tingling shot of renewed proximity.

The only thing to do now is to play everything cool, to

keep up my end of the conversation until some convenient moment comes round for me to make that urgent trip to the bathroom.

*

'Am I allowed to tell a famous artist he's grown since the last time I saw him?'

'Since Maggie's funeral, you mean?'

Shouldn't have said that. Shouldn't have said her name. Her mother frowns, looking at me. 'Were you at her funeral?'

I nod.

'Ah . . .' She smiles fondly, briefly, before changing the subject abruptly. 'Julian's father is abroad. I know he'll be very disappointed to have missed the show.'

Talking to Maggie's mother is having an unpredictable effect on me. It's underlining the undeniable: how dead she is. This elderly lady, reeking of rosewater, with Maggie's chin and Maggie's nose, is making this whole evening ridiculous. What am I trying to prove? What good can it possibly do?

It's pathetic, really. I'm pathetic.

*

'An English teacher?' Spencer grins at me, as though I've told a joke. 'That's terrific.'

'I enjoy it,' I respond evenly, trying not to look at Adrienne, trying not to be side-tracked by the thought that the passing on of learning is a slightly more useful occupation than the making of violent, pro-war thrillers. I have nothing to be ashamed of, I remind myself, facing Spencer squarely.

'Hey, someone's got to do it,' he says.

Adrienne slips her arm round her husband's waist and the intimacy of this gesture exposes a truth that no number of expensive haircuts can hope to change: that it's the guys like Spencer who get the girls like Adrienne. Not, I remind myself, that I'm interested in girls like Adrienne any more.

Trying to think of something to say, I ask her how her mother and Spencer get on.

'Oh, they *love* each other.'

So that's it, then.

*

With the contrast so starkly drawn – breathe *calmly*, Adrienne – it's not difficult to see why Spencer's the guy I ended up with. He's got WINNER stamped across his forehead. Looking at Julian, I try to imagine him in New York, yet another gangly Brit with bad hair – speaking of which, what's he done to his hair? It used to be so beautiful, tousled and kind of bashful, not all that clean. Adorable. Now there's hardly any of it left and it's covered in gunk.

It's not like I lost out by marrying Spencer – Spencer, the man I love, the father of my child. It's not like I'd wish us unmarried, even if time could be rewound, which it can't be, which doesn't matter anyway because I'd make the same choice all over again.

I *love* my life, I decide. I *love* being Spencer's wife.

*

Somehow I get away from Maggie's mother. Somehow I make it into the back office, which a strong scent of *L'Égoïste* tells me has recently been vacated by Hank. This is a relief. So is the fact that Hank obviously didn't brief the catering staff correctly, since I've just asked for (and been given) a bottle of cold champagne.

Champagne's not easy to drink quickly. The bubbles

lacerate your throat. But this isn't a moment to worry about creature comforts.

I pop the cork and watch it froth, licking the spillage.

*

'Julian Ogilvie, isn't it? I never forget a face. Long time no see.'

Benedict Chieveley is moving towards me, trailed by a woman with TV-presenter hair who's holding tightly onto his right arm and being dragged through the crowd behind him, like a child's teddy bear. He's fatter than he used to be; his cheeks have filled out in tandem with his belly; he looks like he smokes cigars now.

Watching Benedict huff towards me, clearly in a rage he's trying only *quite* hard to disguise, I wonder where Jake is. This should be a pleasantly nasty surprise. I scan the horizon for him but predictably he's nowhere to be seen and in the meantime I've got more immediate concerns, like how to cover my crotch while simultaneously holding a glass of champagne and shaking Benedict Chieveley's outstretched hand.

'How the hell are you?' I exclaim, affecting bluster.

'Need the bathroom, guy?' asks Spencer.

*

Chieveley arrives in a stinking mood. I watch him on the video screen while working my way through the bottle of champagne, wishing I'd made things easier on myself by laying in some vodka beforehand. Fuck Hank and his holier-than-thou coke habit. Fuck John and all that bullshit about rehabilitation. There *isn't* any rehabilitation. Life *doesn't* get better. There's only conclusion and symmetry and honouring the dead.

Chieveley's got his wife with him. From the look of her –

blazing smile, knuckle whites showing where she's grabbed his hand – they've had a bust-up in the car.

I try to imagine Maggie here, with me. Laughing. Conspiratorial. I summon her image and wait expectantly to be told how funny it is, seeing everybody again, how funny *they* are. But her image won't come. I'm left with mangled snapshots of memory. The nape of her neck. Her limbs twisted in sleep. The circled imprint of her teeth on my hand.

I steady myself, or try to, by fingering the torn envelope in my pocket. I even take it out, watching my mother's handwriting blur. *Dad and I think your great.* The relic has an aura of neglect. Its tattered folds whisper age, irrelevance. It doesn't work like it used to. It doesn't fill me with hatred or even rage.

*

Then Benedict Chieveley arrives, and *then* when it turns out he and Spencer are old buddies, it occurs to me I've had about as much of this as I can take. I excuse myself, pretending to need the ladies' room, actually slipping out of the main doors of the gallery, hoping no one's seen me.

You want to know how I'm feeling? How would you feel if you were me?

I came to England to get away from my husband for a few days: Mission Impossible. Then there's Julian, who I'm mad with for being such a push-over, for letting Spencer prove himself so easily. Maybe a *tiny* bit of credibility would've been nice, a little shred of evidence that the first guy I ever fell in love with wasn't a total loser. Instead of which he turns up, dressed like someone in a British Airways commercial, with this, like, *stain* on his crotch which everyone, myself included, pretends not to notice while he holds his hands in front of it, basically *advertising* its existence.

And the only thing he asks me all night is: how do Spencer and Momma get on?

Like a house on fire, I told him.

*

'Wine, wine. Ha ha. Wine.' For some reason I can't even frame a sentence around the truth. I try again, with less conviction. Looking up, I see that the group's attention is being taken up with the woman Benedict's been dragging across the room, whom it emerges is his wife. No one's looking at me; Adrienne's eyes are on the floor; Chloe Chieveley seems awfully excited to be meeting her.

This is not a time to be where other people are.

Adrienne nods at Benedict, shakes Chloe's hand, smiles at her husband, barely looks at me and turns away, in that order. I head for the loo, head buzzing. Standing with one leg on the sink, crotch under the stainless steel electric drier, I am reflected full-length in the mirror on the facing wall. Self-worth wise, it's not a good moment. I have a full two minutes to consider myself until my groin starts sweating and I abandon the charade that I'll ever be cool – in either sense of the word – or dry.

I can almost hear Maggie laughing at me; I'll bet she's pissing herself in heaven.

*

All I am is empty.

I sit in the back office, considering this fact. For the last eight weeks I've worked like a maniac to make this show. For the month before that, only the thought of tonight sustained me. Now tonight is here and – I drain the dregs of the champagne – I've got nothing to say to it.

I sit at Hank's desk, cradling this thought.

*

Adrienne hasn't rejoined the group and she's nowhere to be seen inside. Has she escaped? Has she wanted to? The merest possibility that she, at least, is finding all this as excruciating as I am is enough to make me feel better, until I consider the fact that if she's running away from anyone, it's probably not from her rich, powerful husband; it's probably from me.

To tell the truth, the realization upsets me. It's one thing, after all, to decide that I don't want Adrienne in my life; it's quite another to see that she's made exactly the same decision about me. It would have been nice of her at least to acknowledge me properly, I think, deciding to keep my moistness to myself and walking through the open doors of the gallery; it would have been nice at least to have been asked how I've been. Surely she could have shown a passing interest, however feigned, in my well-being; would that have been too much to hope for?

The photographers have gone home or given up, but there are still party-goers and their hangers-on loitering on the pavement, the kind of people who clearly think this sort of thing is fun. My mood worsening, I turn down a side street, cursing my mother, whose presence means I can't leave, can't seek the solace of a comfortable chair and a bottle of wine; two bottles of wine. I must return shortly and get her; I must, as ever, be dutiful.

Ahead of me, in the shadows, a girl is leaning against the wall.

*

There are too many people standing around outside the gallery and I need to be alone – thank God there's a dingy side alley. It's the kind of place distraught women in the movies smoke cigarettes in, but since I'm pregnant I can't even do *that* and maybe it's the thought of smoking, maybe it's seeing them all again tonight, but suddenly I wish Maggie were here.

Maggie, Maggie, why did you leave us?

I imagine her sitting on the wall beside me, lighting a joint (God it's been a long time since I smoked one of those), laughing about Benedict Chieveley's wife, this careful blonde chick who's, like, over the moon to be one of Petrol's Power People, whatever that is.

I'm halfway between laughter and tears, as usual unable to decide between either, when I notice a shadow. Someone's blocking the light from the street, obviously about to mug me or rape me.

'Get the fuck away!' I scream, sounding totally unlike myself.

The guy backs off.

*

Uh *huh*. Time for a U-turn, a blistering backtrack; because seconds after I recognize the girl as Adrienne, she screams at me, her voice high and rasping, blazing fury, telling me, essentially, to get lost.

So that's how things stand, is it? Fair enough. I retrace my steps, into the light of the street, trying not to shake, trying to recall my images of her that morning, the morning after Maggie died – sneaking out of my room with the keys to the punt shed. The problem is, the scene refuses to come. Instead, all I can think of is that first night: the creak of her door at St Botolph's, the wait for the homesick farm girl, the revelation of Adrienne. And then I think of the way she looked at me that day in the rain when it ended, when we ended, and of how all she said, very quietly, was 'Can I call you sometimes?'

*

Spencer moves out of range of the CCTV camera. The last bubble of the last drop of champagne scorches the back of my throat. The welcoming refuge of drunkenness beckons. I want more booze. Lots more booze.

But I don't want any more of this evening. The whole enterprise is ludicrous. *I'm* ludicrous. Ridiculous. Everyone looks so old, so much *older*. Only Maggie's stayed young.

I stagger to my feet.

Must find Deborah.

*

Would you believe it, the guy comes *back*, and suddenly it occurs to me how dumb it is for a pregnant woman to be standing alone in a dark alley at eleven o'clock at night, how dumb *I* am for getting myself into this situation. The perfect end to the perfect weekend – ruthless romance from Spencer, followed by mugging and rape in central London.

The light's behind him and I can't see his face, but I can see he's moving slowly, almost creeping towards me – kind of hesitant, like he thinks I haven't seen him.

It's only when he shifts his head that I recognize him, or at least his nose. It's Julian.

*

What do you say? What should *I* say? I don't want her to get the wrong idea, or to provoke her in any way to repeat the scream performance. But I do want . . . What do I want? I do want to talk to her, to find out how she is, what her life is now.

*

Where the fuck is Deborah? Where the fuck fuck *fuck* is Deborah?

I take a glass of champagne from a passing tray and down it.

*

'I'm glad to see you looking well,' he tells me.

Looking well. That's so Julian. We meet again, thirteen years on, and he can't even find it in himself to tell me I look 'good'. What kind of a compliment is it to tell a thirty-two-year-old woman who works out five times a week, drinks hot water in the mornings and lives mainly off green vegetables and nuts that she looks *well*? Of course I fucking look 'well'.

He smiles. That classic, goofy Julian smile, no competition for Spencer's, and I fill the resulting silence by telling him he's in pretty good shape himself, a point which isn't strictly true but seems appropriate.

More silence.

*

I've just realized that Deborah is probably in the corridor with the light switches, when the lights go out and prove that she is. Or was. I can see her now, pushing her way through the room. She wants a good view. There's a half-hearted shriek, then silence. The gallery's in darkness, but the tank's interior lights are on. Meaning that WE KNOW IT WAS YOU is shining out across the room, the colour of blood. Someone on my right (Hank?) starts to clap. Others follow, falteringly. I move to where I can see Chieveley. He's looking at the words, frowning. Trying to place a distant memory. His wife joins in the clapping and looks at him crossly, which seems to trigger something.

In the darkness I watch his shoulders start to shake.

*

'Thank you,' she says, with an edge to her voice. 'You're not looking too bad yourself.'

The edge isn't good, but the compliment's touching and I smile at her for a moment, trying to see her eyes in the darkness. She's wearing a long, flowing blue-green dress; I had forgotten how unlikely she is, how improbable the effect of her is.

It's Adrienne who breaks the silence. 'Give me another six months,' she says, wryly.

*

Chieveley's *laughing*.

He doesn't laugh quietly, either. He throws his head back, drooping at the knees and roars. The clapping stops and there's an icy silence in the room. I move closer to him and see his wife say something through pursed lips. She's clearly mortified. Her mouth is narrow, like a crescent moon. Sharp at the edges. She tugs at his sleeve, hissing something sibilant. On and on Chieveley laughs. A fleck of spit catches the red light from the wall and settles on his wife's chest.

Chloe Chieveley turns on her heel and marches out just as the lights come on. The room breaks once more into nervous applause. The hubbub of conversation resumes. Chieveley helps himself to a drink and watches laconically as his wife runs into the street to hail a taxi. He finishes his champagne and wipes his hand across his mouth. His smile settles, then firms. He puts his glass down and starts after her.

*

Adrienne's pregnant.

She's pregnant with Spencer's baby.

I do my best to maintain composure as this fact registers, sinking through my head like lead weight. No wonder she needed some air after that hot, stuffy room; no wonder she stepped away from the party for a moment. She's pregnant.

She's fucking *pregnant*.

*

The taxi containing Chloe Chieveley is just disappearing at the end of the road when Chieveley emerges from the gallery. He hesitates, looking up and down the street, making a decision. With an impatience that suggests his earlier rage is reigniting, he fumbles in his pocket for car keys. He looks like he's been drinking. I knock back the vodka I picked up while following his progress through the room.

I'm feeling much more myself now. Much more clear-headed with a few drinks inside me. My mother's letter crinkles in my pocket, reminding me of its presence. I watch Chieveley begin walking to his car. It's taken him only thirteen years to reach middle age. The arrogance of his strut has become haughty. Heavy. A pillar of the fucking community.

I grab one more drink and follow him.

*

It goes on like this for a while. I am totally handling this interaction, by the way. Julian's explaining what it's like being a teacher, how he's considering writing a small book of verse,

I'm saying 'how great', not really meeting his eyes, but otherwise one hundred per cent fine, concentrating on my breathing.

*

'Congratulations,' is all I say, trying to mean it. Now she's telling me that she and Spencer try to get away together at least once every two months, just a weekend, 'someplace nice'. That's what this impromptu trip to London is: a romantic excursion with the father of her child; the possibility of seeing me obviously never entered her head.

'You seem happy,' I murmur, wondering what the correct response is to this news. It might sound truculent to tell her I haven't had a holiday for two years, and that the last time I went anywhere it was to Le Havre on a day trip to buy wine. Our anecdotes, it occurs to me, don't mix.

I'm quite unprepared for what she does next, which is burst into tears.

*

Why am I crying?

I'm *crying*, goddammit, because pregnant women cry, because *I* cry. I'm crying because I'd rather not have seen Julian at all, I'd rather have left him a memory, than have him stand here and make small talk to me. I'm crying because I've come all the way to England to find a man who has nothing to say to me.

*

Instinctively I pull her towards me, burying my face in her hair as she sobs.

*

He leans towards me, awkwardly, and awkwardly puts his hand on my shoulder. I can tell he's embarrassed and I try to stop but, you know what, this has been a tough week for me. We stand there for a while, me with the floodgate sign switched to OPEN, Julian silent, neither of us at all certain of what to say. In fact, it begins to seem preferable to me to go on crying indefinitely rather than stop and have to say something, but I can't go on for ever and, eventually, just as the lights in the gallery go off, leaving us in near total darkness, my tears dry up.

The sudden dark makes the moment more illicit than it is, so I pull away from him and we stand there, looking at each other. Part of me wishes he'd just take the plunge and kiss me, the other part is grateful to him for maintaining his cool. I'm a married, pregnant woman with a fabulous husband. Life is *great*.

'I miss Maggie,' I say.

*

Caution, *prudence*, has once again come to my rescue – because it was the extra second's delay on my part, the extra second during which I paused to reconsider the just-made decision to kiss Adrienne firmly, on the mouth, that allowed her to tell me that she misses . . . my sister.

She wasn't crying for me. She doesn't miss *us*. I should've known: it's not as though I haven't had a lifetime's experience in the bit part of second fiddle; it's not as though Adrienne's secret preference is any news to me.

*

I catch up with Chieveley as he reaches his car. He looks up and . . . smiles at me. It's difficult to tell what kind of smile this is. It's not the one I remember. His lips are fatter now, set in jowlier cheeks. The gaunt disdain of his youth has been replaced by – by what? A certain rotund smugness.

'Women!' he exclaims. He stretches out his right hand. 'They say you can't live without 'em. I'm not so sure about that.' The smile becomes a laugh. He wheezes in front of me, shifting from foot to foot in merriment. Benedict Chieveley is laughing and trying to shake my hand? This is bewildering. It's almost, as a matter of fact, touching. I shake hands with him. He wrings mine heartily, clapping me on the shoulder with his left hand. He's still laughing.

'Lemme buy you a drink,' he says, opening the passenger door of the car. 'For old time's sake.'

Old time's sake?

He's already pushing me into the seat and this alone is so mesmerizingly strange I don't protest. Soon I'm smelling leather and he's at the wheel, still chuckling. He starts the car and swings sharply off into the traffic.

*

We're walking back down the alley, towards the front of the gallery. After this moment – was it a moment? – that then wasn't a moment, we're both feeling edgy. At least *I'm* feeling edgy and the thing is, the weird thing is, I can't get that phrase about speaking now or forever holding your peace out of my head.

*

'I shat myself for a few weeks back then in Oxford,' Chieveley tells me jovially. 'I don't mind admitting that. I mean, coming to in the car, seeing all that blood – who wouldn't? I didn't hang around to examine things, either. I just drove straight back to Bridwell and went to bed. I was pretty out of it. But when I read that article I thought, you know, maybe I'd killed someone, maybe I was going to spend the rest of my life in prison. Do you know how many men get raped in prison? I hardly slept for a month – till I went to the coroner's office and checked up on any recently dead schoolgirls in the Headington area.'

He takes his eyes off the road to look at me. His smile narrows. He's more like the schoolboy I remember. 'They keep records, you know. I spent an entire week of that vacation combing the crime reports, mortalities, cases pending. Nothing.' His smile twists. We approach an intersection just as the lights are changing. Chieveley puts his foot down and takes the red light. Without looking at me, staring straight ahead, he continues, almost reflectively: 'It took a few days for the relief to die down. Honestly. I was so grateful to have it over, to be able to forget the whole thing.' He takes an abrupt left turn, indicating at the last moment. A horn honks behind us.

'But when the relief had died down,' he goes on, 'and it did die down, I got round to wondering who was playing with my fucking head like this, who'd been creeping round my room and into my life.' He shifts mood and gear and turns to me, grinning. 'That was the worst part of it, actually. Not knowing who was doing it, trying to work it out.' The car leaps forward. 'I never even considered old 'Itchins.'

*

Once she's calmed down and dried her eyes, examined them in the mirror of a tortoiseshell vanity compact, she stands upright and we both start walking back to the gallery, neither of us speaking.

Game over, I tell myself. I had my chance thirteen years ago and I 'blew it' (as Spencer would say) and now Adrienne's married to him and about to be the mother of his child.

Was I entirely wrong back there?

*

Two facts become agonizingly clear as we walk together:

1. If I kiss him now, he'd kiss me back.
2. If Julian and I reach the lighted street and then the gallery, the party, Spencer, we'll say goodbye to each other in about fifteen minutes and I'll offer him a bed anytime in New York and he'll say, 'Absolutely. If a floor in Fulham ever appeals . . .' And then: nothing. Finito. I'll never see him again.

*

'Who would've thought it. 'Itchins!' Benedict chuckles again, then giggles. His eyes are watering. He glances at me as though sharing a joke, then back at the road, then back at me. Something about the way I'm staring at him sets him off every time he does this. He claps his hand on my thigh.

'I'm so glad it was only you!'

Epilogue

It ended, though only Adrienne and Julian suspected the details, with all the trappings of a seventies movie watched on a Sunday afternoon. The sleek, fast car. The furious struggle for control of a moving vehicle. The quick, half lovely moment when a game becomes life – and then death.

Though no one knew this but Jake, Benedict Chieveley was laughing throughout. In fact, it was the paralysis of laughter, of pure, unfeigned hilarity, that made it possible for Jake to pull his hands free of the steering wheel. Benedict had always been the stronger of the pair. Now he laughed and made himself weak with it. He laughed and laughed and laughed until his head hit the windshield. That silenced him.

Jake, whose body was found some distance away, having hurtled from its seat at the moment of impact, had been calm in the car. He had had a strong sense of the ludicrousness of their situation. 'Ludicrous', from Latin *ludicer*, meaning 'playful', he had thought, when he saw how he would die.

He wondered whether Maggie would have approved.

Acknowledgements

The fact that this book has seen the light of day owes a great deal to the love, care, sage advice and practical support of many people and institutions. Among them are: Benjamin Morse; Jane and Tony Mason; Jenny Mason; the Revd Rob Gillion, Janine Gillion and all at St Saviour's Church; Paolo Landi, Elisabetta Prando, Monica Faggin, Lisa Martelli, Angela Quintavalle and my many other friends at Fabrica; Adam Broomberg, Olly Chanarin and the staff of *Colors* magazine; His Excellency Alessandro Stassano, the Italian Consul General in London; Antonio Caramadre; Dr Giuliano Soria; the Associazione Premio Grinzane Cavour; Dr Kay Redfield Jamison; Prof. Guy Goodwin; James Holland; the Revd Jane Shaw; Sarah Ogilvie; Sophie Orde; Plum Sykes; Geordie Greig; Hermione Eyre; Lorna Maclean; Eleanor Rees; G. Colin Crawford; Madhavi Nevader; Louie Stowell; Emma Dummett; James Hardy; Rebecca Saxe; Randy Watson; Christopher Fremantle; Adelyn Jones; Phil Walker; John McMully; the late Virginia Wynn-Jones; Prof. Tony Nuttall; Monica O'Kane; Eric Smith; Domitilla Sartoga; Emma Sergeant; Andrea Canobbio, Paola Novarese and Chiara Stangalino at Einaudi; Kathy Anderson at Anderson/Grinberg Literary Management, New York; Peter Robinson and Diana Mackay at Curtis Brown, London; Anoukh Foerg at Agence Hoffman, Munich; and last, but by no means least, Kate Barker, Tom Weldon and Juliet Annan at Penguin.

From Desmond M. Tutu.
Anglican Archbishop Emeritus of Cape Town

Dear Richard

Thank you for coming to see me. I am very pleased to be patron of the Kay Mason Foundation and I commend you most warmly for your initiative in wanting to make a difference in the lives of young South Africans.

Sadly a very small minority of children in South Africa have access to quality education. Education is the key to the future. The Kay Mason Foundation seeks to change the lives of just a few young people, to enable them to realise their potential and to unlock the leadership capacity within them. It is focused assistance around the needs of a selected few. The personal contact between the benefactor and the beneficiary is a tremendous bonus to the programme, a relationship in which I believe both parties will find that they are greatly enriched.

The world has been changed by individuals. We have a role model in former President Mandela. I am convinced there are others if they only had the opportunity. I urge our international friends to join you in transforming the life of a young person. What could be more worthwhile?

God bless you.

The Most Revd. Desmond M. Tutu, Archbishop Emeritus of Cape Town

KAY MASON FOUNDATION

Patron: The Most Revd. Desmond M. Tutu, Archbishop Emeritus of Cape Town

Dear Reader,

I spent my childhood in a country heading for disaster. The South Africa of the seventies and eighties was in the midst of a great struggle against Apartheid and the future seemed hopeless. My parents, anti-Apartheid activists, left the country in 1987 and brought me to England, where I spent the nineties watching my homeland being saved from self-destruction by the inspired example of Nelson Mandela and Desmond Tutu.

When my first novel, *The Drowning People* (Penguin), was published in 1999, I decided to use some of the money to send four children to school in South Africa. One of Apartheid's few worthwhile legacies is a tier of excellent (formerly white-only) schools which are now open to all – though, in practice, few from disadvantaged communities can afford to go to them.

My four kids are now in their last year. Three of them are prefects; two are also heads of their houses; and one is head of day girls. Inspired by their achievements, I decided to set up the Kay Mason Foundation (in memory of my sister, Kay, who died when I was a child), to allow others to taste the joy I had experienced in helping such exceptional children.

Desmond Tutu's example taught me that individuals *can* change the world. I wanted to find others who could, and to help them if at all possible. Under his patronage, the Foundation has thrived and we now help thirty kids to receive the education they deserve.

Royalties from my books cover the Foundation's running costs, which means that **100 per cent of anything you give goes to the children who need it**. For as little as £3.00 per week, you can change a child's life and unlock a country's future. Visit www.kaymasonfoundation.org and click on a scholar's face to read all about them in their own words – because they tell their stories far better than I could.

If you'd like to help, donations can be given on line or cheques made out to the Kay Mason Foundation can be sent to me, c/o Penguin Books, 80 Strand, London, WC2R ORL.

There's no saying what a little random kindness let loose in our dark world can do.

With all good wishes,

RICHARD MASON

Kay Mason Foundation, Registered Charity Number 1094073 (UK), IT2782/2003 (RSA)

RICHARD MASON

THE DROWNING PEOPLE

'My wife of more than forty-five years shot herself yesterday afternoon. At least that is what the police assume ... of course I know that she did nothing of the kind ... It was I who killed her'

It is twenty-four hours since the death of James Farrell's wife at Seton Castle and as it grows dark he tries to make sense of a life only recently understood; and to explain how he, by no means a violent man, has come to kill in cold blood after half a century of contented married life.

But answers don't come easily. And explanation involves a return to the events of five decades ago, when as a talented young violinist he fell in love with Ella – his wife's cousin – and she with him. He must remember their love in all its power and fragility; and he must try to understand the test she set him and the tragic consequences of his success for them both.

'If you want to be au courant with modern fiction, you will need to read it ... A truly extraordinary novel' *Sunday Telegraph*

'A sweeping, romantic thriller ... glamorous, ghostly and decadent' *Vogue*

'Redolent of early Evelyn Waugh ... perceptively and powerfully done' *Express*

'An exceptional achievement' *Guardian*

'An addictive emotional thriller' *Independent*

'Irresistible ... readers will adore it' *Scotsman*